SHERLOCK HOLMES
MYSTERY MAGAZINE

VOL. 9, NO. 4   I0685932   Issue #34

"NO, HOLMES IS NOT ON A CASE. AFTER MRS. HUDSON CLEANS OUR ROOMS, HE INSPECTS FOR DUST."

MARC BILGREY

STAFF

Publisher & Executive Editor: *John Betancourt*
Editor: *Carla Kaessinger Coupe*
Assistant Editors: *Sam Hogan, Karl Würf* and *Steve Coupe.*

Sherlock Holmes Mystery Magazine is published by Wildside Press, LLC. Single copies: $13.00 + $3.65 postage. Subscriptions (U.S.A. only) are available for $39.99 for the next 4 issues in the U.S.A., from:

Wildside Press Subscription Dept.
7945 MacArthur Blvd, Suite 215
Cabin John, MD 20818

Available as an ebook ($3.99) through all major online stores or as an instant download from wildsidepress.com.

FROM WATSON'S NOTEBOOKS

My friend Sherlock Holmes famously said "No ghosts need apply," but as I've aged I wonder if that is strictly true. After all, our Literary Agent firmly asserts that there is a world beyond our mortal senses, waiting to be explored. He could be right, as much of this issue suggests.

Paula Hammond introduces us to a remarkable young woman whose extraordinary talent and bravery help resolve a horrifying series of murders in "A Very Curious Occupation." S. Brent Morris, on the other hand, explores the actions of Sir Charles Warren, the Metropolitan Police Commissioner during that dreadful period in 1888 when the Whitechapel murders terrorised London. One day I will be allowed to relate Holmes's part in that investigation, along with the shocking revelations about the perpetrator, but I'm afraid there wasn't even a whiff of the supernatural in that particular incident (much to the disappointment of our Literary Agent). This was also true in the indelicate and distressing case of "The Surgeon's Swindle," ably reported by Jeffrey A. Lockwood.

In "Screen of the Crime," the inestimable Kim Newman recommends two televised programmes with a strong otherworldly flavour, as well as several others that will surely pique the interest of our Readers. I clearly recall the incident Mrs Hudson relates in her column, however, the case itself, despite the outward trappings of clairvoyance, was a simple one of financial chicanery and greed. I am happy to report that, because of our actions, 'Mrs Tottenham' received the monies due her and that she and her daughter now live in comfort and security. I did have to buy a new hat, however.

Speaking of new hats, I find it necessary to replenish a few articles in my wardrobe, including a hat. Perhaps I will try a fedora for a change…. In the meantime, here is Our Editor to talk more about the contents of this issue of *Sherlock Holmes Mystery Magazine*.

⚓

This issue of *SHMM* includes several stories and viewing recommendations with supernatural themes, from gods and goddesses to creatures of the night, from beings from sea lore to cryptic messages from the ether. And just to shake things up a bit, we include references to the animal kingdom, with frogs and butterflies both making an appearance.

We don't neglect crimes, however, whether they take place in Renaissance Italy, present-day small-town America and Canada, Victorian London, or in the chaotic world of the music scene. Along with our usual columns and cartoon, we've included "The Adventure of the Solitary Cyclist," a case where threats against a young woman are all too real.

Happy reading!

Canonically yours,
Carla Kaessinger Coupe

Not a subscriber yet?
Send $39.99 for 4 issues (postage paid in the U.S.) to:

Wildside Press LLC
Attn: Subscription Dept.
7945 MacArthur Blvd, Suite 215
Cabin John, MD 20818
You can also subscribe online at wildsidepress.com

ASK MRS HUDSON
(Mrs) Martha Hudson

My Dear Readers,

The other morning, as I was serving Dr Watson his poached eggs and coffee for breakfast, he asked if I was still writing my "little column." I replied that yes, I was, and that I had one due to the publisher in a week's time, but had no idea of what I should write.

At that very moment, he dropped a large piece of egg down the front of his waistcoat. "There's your subject," he said, laughing. "Stain removal. Heaven knows Holmes and I bring home plenty of those! Or create them here. Sorry about the sitting room carpet last week."

"Perfectly all right," I told him. "I shall just add the cost of cleaning to your next month's rent. And that is a brilliant idea. Now give me your waistcoat, and go put on a new one."

A few minutes later, he was off to a full office, and I sat down at my desk to begin my article. Where was Mr Holmes, you ask? Heaven only knows. Inspector Lestrade had sent for him the day before, and he'd run out before I could ask where he was off to.

I have not had much formal schooling; certainly not as much as my lodgers, but I've heard their stories of writing exams and finding themselves stuck in the middle of one, with no idea of what to put next. I wrote a few lines, crossed them out, then wrote another, which met the same fate. This went on for over an hour before I heard the day's first post come through the letter-box. Grateful for a distraction, I went to fetch it. The first letter was addressed to me, and by the time I'd finished reading it, I'd forgotten all about stains.

Here, Readers, is the letter:

✗ ✗ ✗

Dear Mrs Hudson,

I don't mind telling you, I have had a time of it lately. Worries for my grown children, worries over money, worries about my own health—all are more than this widow can bear! Last week, I found myself discussing my woes with a dear friend, and she suggested that I consult a clairvoyant. She told me that she had been going to see a Madame Delaroux in Conduit-street, and not only did that lady tell her where to find her lost watch, she also warned her not to partake of the prawn sandwiches at her great-aunt's tea, which proved prescient as everyone but my friend became violently ill that evening. Now I will say that my late husband revered the sciences. He would never have countenanced such a thing, but I decided it could not hurt to go with my friend just the once.

I imagined that Madame Delaroux's rooms would be dark and spooky, but in fact her parlour was well-lit and tastefully appointed, with the only hint of her occupation a crystal ball and a deck of fantastically-decorated cards on a large round table in the centre of the room. She first examined my palm, then, not liking what she saw, said that she would like to consult her cards. They were frightening-looking things, Mrs Hudson, and I thought they seemed devilish, so she said that she would look into her crystal instead.

I have never believed in such things as fortune-tellers and ghosts. I am a level-headed, practical woman who attends church most Sundays in good weather when my health allows. Before our visit, my friend instructed me not to tell Madame anything about my life; yet, when that woman looked into her crystal ball, she was able to see everything! She knew that I had come down in the world, and that I was a widow with a delicate constitution. She told me that my son is in India with his regiment, and that my daughter suffers from a debilitating condition which makes her unlikely to marry. She knew that I was wearing my only pair of boots, and that they were much-repaired. Then, as I looked at her in wonder, she stared directly into my eyes and told me how my dear Roger had died—even though we had managed to keep that out of the papers. She then stopped and looked around the room, as if she were searching for someone. "I smell a cigar," she said, "Don't you? But it's not a regular cigar. It has a lovely bouquet…like some tropical island…." She trailed off, but I was stunned. My Roger had few indulgences, but one was his insistence on Cuban cigars instead of the everyday Indian cheroots. But it was not only that—after a moment, I could smell it, too!

I was so overwhelmed that I ran from the house in tears, my friend calling after me. The next day, I received a letter from Madame Delaroux, asking me to return—that my husband had an urgent message for me and that he would give her no peace until she delivered it to me in person. I do not know what to do. My friend says that I should go, that perhaps it has to do with money. As to that, I could not afford the two shillings I gave her the first time, and while I do want to know what Roger wishes to tell me, I must admit that I am also afraid. What if he appears before me? I loved my husband, Mrs Hudson, but I do not want to see his ghost. I would die of the shock, and then who would care for my daughter? I asked my poor Violet what she thought of all this. Although she is often confined to her bed, she is an avid reader of all sorts of stories, with Dr Watson's tales being her favourite. She said that the solution was obvious—that I should consult Sherlock Holmes, and that he would know what to do.

Asking for your help, I am,

Yours sincerely,
Mrs. Roger Tottenham (Agnes)
London

Readers, I have seen many sad, desperate people in my years as Sherlock Holmes's landlady; still, Mrs Tottenham sounded so frantic, and as a widow myself, I knew how she felt. Although the pain is old and faded, I still miss my sailor husband—and I do *not* want to see him appear in my parlour! Just then, there came a pounding on the front door, which made me jump nearly out of my skin! I answered it with some trepidation—to find my lodger standing there on the step. Mr Holmes had once again forgotten his key. After supplying him with tea, I showed him my letter. He gave me his opinion, and I sat down at my desk to reply.

My Dear Mrs Tottenham,

I write this knowing full well that Tottenham is not your real surname. Upon reading your letter, I was quite alarmed and immediately turned it over to Mr Holmes, who unfortunately believes your reputation, finances, and quite possibly your life might be in grave danger. He sent for Dr Watson, and the two of them are even now on their way to your lodgings. Although you provided no information but "London," Mr Holmes was able to deduce your address by the postmark on your letter, a bit of dust in the envelope, and a whiff of the stationery.

As he waited for the doctor to arrive from his practice, Mr Holmes told me what he suspected. "Write this down, Mrs Hudson," he commanded, "and have it printed in your column, for there are many Agnes Tottenhams in this world, and just as many 'Madames' seeking to take advantage of them.

"There is no such thing as a true clairvoyant," he continued. "It is human nature to seek reassurance in uncertain times, and people such as Madame Delaroux can make a nice sum by pretending to see the future and talk to the dead. I know who this 'Roger Tottenham' was, and how he died. No, no, I will not divulge that to you, but his widow's dire situation arose from it, and I quite understand why this psychic might use circumstances to lure the poor woman into her web."

I gasped at that, and he nodded. "Yes, I believe their meeting was planned from the beginning. Some clairvoyants truly believe that they have certain 'powers,' but Madame Delaroux is not one of them. Delaroux is not her name; she is not even French. Born in Bermondsey, I believe. And while I do not presume to know how we will employ ourselves after death, I should be very surprised if we whiled away eternity knocking on strangers' tables whilst emitting various scents."

I giggled at that, and he gave me an irritated look.

"At first," he continued, "I believed this to be a simple case of 'cold reading,' whereby a fortune-teller or con artist uses his powers of observation to discern facts about a potential victim."

"So, deductions, then," I said.

"No, not deduction. I am not a fortune-teller or con artist, Mrs Hudson," he said, dreadfully affronted.

"Of course not."

"It would be mere child's play for someone skilled at cold reading to see that Mrs Tottenham is a widow in reduced circumstances by her clothing alone—she likely continues to wear black in some form, along with her wedding ring and, as she wrote, her attire is shabby. Her shawl, a bit of jewellery, even a feather on her hat might reveal a son abroad, and most people who care for invalids carry the odour of the sickroom wherever they go. I quickly realised, however, that 'Madame' has a much more obvious—and accurate—source: our client's friend. No doubt the woman's concern for her friend has spilled out in her own conversations with this clairvoyant, and given Madame an idea of how she might add to her coffers."

"With more sessions, you mean?"

"Yes," he said impatiently, tapping his foot and glaring at the front door, where Dr Watson refused to appear. "Readings, or good luck charms, or money spells. Remedies for her daughter. Blackmail. Perhaps even murder." He threw out this last as nonchalantly as I give my order to the butcher.

"Murder!" I exclaimed.

"My dear Mrs Hudson," he said, "The number of professional confidantes—clergymen, companions, psychics, even physicians—who turn up in the wills of those who die suddenly is far higher than one would imagine." At this, we heard Dr Watson's key in the lock. As he entered, Mr Holmes spun him 'round and pushed him right back out the door with his customary cry, "Come, Watson! The game is afoot!" As I finish this letter, I have no doubt that my lodgers are in your parlour, and whatever Madame is up to, her plans will be thwarted.

Yours most sincerely,

Mrs Richard Hudson (Martha)

Those lodgers returned to their flat at dawn, some four days later, bedraggled and covered with soot, but quite exhilarated. Dr Watson's hat was covered with a sticky white substance that I cannot seem to remove. When I asked what happened, he refused to tell me. "I must pay the rent, after all. Your readers must wait for it all to come out in the *Strand*. It will be a real rip-snorter, too! All came out well, I assure you."

Of course it did. Sherlock Holmes was on the case.

⚹

Now, Dear Readers, I will finish up with another letter. Do you remember young Master Alfred Higgs, the boy who would not eat his vegetables? Well, I recently received this in the post:

⚹   ⚹   ⚹   ⚹

Dear Mrs Hudson,

I have been remiss in writing; do forgive me! I am Consuelo Higgs, the mother of Alfred, who wrote to you some time ago regarding his dislike of vegetables and other healthy foods. He was thrilled to see that you answered him in your column, and he did indeed like the oyster omelet recipe you provided. In the interim, I have read as many cookbooks as I can get my hands on to find more palatable dishes. I thought I would share two simple ones with you—and possibly your readers. I think the lemon makes the difference. Mr Higgs and Alfred say it is the nutmeg.

With many thanks,
Consuelo Higgs
Bailey Cottage
Salford

Alfred's Vegetables

First, dice an onion very fine. Sauté with butter until just brown, then add your preferred (chopped) vegetables. Add pepper, salt, and some grated nutmeg. Add any stock you have on hand and let the vegetables simmer until done. Alfred likes carrots and turnips best. He will tolerate parsnips this way, but still steadfastly refuses to try swedes.

If you have time and wish a more filling dish, place your cut-up vegetables in a saucepan and add salt, pepper, chopped parsley and grated nutmeg. Toss all with butter (I use quite a lot), then add just enough water to keep the dish from burning. Separate an egg and beat the yolk with lemon juice. Stir this into your vegetables when they are done. I think that either of these recipes could be a meal unto themselves, but my husband and son still want a nice chop or joint on the table.

Editor's note: The originals of the two above recipes can be found in *Round the Table: Notes on Cookery and Plain Recipes with Selection of Bills Fare for Every Month*, by "C. G.", published in 1873 by Horace Cox, London.

SCREEN OF THE CRIME

Kim Newman

A Ghost Story for Christmas: "Lot No. 249" (2023)

The BBC-TV tradition of airing a classic ghost story over the Christmas Holidays began with "The Stalls of Barchester" in 1971 and ran throughout the 1970s, then went on hold until the 21st century, though it's currently an annual tradition again in the hands of genre specialist Mark Gatiss who has devoted a career to homaging and rebooting the creepy things he loved as a lad in the '70s. The slot hasn't exclusively been devoted to M.R. James—after a run of James ghost stories, the BBC mounted Dickens' "The Signalman" in 1976—but the author has dominated. Seven out of the nine 21st century *Ghost Stories for Christmas* have been James stories. However, in 2023, tying in with a three-part documentary about Arthur Conan Doyle, Gatiss rang the changes with a version of Doyle's archetypal "revived mummy" tale "Lot No. 249" (1892) which in typical Gatissian fashion he embroidered with fan service material which (somewhat controversially) tied the spook stuff in with the Holmes canon.

A frame story has Oxford medical student Abercrombie Smith (Kit Harington) arriving in some distress at the rooms of a character archly billed as "a friend" but played with pipe, dressing gown, Sidney Paget-accurate receding hairline and incisive manner by John Heffernan—perhaps best known for *Jonathan Strange & Mr Norrell* but also Jonathan Harker in Gatiss' recent Dracula miniseries. Smith recounts Doyle's story, which involves an effete student of the occult, Edward Bellingham (Freddie Fox), who keeps a traditionally withered mummy (James Swanton) in his rooms. When university folk who have irritated Bellingham are attacked by ragged-bandaged hands, Bellingham deduces that the mumbling which has disturbed his sleep is an arcane chant which has brought "lot 249" to life. The original story sketches the conventions of the 1940s style mummy movies in which a high priest in a fez sends Kharis (Tom Tyler or Lon Chaney Jr) out to reprimand terrified tomb-defilers by backing them into corners where they can be throttled.

Smith and his friend trade lines adapted from "The Adventure of the Sussex Vampire" in which the rationalist takes a "no ghosts need apply" attitude and doesn't accept that there's a murderous mummy on the loose. There's also a nod to "The Creeping Man" which doesn't track—surely, that's one of the great man's later cases?—and some fey business about the friend having his eye on rooms in Baker Street and wondering whether a doctor might not make a suitable fellow lodger. All this is quite sweet and nicely played—Heffernan would be a refreshingly traditional, non-neurotic Holmes—but in the universe of this 25-minute film, the great detective is wrong. There are unambiguously such things. The best thing in the show is Swanton's disturbing mummy, with makeup design by Dave and Lou Elsey, and he's definitely up and about and chasing Smith through a wooded path in an archetypal monster-on-the-loose sequence.

Gatiss plays up the enclosed, male-dominated university world, with the lank-haired, decadent, probably gay Bellingham set against healthy muscular outdoors types. Fox is a splendidly hissable villain. Like M.R. James' Karswell, this Bellingham is a thorough bad hat and rotter even though you might expect a modern adaptation to present a more nuanced, even sympathetic outsider.

Inside Classical *The Hound of the Baskervilles* (2023)

In 2023, composer Neil Brand adapted the Doyle novel into a combination dramatic reading and concert—staged at the Barbican Hall in London, broadcast immediately on BBC Radio 3, with a filmed record of the event televised on BBC4 on Christmas Day. The ubiquitous Mark Gatiss and the worthy Sanjeev Bhaskar make an excellent Holmes and Watson, though Brand takes some weight off Bhaskar (perhaps best known for the very Watsonian role of DI Sunny Khan in the *Unforgotten* serials) by distributing a lot of the descriptive action around a five-actor supporting cast who also do multiple duties in the expected range of roles.

The orchestral accompaniment has a lush, witty, shivery feel, with homages to Universal and Hammer scores—and, of course, a couple of plaintive violin solos when the sleuth is in a musical mood (Gatiss steps aside for these and the first violin effectively plays Holmes). Holmesians shouldn't be lulled by the format into expecting an audiobook with music—Brand has performed radical surgery on the novel (no Laura Lyons, no left-behind walking stick, no Lestrade) to get it into a trim 78 minutes. He also makes some fundamental changes which are liable to prove as controversial as the 1958 Hammer film (which changed the identity of the killer) to purists but arguably shore up a climax which the novel (and most adaptations) don't quite manage.

It's always a disappointment when the spectral hound turns out to be just a big glowing dog, but Doyle could have done better by the unmasked villain—who tends to run off into the bog and be forgotten about in a welter of explanations. Here, Brand radically has Sherlock consult Mycroft while Watson is off on Dartmoor. It comes out that while Sherlock maintains the above-mentioned "no ghosts need apply" attitude to the supernatural, the possibly cleverer Mycroft isn't a complete disbeliever in the occult. This sets up a finish which, admittedly, is a lift from William Hope Hodgson's *Carnacki the Ghost Finder* story "The Horse of the Invisible"—itself a conscious spin on the Baskervilles. After the dog is done away with, the scheming Stapleton finds himself attacked by the real phantom hound. Holmes points out that the villain is also a Baskerville and thus subject to the family curse. The dog, of course, has to be played by the massed strings of the BBC Symphony Orchestra conducted by Timothy Brock—and a fine job they make of it too.

Hundreds of Beavers (2023)

Jean Kayak (Ryland Brickson Cole Tews), proprietor of the Acme Applejack concern in a 19th century American frontier wilderness, is reduced to penury when his business is destroyed by a slapstick combination of gnawing beavers and his own high-on-his-own-supply drunken ineptitude. In a frozen forest, with only the clothes on his back and the teeth in his head, he survives and gets revenge by becoming a trapper—tangling not only with his beaver nemeses but wily rabbits, ravenous wolves, crochet fish, buzzing flies, and a mean-spirited woodpecker. He feeds and clothes himself—and sports a huge beaver-head hat for most of the rest of the picture—and is set a task by a merchant (Doug Mancheski). In order to wed a furrier (Olivia Graves), he must trap and deliver "hundreds of beavers."

Written by Tews and director Mike Cheslik—who worked on the equally odd *Lake Michigan Monster* (2018)—*Hundreds of Beavers* is a tribute to silent comedy and Looney Tunes, made in real snowy forests and on cardboard or CG sets. The relatively small human cast is augmented by a horde of "mascots": mimes in baggy animal costumes of the sort found at Disneyland or supporting sports teams. Even when slaughtered, dismembered or chewed to bits, the mascots are sort of cute and funny…but the fact that there are people inside adds a sneaky undertaste of real horror. This is the wolf-eat-dog, hunter-vs-rabbit, man-against-*kaiju*-beaver world of animated cartoons played out against a real historical backdrop of brutal manifest destiny. Jean Kayak, amiable buffoon and Northwoods Robinson Crusoe, is also a walking eco-catastrophe. Just as many silent comic heroes leave slapstick chaos and destruction in their wakes, Jean is responsible for an enormous amount of devastation.

It's a remarkable achievement which gets past what you think will be its problem—sustaining a spot-gag-based non-verbal comedy for 108 minutes—with ingenuity, deploying one-off jokes which more often than not set up other, even funnier jokes. A trapper's dogs are seen playing poker around a fire, which is funny in itself but the scene gets funnier and darker on successive nights as wolves snatch the dogs one by one—with the last dog glumly playing solitaire. Another running joke is the reason *Hundreds of Beavers* is being reviewed in this column. After he's mastered the Wile E. Coyote method of overly intricate animal traps, the site of one of Jean's kills is investigated by a pair of beavers costumed as Sherlock Holmes and Dr Watson…again, the image seems good for its single solid laugh but the characters come back and intersect with the plot as Jean braves a beaver metropolis and finds himself on trial for mass murder (as it happens, a fair cop—he's even wearing the evidence) and the master sleuth beaver appears as a prosecution witness to interpret marks left in the snow by Jean's mal-functioning but lethal traps.

What's especially funny is that beaver Holmes jumps to wild, wrong conclusions.

Dr Watson and the Darkwater Hall Mystery: A Singular Adventure (1974)

"But you've worked with Mr Holmes on his previous cases. You're his close friend and associate. You must have learned something from him…"

Having ordered Sherlock Holmes to take a recuperative holiday, Dr Watson (Edward Fox) is left to his own devices. When Lady Fairfax (Elaine Taylor) comes to Baker Street with concerns that her husband Sir Harry (Christopher Cazenove) is in danger because local rogue Black Paul (Anthony Langdon) has threatened his life, the doctor feels obliged to take a case. In acknowledgement of Sir Hugh Greene's anthologies—and the TV series based on them—Watson admits his flatmate's success has inspired 'rivals of Sherlock Holmes' to open their own detective agencies, though he isn't sure how to pronounce "Carnacki" and ghost-finding isn't really needed at Darkwater Hall, where earthly perfidy is in evidence.

Novelist Kingsley Amis has a smattering of television script credits, in-cluding episodes of *Comedy Playhouse* ("The Importance of Being Hairy," 1971) and *Softly Softly: Task Force* ("Now See What You've Done," 1974). This Conan Doyle pastiche/critique was evidently something of a lark for Amis, broadcast between Christmas and the New Year in 1974. In 221B Baker Street, a scrap of wallpaper with the bloody word "Rache" written on it is a souvenir of *A Study in Scarlet*. Watson crosses out "The Adventure of the Deadly Cobra" on a manuscript to come up with the less spoilery title "The Speckled Band." Fan-service aside, it's surprisingly subtle. Fox's Watson isn't a comic idiot—he notes anyone who wants to kill Sir Harry would be well-advised to strike just after a known criminal has threatened the magistrate. However, he is constantly teased about his worship of "the great Sherlock Holmes" and imperfect employment of the master's methods. Typical of Amis is the addition of mild sauce: the Fairfaxes enjoy roleplay in theatrical costumes involving masks and whips and Watson's bed is warmed by the Spanish maid (Carmen Gómez).

Like Amis' novel *The Riverside Villas Murder* (1973), this plays games with the classic form of the detective story but privileges character over mystery. The solution is ambiguous, with Watson smugly accepting credit for perceiving something—the obvious—which his puzzle-addicted friend might have ignored in search of a convoluted, satisfying solution…but we wonder whether he's got the right man and if Sir Harry is entirely safe. A streak of anti-snobbishness underestimates Doyle: this complacent Watson tags brutish poacher Black Paul an "unmitigated villain" on sight, while deeming Sir Harry's household above suspicion because of their respectability. Actually, the Holmes stories are full of blackguards of all levels of society—with plenty of well-bred rotters and respectable dastards. But Amis also makes space for obvious suspects to be rounded characters. Sir Harry's louche brother Miles (Jeremy Clyde) seethes that being born a few minutes after his non-identical twin has robbed him of title and wealth, while hanger-on Major Bradshaw (John Westbrook) is self-conscious that his military record doesn't extend to combat and has a long-standing unhealthy romantic obsession with Lady Fairfax which goes back to when she was a child. Clyde enjoys himself as an embittered, absinthe-tippling wit, but when his brother is wounded shows apparently genuine, touching concern. Such contradictions neither Holmes nor Watson are equipped to fathom. Murder they understand—repressed, disappointed rich people, not so much.

Directed by James Cellan Jones (*The Hunchback of Notre Dame*, 1967) and produced by Mark Shivas, this looks like every other 1970s Sherlockian television production—which is as it should be. Carriages clip-clop, trains chuff chuff, studio sets are cosily cluttered or oppressively shadowed, and well-spoken character actors cut fine figures in Victorian costume and coiffure. With Marguerite Young as Mrs Hudson. Amis turned his script into a short story, first published in *Playboy* (1978).

Goluboy Karbunkul (1979)

In modern TV series parlance, "The Adventure of the Blue Carbuncle" is the only "Christmas episode" of the Sherlock Holmes canon. It was the seventh short story, appearing in the January 1892 issue of the *Strand Magazine*—probably on newsstands for Christmas 1891—and Arthur Conan Doyle may have been trying to get some variety into the series even this early on. "The Blue Carbuncle" is free of grim, gruesome elements (unless you're a goose, of course) and ends with Holmes showing unusual forgiveness to a fairly rotten crook. And we get Christmas at Baker Street. Having done it once, Doyle never felt the need to write more holiday episodes—though he reworked the story's basic premise for "The Six Napoleons," which cannily approaches the mystery from a different angle. It's not one of the more often-adapted stories, perhaps because it's amusing and charming when the current fashion for Holmesiana is psychological and sinister.

In 1980, Soviet television broadcast the first episodes of an outstanding series of Sherlock Holmes dramas starring Vasily Livanov and Vitaly Solomin as Holmes and Watson. Even before the Jeremy Brett series at Granada, this Russian Sherlock set the tone for Holmes adaptations of the 1980s and beyond. However, a few weeks before that debuted, another Russian Holmes adaptation presented a very different approach. Broadcast on January 13—the Orthodox New Year—*Goluboy Karbunkul* is a comedy musical revolving not around Algimantas Masiulis and Ernst Romanov as Holmes and Watson but Boris Galkin as hapless jewel-snatcher James Ryder. Galkin—who is still working today as an actor and director—is known for tough military roles, as a Soviet paratrooper in *V Zone Osobogo Vnimaniya* (*In the Zone of Special Interest*, 1978) and as ex-Spetsznaz hardnut Dedov in a popular series of action dramas which began with *Ostavnik* (2009). For Russian viewers, seeing Galkin clown about in silly disguises as a blithering idiot must be like watching Michael Caine or Sean Connery in their occasional ventures into comedy. He's not a natural funnyman, which might well be the point.

The TV special opens with an animated history of the eponymous "brilliant," which involves murky deeds in India, and then launches into an *Oliver!*-style production number staged on the streets of London with caricature Victorian Brits having a right old knees-up. Callow youth Ryder is tempted by maid Katarina (Irina Pechernikova) to steal the gem from Countess Morcar (Valentina Titova) and—more reprehensibly—frame a suitable patsy for the crime. All this is explained late in Doyle's story, but writer Anatoli Delendik and director Nikolai Lukyanov tell the tale from Ryder's bumbling point of view. When he needs to find a frameable crook, Ryder goes out on the streets with a wallet stuffed with newspaper pinned to his jacket and does his best to attract a pickpocket by brushing up against likely characters. He also falls in (and out) with a gang of proper criminals, who might be the last of Moriarty's gang (a portrait in their lair could be the Professor). It's mostly played for broad comedy, with amiably silly touches like a portrait of an Indian prince on the jewel case showing different expressions every time the camera goes back to it.

With all this to-do, the second half of the show has to rush through the actual story of goose-losing Henry Baker (Edgars Liepins) and the singing, smug detective's search through London's markets, pubs and back alleys to solve the mystery. Unlike all Western depictions of Victorian Christmas, there's no snow—you can imagine deep-frozen Muscovites scorning *A Christmas Carol* with "you call that snow!"—but there are paper lanterns and a lot of on-the-streets jollity. Western television might not be quite so keen on manhandling live geese and the mix of Russian anglophilia with communist disapproval of bourgeois imperialists is very particular and might be tiresome to some (though Doyle, vocally in favor of the British Empire, still dwells an awful lot on the misdeeds of colonizers and exploiters in the far corners of the world). The Lithuanian Masiulis was known for playing German baddies in WWII-set propaganda films and elders in other Russian riffs on oft-told British tales—Squire Trelawny in *Treasure Island*, Sir Guy in *Robin Hood*, Prince John in *Ivanhoe*. He's a white-haired, somewhat plump, fairly sneery, late middle-aged Holmes, with Romanov's Watson admitting to tidying up his character in published accounts. Holmes's singing voice apparently belongs to someone else (Anatoly Kuznetsov).

Anyway, completists—it's on YouTube at the time of writing.

Kim Newman is a prolific, award-winning English writer and editor, who also acts, is a film critic, and a London broadcaster. Of his many novels and stories, one of the most famous is *Anno Dracula*.

IS THE FROG OK?
O'Neill Curatolo

"This splinter of wood, which I have every reason to believe to
be poisoned, was in the man's scalp where you still see the mark."
—Arthur Conan Doyle, *The Sign of the Four*

In *The Sign of the Four*, Holmes and Watson come upon the body of
the murdered Bartholomew Sholto. They observe that his muscles are
"as hard as a board," and his face is contorted into the "*risus sar-
donicus*," which is characterized by a wide grin and raised eyebrows.
Watson says that this contracted face suggests "Death from some
powerful vegetable alkaloid, some strychnine-like substance which
would produce tetanus." They discover a thorn in Sholto's scalp, and
the thorn has "some gummy substance" dried on its point.

As the story develops, it becomes clear that the thorn was shot from a
blowgun by Tonga, an aboriginal native of the Andaman Islands.

The Sign of the Four was published in 1890, and it is interesting to spec-
ulate how much Conan Doyle might have known about subjects like dart
poisons and the people of the Andaman Islands. In fact, vegetable alkaloids
were well known in Conan Doyle's time. Strychnine, for example, was discovered by French scientists in 1818. In general, alkaloids comprise a large
number of related chemical structures—hundreds and perhaps a thousand—
including widely known compounds like atropine, coniine, colchicine, and
cocaine.

While little is known about how poisonous blow darts were used in the
Andaman Islands, quite a lot is known about their use in the Neotropics, i.e.
Central America and South America. In this region, the source of alkaloid
poison for darts is the skin of amphibians known colloquially as poison dart
frogs. This is well-plowed scientific turf, and there have been more than 800
frog skin alkaloids identified. It is generally accepted that the purpose of the
skin alkaloids is to discourage predators from eating the frog. In general, the
frog species that possess skin alkaloids are also brightly colored—to warn
predators to stay away. Bright coloration is an example of aposematism—the
use of warning signals to convey to predators the risk of attacking.

John W. Daly of the US National Institutes of Health spent a career
lifetime investigating the species distribution, activity, and biosynthesis of
a wide variety of alkaloids and other poisons (see for example, Daly, J.W.
(1995) *Proc. Natl. Acad. Sci.* 92, 9-13). From this enormous body of work,
we choose to focus here on one class of alkaloids, the batrachotoxins. The

prefix "batracho-" is from the Greek word for frog, *batrachos*. Batracho-toxin is secreted from glands on the back of frogs of the genus *Phyllobates*, and these secretions have been used to poison the blow darts of indigenous peoples in the Neotropics. While poison darts play a role in sensational fictional stories about human murder, their real use has largely been in the hunt for large prey for food.

Poison dart frogs generally retain their alkaloid poison in various organs, with a particularly high concentration in the skin. Biochemical studies of these frogs have revealed an inability to synthesize alkaloids. A clue to the mystery of the source of the alkaloids was revealed when it became apparent that frogs of these species did not possess alkaloid poisons when raised in captivity. Thus, these alkaloids must be obtained from the frog's environment in the wild. It turns out (again from Daly's work) that batrachotoxin and related alkaloids are commonly present in various insect species such as melyrid beetles, formicine ants, and oribatid mites. Preliminary studies suggest that these insects may obtain the alkaloids from bacteria that live on them or from plants they eat. Frogs almost certainly get their batrachotoxin from insects that they eat. There are other toxins carried by poison dart frogs, such as pumiliotoxins and epibatidine, and these toxins are also obtained by eating insects which possess these compounds.

It is a bit shocking to consider just how toxic batrachotoxin is. The LD50 in mice is about 3 microgm/kg. By comparison, morphine is greater than 100,000-fold less toxic, with an LD50 of 400 milligm/kg. Generally, one poison dart frog contains enough batrachotoxin to kill 10 humans.

How can a frog live with all that poison in its body? Batrachotoxin works by inhibiting the closing of sodium-ion channels in the cell membranes of nerves and muscles. These acetylcholine receptor-triggered ion-channels are critical for operation of the lungs, heart, and other organs. Animals that eat poison dart frogs (or who are shot with poisoned darts) generally die quickly from paralysis of various physiological systems. Other poison dart toxins like epibatidine and pumiliotoxins operate similarly to batrachotoxin. Rebecca Tarvin (of UC Berkeley) and colleagues studied resistance in frogs to the toxic alkaloid epibatidine which sequesters in the frog's skin and other organs. Single amino acid changes, i.e. mutations, in the frog's nerve cell acetylcholine receptors make a small change in the shape of the receptor, thus preventing binding of epibatidine, rendering the alkaloid harmless to the frog.

There are likely other elements involved in protection of the poison dart frog. For example, saxitoxin is another alkaloid poison that is found in the skin of certain frogs. These frogs also possess a protein in their circulatory system called saxiphilin. This protein is a "toxin sponge" that binds saxitoxin, preventing it from interfering with the frog's neural and muscular sodium-ion channels. Saxiphilin sequesters saxitoxin until the toxin can be deposited in the skin where it can protect against predators.

So what was the poison on Tonga's dart in *The Sign of the Four*? Watson didn't know, and neither do we. The dart may have been directly treated with a vegetable alkaloid as Watson suggested, or it could have been treated with the skin of a frog who ate an insect who ate an alkaloid-containing plant.

O'Neill Curatolo is a biophysicist who holds 36 US Patents. His suspense novel *Campanilismo* (2013) chronicles the activities of drug industry physicians and scientists in ethically murky waters in New Jersey, Kuala Lumpur, and Malaysian Borneo. He published a sequel titled *Too Many Hats: Herbal Medicine and The Mob* (2018), about which Kirkus Reviews said, "An entertaining and illuminating romp through interconnected and delightfully suspect organizations."

LESTRADE'S BOSS:
Sir Charles Warren, KCMG, KCB
S. Brent Morris

Sherlock Holmes described Inspectors G. Lestrade and Tobias Gregson as "the pick of a bad lot. They are both quick and energetic, but conventional—shockingly so." Lestrade had been a Scotland Yard detective for some 20 years when Holmes gave his blunt assessment in 1881 in *A Study in Scarlet*. Lestrade went on to serve for at least another 20 or more years, as he appears in the early-1900s stories, "The Six Napoleons," "The Three Garridebs," and "The Disappearance of Lady Francis Carfax." From March 1886 to November 1888, Sir Charles Warren was the Metropolitan Police Commissioner and thus "Lestrade's Boss."

Charles Warren was born in Bangor, Wales, February 7, 1840, and attended the Sandhurst and Woolwich military academies. He was commissioned a Second Lieutenant in 1857 in the Royal Engineers. As an agent of the Palestine Exploration Fund in 1867 (at age 27!), he surveyed Herod's Temple and conducted excavations in Jerusalem, recording his discoveries in two books: *The Temple or the Tomb* and *Under Jerusalem*. Today the large tunnel under the Temple Mount is known as Warren's Shaft. It is believed to have been used to bring water within the city. He also discovered the "Moabite Stone" with an inscription of 34 lines, the most extensive inscription ever recovered from ancient Israel[1]. It was set up by King Mesha of Moab as a record and memorial of his victories in his revolt against the King-

---

1   en.wikipedia.org/wiki/Ancient_Israel

dom of Israel[2], which he undertook after the death of his overlord, Ahab[3].

Inspector G. Lestrade of Scotland Yard first appears in A Study in Scarlet, which Les Klinger in his book *The New Annotated Sherlock Holmes* dates to 1881, and Lestrade is mentioned in fourteen of the adventures. Lestrade said to Holmes in "The Adventure of the Six Napoleons," "We're not jealous of you down at Scotland Yard. No, sir, we are damned proud of you." Watson notes in passing that this little comment is one of the few instances where Holmes is visibly moved. Holmes returns the compliment in his laconic style when he commented to Dr. Watson in *The Hound of the Baskervilles* that Lestrade "is the best of the professionals, I think."

The paths of Warren and Lestrade crossed soon after Lestrade first came to Holmes's attention. In 1885 Charles Warren, now Major General, lost a close election to Parliament, and in March 1886, he was appointed Metropolitan Police Commissioner. Warren's predecessor, Sir Edmund Henderson, had resigned because of his mishandling of the Trafalgar Square Riot. Sir Charles was selected because it was now thought the Commissioner should have more military experience.

Warren's tenure was rocky, and he received considerable criticism from the press. He wore an elaborate military uniform and insisted that his constables have fine and well-polished boots. This was dismissed as a military man's affection for fine "kit," but his men walked up to 20 miles a day, and good boots were essential to their well-being. Warren was Lestrade's ultimate boss, and no doubt occasionally heard of Holmes's adventures through Lestrade's reports. It is reasonable to assume that Warren encouraged Lestrade to take advantage of Holmes's skills and to cooperate with him whenever possible.

Warren's greatest crisis during his tenure as Police Commissioner came during 71 days in 1888 when a series of grisly murders of prostitutes occurred in Whitechapel. Eventually five of these murders, involving horrible mutilation of the victims, were attributed to a madman who identified himself as "Jack the Ripper."

The generally accepted Ripper victims from among the Whitechapel murders are:

•Mary Ann Nichols, August 31, 1888

•Annie Chapman, September 8, 1888

•Elizabeth Stride, September 30, 1888

•Catherine Eddowes, September 30, 1888

•Mary Jane Kelly, November 9, 1888

2   en.wikipedia.org/wiki/Kingdom_of_Israel
3   en.wikipedia.org/wiki/Ahab

Warren's most famous action during this crisis was to wash a wall. After the two murders on September 30, the following graffiti was found on a wall on Goulston Street:

The Jewes are
The men that
Will not
be Blamed
for nothing

Here is Warren's report to the Home Secretary on November 6, 1888, explaining his action of washing the wall some 6 weeks before.

4 Whitehall Place, S.W. – 6th November 1888

Confidential
The Under Secretary of State
The Home Office
Sir,

In reply to your letter of the 5th instant, I enclose a report of the circumstances of the Mitre Square Murder so far as they have come under the notice of the Metropolitan Police....

On the 30th September on hearing of the Berner Street murder, after visiting Commercial Street Station I arrived at Leman Street Station shortly before 5 A.M. and ascertained from the Superintendant [sic] Arnold all that was known there relative to the two murders.

The most pressing question at that moment was some writing on the wall in Goulston Street evidently written with the intention of inflaming the public mind against the Jews, and which Mr. Arnold with a view to prevent serious disorder proposed to obliterate, and had sent down an Inspector with a sponge for that purpose, telling him to await his arrival.

I considered it desirable that I should decide the matter myself, as it was one involving so great a responsibility whether any action was taken or not.

I accordingly went down to Goulston Street at once before going to the scene of the murder....

There were several Police around the spot when I arrived, both Metropolitan and City.

The writing was on the jamb of the open archway or doorway visible *in the street* and could not be covered up without danger of the covering being torn off at once.

A discussion took place whether the writing could *be left covered up* or otherwise or whether any portion of it could be left for an hour until it could be photographed; but after taking into consideration the excited state of the population in London generally at the time, the strong feeling which had been excited against the Jews, and the fact that in a short time there would be a large concourse of the people in the streets, and having before me the Report that if it was left there the house was likely to be wrecked (in which from my own observation I entirely concurred) I considered it desirable to obliterate the writing at once, having taken a copy of which I enclose a duplicate....

I may mention that so great was the feeling with regard to the Jews that on the 13th ulto. the Acting Chief Rabbi wrote to me on the subject of the spelling of the word "Jewes" on account of a newspaper asserting that this was Jewish spelling in the Yiddish dialect. He added "in the present state of excitement it is dangerous to the safety of the poor Jews in the East [End] to allow such an assertion to remain uncontradicted. My community keenly appreciates your humane and vigilant action during this critical time."...

I do not hesitate myself to say that if that writing had been left there would have been an onslaught upon the Jews, property would have been wrecked, and lives would probably have been lost....

I am, Sir,

Your most obedient Servant, – [*signed*] C. Warren[4]

Warren resigned on November 8, 1888, two days after submitting this report, and one day before the murder of Mary Jane Kelley. His military skills were not sufficient to meet the needs of civilian policing and the infor-

---

4   *Ars Quatuor Coronatorum,* Transactions of the Quatuor Coronati Lodge No. 2076, London, vol. xl (1927), pp. 43-4.

mal oversight of the London press. He returned to military service and later commanded the British defeat in 1900 at Spion Kop in South Africa during the Boer War, where 250 British soldiers were killed and 1,250 wounded or captured. He was soon recalled to England, never again to have a field command. Despite the loss at Spion Kop, Warren was promoted to Lieutenant General and became a Knight Commander of Michael and George and a Knight Commander of Bath. From 1908, after his retirement, he actively supported Lord Baden-Powell in creating the Boy Scouts.

Sir Charles Warren died of pneumonia brought on by influenza on January 21, 1927. He had a military funeral in Canterbury and was buried in Kent, next to his wife.

Epilogue

Warren was an active Freemason and the third District Grand Master of the Eastern Archipelago (that part of Malaysia in the area of Singapore). He was elected Founding Master in1884 of Quatuor Coronati Lodge No. 2076, a lodge devoted to the "authentic school" of history as opposed to the "romantic school." The lodge warrant was granted on November 28, 1884, but, due to his departure to Buchuana, Africa, the lodge did not meet until after his return at the end of 1885. He was installed at the first regular meeting on January 12, 1886, when the lodge was consecrated. Quatuor Coronati publishes annually a volume of several hundred pages with papers devoted to the history of Freemasonry.

On November 8, 2007, I was elected the Master of Quatuor Coronati Lodge and successor to Lestrade's boss, Sir Charles Warren. I immediately searched the lodge archives for any records of correspondence between Warren and Lestrade, hoping that Lestrade may have been a Mason himself. Much to my regret, our lodge records contain no such correspondence, and thus establishing the Masonic membership of Lestrade will require further research.

References: Colin Macdonald's e-biography, *Warren! The Bond of Brotherhood*, highlights Warren's Masonic connections.

✗

S. Brent Morris retired in 2021 as managing editor of the *Scottish Rite Journal*, the largest-circulation Masonic magazine in the world. He has published widely on Freemasonry and in 2000 retired as a mathematician with the federal government. He has taught at Duke, Johns Hopkins, and George Washington Universities.

A VERY CURIOUS OCCUPATION
Paula Hammond

Mama still calls me her baby although I am fourteen now. A woman in law, and of marriageable age. Not that I ever shall marry, of course, for it seems a foolish thing for a woman to do: make herself slave to another.

My sisters are all older than I and say that I still have much to learn about the ways of the world—and maybe that is true. But when I hear them now, their music plays a different tune. Sadder, somehow, with a dark edge that I've come to know and dread.

I have always been able to hear the music. The soul songs.

As a child, I would lie on the floor of the nursery, my nose pressed against the weave of the Turkish rug, listening to the quick staccato whistles and pops of mice under the floorboards. Sometimes, I would catch Cook's lazy melody as she slept in the kitchen below. Or Papa's roaring, angry rhythm, intertwined with my mother's more balanced harmony. I would hear visitors arrive and, while they waited for the maid to open the door, I'd amuse myself by unpicking their songs to get at the marrow of their personalities.

It wasn't until I was older that I realized no one else could hear the music. It was my gift, alone.

Thank goodness we live in an age of reason and science. At least I do not have to worry about being branded a witch. Still, I keep my counsel and only use my talent in small ways—although perhaps I have been incautious. I can see no other reason that an officer from Great Scotland Yard should appear at Papa's door, requesting an interview.

⚹ ⚹ ⚹ ⚹

It's a requirement for all policemen to be at least five feet seven inches tall, but Detective Anderson stands another six inches above that. With his wild red hair and piercing green eyes, he makes a formidable sight. His music, however, reassures me as to his true nature: strong, and as steady as a metronome. He meets me with a smile and a look of surprise.

"Forgive me, Miss," he says, in a lilting Highland accent that seems at curious odds with his slow, steady soul song. "I wish to speak to you on a matter of some delicacy, but I was not expecting such a young lady. Perhaps you would prefer your father be present before we begin?"

Had I known then what I know now, I would have agreed, but it rankled to be treated as a child. "I may be small of stature, but you can speak to me as an adult," I said, with more confidence than I felt, "for in truth, that is what I am. And, as for my gender, why, we have a new queen who is already proving that women do not need a man to speak for them."

The detective smiled and, motioning me to sit, replied in a tone of heavy dignity. "Well, then, Madam Kidd, if you would be seated, we can get straight down to business."

His tone made me blush and laugh. I was sensible enough to realize how pompous I had sounded. "Thank you, Detective. And please do call me Kitty—everyone else does."

The detective chuckled, his soul song skipped along with the laughter, then settled back to its familiar tick-tock. "And you, young Miss, may call me Dougie."

I spoke before I could think—Mama will tell you that is one of my defining qualities. "Oh, I couldn't possibly. I will call you Detective, if you do not mind?"

He laughed again. "As you wish, Miss Kitty."

"I believe," he began, "that we have a mutual friend in Tilly Whitlock? It was she who suggested that you may be able to help. You see, while the Metropolitan Police were only formed eight years ago, London has always had its own special detectives. Those who deal with the city's more, shall we say, 'unusual' occurrences. Until a few years ago, we operated under the direct control of the Crown. But, as you pointed out, our queen is a singular lady, and it was she who suggested that we should be incorporated into the regular force. As a sort of short-hand, the Home Office calls us C-Division, but the wags have a better name for us: The Curious Crime Squad."

⚔ ⚔ ⚔ ⚔

Matilda Whitlock was one of my oldest friends and, now I looked, I saw a family resemblance between Tilly and this ruddy-haired detective. Why I was of interest to either him or his Curious Crime Squad quickly became clear.

"Tilly is my sister's child and, while my work takes me away for many months at a time, I always catch up with her news when I'm back in town. She often speaks of you and your special… gifts?"

"Why, I'm sure I don't know…" I started to say, but realized my protests wouldn't wash. Had I let Tilly in on my secret? Not knowingly perhaps, but I had reveled in teasing her. In 'knowing' things I should not. In making little predictions and watching her marvel at my cleverness.

"We have a monster at large in the city," the detective began. "As long as he doesn't know we're on his trail, we have a chance of bringing the beast to heel. So far, we've managed to keep the business out of the press but it's just a matter of time before the hacks get wind of it and, when that happens, we fear he will flee the country. Maybe to continue his terror elsewhere. I believe your special skills may be of use."

I wondered, then, what special skills of his own the detective might have. Why he had joined C-Division. When I asked, he would not say beyond the fact that he had his own reasons for choosing such a very Curious occupation. What he did relate were the facts of the case, along with his suspicions and fears.

From the way he spoke it seemed that Tilly had given him to believe I could achieve all manner of wonders. I fully expected that, once I had explained the truth of things, he would no longer be interested in little Kitty Kidd. I was wrong.

He listened as I told him about the music. How every living thing, even the Earth itself, has its own song. And how those songs sometimes change.

I know by their song when people are lying. I can hear sickness, whether in the body or mind. I can even tell when danger is near, although that is the hardest part of my gift to explain. I think maybe the music is tied to our deepest and most instinctual selves. Just as animals feel fear when they're taken to market, without understanding exactly what is happening, so our soul music changes in response to things we don't consciously perceive. And sometimes, just sometimes, I hear what I call the music of fate. When something *big* is about to happen.

As the detective spoke, I could hear it—fate's distinctive air bobbing beneath his words. A strange, hypnotic beat that both thrilled and alarmed me. What could I do but say yes?

⚔ ⚔ ⚔ ⚔

The detective was right. There was a beast loose in London town.

A beast who had, so far, killed four men. The manner of their deaths was certainly curious enough to fill the remit of C-Division.

The bodies of all four victims had been thrown into the Thames. They would, perhaps, have gone unnoticed amongst all the suicides and accidents had not their heads been left embedded on spikes in apparently random locations throughout the city.

The victims were all men of property, although virtual unknowns in society. It had taken weeks to identify them, for their clothes carried no formal papers and no missing person reports had been filed. All were of indeterminate age with no signs of illness or disease. And, in each instance, the victim's mouth had been filled with a holy wafer of the kind used in the Catholic Eucharist, then sewn shut.

Daguerreotypes of the scene, along with images of the victims had been taken and, after much arguing, I eventually persuaded the detective to let me view them. I wish I hadn't.

Death is a familiar part of life. We have all seen departed family members laid out for burial, but to see bodies treated in such an unholy way was shocking.

I pored over the images until I no longer flinched. But, while even the oldest paintings are imprinted with the soul-songs of artist and sitter, these images would not sing.

For a while I despaired. It seemed that the detective expected some kind of magic from me, but without the music as my guide, I felt lost. Still, I reminded myself that I had more than one gift. I was well-schooled, sharp-eyed, and quick-witted.

The spike used to impale the latest victim had been found high on the muddy banks of our city's great river—the Thames. This seemed a sensible precaution. The river is tidal. Its waters flow cold and fast, washing away anything or anyone caught in its path. The wharves and river walls would also throw up enough shadow to hide the monster's grizzly work. It was there, stamped in the black slime of the polluted river, that I found my first piece of tangible evidence. There, amongst the chaos of feet coming and going, amongst all those heavy police boots and workman's hobnails. An imprint that was deeper than the rest, as though its owner had been carrying something heavy.

The closer I looked, the more singular the foot-prints seemed: wide, with a round toe and heel and a smooth sole. It took me a while to identify them as sand shoes. The imprints were small, too, which struck me as even more remarkable.

The victims' bodies had all been found upstream. As heavy objects will sink into the mud, whoever our murderer was, had to be strong enough to throw the bodies into the deepest part of the flow. Yet the prints did not match the character of someone large and well-muscled. No, our monster was surprisingly petite. A gentleman—or woman—certainly, for sand shoes are expensive. Furthermore, the rubber on the soles of this type of beach wear scuff easily, becoming pitted as grains work themselves into the tread. These soles were not worn, so the shoes had been bought recently. Nor could the owner have walked very far without the proof of it being found on the soles.

The latest spike and its sickening appendage had been discovered near the York Watergate. This grand stone arch leads directly into the Thames, and dates from a time when London's most desirable residences on the Strand used the river for their everyday travel.

So here were my clues. Someone petite but athletic, with a penchant for expensive shoes, and a possible link to London's high society. It wasn't much, but it was enough to give our investigation a starting point. Had I had been able to hear my own soul song, I felt sure it would have been playing a merry jig as I reported my findings to the detective with an unfamiliar rush of pride.

⚡   ⚡   ⚡   ⚡

While the detective's colleagues did what he called the 'legwork,' questioning shop-keepers and checking their records for sales of sand shoes, we headed to the scene of the crime. I'm embarrassed to say that the phrase gave me a distinct thrill.

Between the Strand and the riverside can be found the homes of some of England's great noble families. Nearest to Temple Bar, the Devereuxes, Earls of Essex; then the Howards, of the ducal family of Norfolk; then the Cecils, Earls of Salisbury and Exeter; then the Percy family, Dukes of Northumberland; and finally the Villiers, Dukes of Buckingham. The York Watergate is also known as the Buckingham Gate as it carries the family crest, so it was to the home of this illustrious family that we headed.

The Strand has ever been a busy thoroughfare linking, as it does, the City of London with the City of Westminster. But for all the crush of people, carriages, and horses, I find it one of the most beautiful parts of our great metropolis. The houses, theatres, taverns, and churches that line this stretch of riverside carry with them the weight of history. Some are wooden, wattle and thatch, dating back to the time of Shakespeare. Others, built with white Italian stone in Greek style, are from the time of King Charles. In between, it seems like the whole world has come to trade their wares. There are butchers, bakers, bookbinders, tailors, and merchants dealing in all manner of exotic items from Africa to the Indies. Yet what I really love is the most surprising aspect of this grand trunk road. Should you glance through the alleys and lanes that gently slope down towards Old Father Thames, you will catch glimpses of a myriad of bridges, hop-scotching across the river. And, in the distance, boats, barges, and patchwork meadows where cattle graze and windmill sails gently spin in the breeze. It is all quite beautiful, in a crowded and dirty sort of way.

* * * *

The new Duke of Buckingham isn't exactly what Mama would call a social butterfly. Little is known of him, and few have seen him since the previous duke's sudden death last year. By all accounts he was a very distant relative and even the scandal sheets have been unable to discover anything of note about his origins or habits.

Considering the gruesome cargo which had been laid on the ducal doorstep, the detective didn't feel the need to arrange an appointment. Instead, we announced ourselves at the door and were ushered into the day room where we waited, with some trepidation, for the duke to receive us.

"Between me and you Miss Kitty," the detective whispered, "this is the worst part of the job. These old families have more skeletons in the cupboard than waistcoats. It has a tendency to make them difficult where the law is concerned. We'll need to play this very carefully."

The duke materialized—that really was the only way to describe it—a few moments later, preceded by the butler who drew the drapes and left us in the peculiar half-light of a summer day filtered through heavy velvet.

With the duke's arrival, the detective's soul song suddenly spiked. It was the musical equivalent of the hairs on the back of your neck prickling. This was so odd it took me some time to realize that, now the butler had retreated, it was the only music I could hear.

I kept my peace while the duke played host, offering tea and refreshments. At first I was so unnerved I could barely hear what was being said. Finally, I shook myself awake and began to take stock.

The detective ran through a series of questions about the victim whose head had been used to make such a terrible riverside ornament. The duke replied to each query in a quavering whisper, stopping occasionally to adjust his chair, gradually turning away from the windows so that his form was eventually enveloped in deep shadow. He apologized, claiming a sensitivity to the light. I didn't believe him, nor, I thought, did the detective. Although I could hear his voice, steady and respectful, the wavering notes of his soul song told a different story.

I sat searching for some answer to this weird turn of events but could find nothing to explain what was happening. I could see His Grace's pale hands twitching in the half-light. Could sense his discomfort—but only in the usual way that one sentient being senses the distress of another. Beyond that was a sickening emptiness.

The duke had no soul song at all!

The detective finally exhausted his questions and rose to leave as the duke remained seated. I jumped out of my chair—a little inelegantly if truth be told—for I was eager to be away from this eerie nothingness.

As we reached the door Detective Anderson suddenly asked, "Why here? Why do you suppose he choose to leave his trophy here?"

I suspected the question wasn't occasioned by any sudden insight. I wasn't even sure that it was directed at His Grace. The detective merely seemed to be thinking out loud, but My Lord Duke did answer.

"Why, it's a warning of course. What else could it be?"

The detective stopped in his tracks. "I'm sorry, Your Grace? A warning from whom? Do you fear for your life?" But it was clear that the duke had also spoken his thoughts out loud and wasn't about to repeat his comments. So, with more questions than answers, we left Buckingham Hall, emerging on the Strand, where I was pleased to welcome back the deafening buzz of humanity's song.

✗   ✗   ✗   ✗

The area west of the Strand is being cleared to make way for a great public square, to be named Trafalgar for Nelson's famous battle, and I found myself bobbing through the crowds that such works inevitably create. As we walked, the detective could hardly contain his excitement.

"A warning. Damn! Sorry, Miss Kitty," he apologized. "Why didn't I think that? It's so obvious."

I was practically cantering to keep up with his long stride, but he seemed oblivious to my predicament.

"And you, Miss Kitty? You've been awfully quiet. What insights can you give us? Anything you can think of which might help us keep the duke alive?"

"Ah, that's the problem, you see," I finally answered, red-faced with the effort of keeping pace in skirts and heeled boots. "I've been thinking it through and there's only one explanation. He's not, you see—the duke. He's not alive at all."

"What?" The detective stopped in his tracks and looked at me as though I had lost my mind.

"It's true. And you know it too. Or at least part of you does." I explained about the soul song. The duke's and his own. How his music had responded to the abomination of a walking, talking dead man. He listened in silence, hummed, then turned and resumed walking, if anything faster and with more purpose than before.

We crossed the square towards Admiralty Arch, where the detective left me for a moment to speak to his colleagues at Great Scotland Yard. Then we retraced our steps and turned towards the church at St Martin's-in-the-Field whose Roman frontage—once hidden behind mean little watch-houses and squalid alleyways—was slowly re-emerging from the clearances, like a phoenix from the flames.

Without a word, the detective hailed a cab. It was one of the new two-seater hansoms, where the driver sits to the rear. The hatch in the roof was open, allowing the detective to direct the driver to the British Museum. It was my first time in such a carriage—Mama considers them indecent—and the ride was agreeably smooth, although too loud over cobbles to talk.

The detective handed our fare through the hatch, which was the signal for the doors to be unlocked. Thus released, I followed the detective into the King's Library, feeling for all the world like a fully-fledged police inspector and not a young girl horribly out of her depth.

✗   ✗   ✗   ✗

The Library, which occupies the ground floor of the Museum's new East Wing, was not open to the public, but it appeared C-Division had privileged access. The space contains the personal collection of George III, comprising books, pamphlets, and assorted maps and charts. Detective Anderson was clearly in his element, pulling files from boxes, and ordering subordinates to bring him maps.

Finally, I could take it no longer. "For heaven's sake, Detective. What's obvious? What have I missed?"

"Oh, my dear Miss, please forgive me. I get like this when the chase is on. The duke spoke of this as a warning, which implies he knows the murderer. Indeed, for all his denials, I'll stake my reputation that he knew the other victims, too. And your clue—the sand shoes...." He motioned to the map. The spikes had been placed in a rough circle around Covent Garden.

"But the victims? You said they weren't society people. They were recluses."

"Indeed. Just like the duke himself. But all four were wealthy men.

Where do wealthy men like to spend their evenings: the Garden. Covent Garden, home of the Theatre Royal and other, shall we say, less savory entertainments."

"Oh," I said, blushing.

Detective Anderson didn't seem to notice my embarrassment and continued in the same frank way. "Even recluses have their vices. Let us suppose that these men shared more than the manner of their deaths. They were members of some secret society, perhaps? A modern-day Hell Fire Club? But the manner of their deaths... why warn your victims? No, not a warning, but a threat...." He trailed off as though tangled in his own reasoning, then continued. "I have my men checking with the Theatre and the hawkers around the Garden. Maybe someone knows more about the victims and their habits than we've been able to glean from their loyal retainers. We're also cross-checking the list of sand shoe purchases against members of the Theatre's troupe."

"An acrobat?" I asked, catching his enthusiasm.

"I suspect so. Although if we're correct, then we don't need a name. Our murderer clearly has at least one more victim on his list—the duke. Which means we have a chance to catch him in the act."

"But the duke," I spluttered. "What about the duke?" The very thought of that unnatural creature filled me with horror.

"He's a puzzle and no mistake. Are you sure you heard nothing? He seemed unwell. Maybe..."

I cut him off with a firm shake of my head.

"Well, Miss, I've known stranger things, but he's an Englishman and a peer of the realm. It's my job to ensure his safety. Now, strictly speaking, I should send you home." I frowned and he offered me a reassuring smile. "But don't worry, Miss, I wouldn't dream of it. That's assuming you would like to be in on the kill?"

The phrase made me feel distinctly unwell, but I was determined not to play the fainting damsel now. Not when the detective had allowed me a glimpse into a much bigger world than I had ever imagined. I eagerly agreed.

"Superb. I was hoping you'd be game, but..." and here he stooped low and fixed me with a steely stare, "...one thing. You must do exactly what I say. When I say. No heroics. You are not to risk yourself in any way. Am I clear?"

His soul song was strong and steady but running deep was a refrain that I hadn't heard before. It was a note that was low, discordant, and hinted at things hidden and dangerous. For the first time since this impossible adventure began, I felt afraid.

✗ ✗ ✗ ✗

I told Mama I would be staying with Tilly for the week, helping her plan a coming-out ball for her cousin. It felt wicked to deceive her so, but it was not a compete falsehood. I *would* be staying with Tilly, and we *would* be planning the ball but, between sun-set and sun-up, I would be part of the detective's team. My job was to give him advance warning, as only I could, as to when our murderer was near.

Upon our arrival at the duke's residence, the butler informed us that His Grace would be remaining in his private quarters until our investigation was concluded. I had no idea where that might be. The house was large, dusty, and full of locked doors and shuttered windows. For all I knew, he slept in a coffin in the family crypt. The very lack of his presence disturbed me, I think, more than if he had been lurking in the shadows watching us work.

For the first two nights, nothing untoward happened. It was on the third night, when I was beginning to worry we had missed something, that I heard it. A soul song so jarring, so utterly wrong, that I almost cried out. Instead, I grabbed the detective by the arm and nodded in the direction of the day room.

He nodded his reply and, motioning me to stay, began to creep towards the room where we had first encountered our not quite dear-departed duke.

Now, I know I made a promise. I'm ashamed to say I broke it without a second's thought. I followed the detective.

I was only moments behind him. The door was still ajar, and I squeezed through the gap as quietly as I could. The music was deafening now. Its roaring, lurching tune sounded exactly like a fairground steam organ. But there was something else, too. Beneath the tumult, something else sang, quiet and gentle. It was almost lost in the chaos, but I could hear it all the same and—with a rush—I knew what it was.

My thoughts were interrupted by the sudden flare of a lantern. And there we were. Myself, still beside the door. The detective in a comical half-crouch about four feet ahead of me. And our beast. Little more than a boy, really—flushed and fevered—the open window behind him, his frightened face illuminated by the glow of the lamp.

For a moment he just blinked at us, then he raised the lamp as though to throw it. The detective took aim with a small, strange-looking pistol.

I could hear it now, the music of violence, of fear and, while I should have waited, I was here to do a job. I would never forgive myself if I let the detective shoot an innocent man.

"Stop!" My voice sounded clear and strong, 'though I was shaking enough to make my shadow waver. The detective spun 'round and, as he did so, our would-be murderer hurled the lamp at him. The detective batted it away, swearing loudly—and the boy was on him. He moved like quicksilver—like a dancer—leaping the distance between them effortlessly. His legs hit the detective full in the chest, and they both went sprawling.

The detective rolled, trying to use his weight and size to trap his assailant. The boy was too fast. He bounded to his feet, using the prone detective as a springboard to propel himself towards the door. I noticed his feet and their dainty little sand shoes as he landed just a few inches in front of me. For a moment we locked eyes, then I made a beginner's mistake. I lunged forward, arms flailing. As I struggled to keep my balance, he slipped past me, out into the hall.

I grabbed the detective's pistol and gave chase.

His music was like a beacon, but he ran like the very Devil. By the time I'd reached the stairs, he was already on the first floor. I could hear him pounding across the creaking floorboards. There was a deadly purpose in his tread. He seemed to know exactly where he was going.

I made to follow him but, by then, the detective was at my elbow, hissing for me to stop. Despite the warm night air, there was something about his voice that chilled me to the bone.

I turned. For a moment everything froze. Towering over me, yellow eyes burning in the gloom, his face horribly deformed into that of a snarling beast, hands now gigantic paws tipped with glinting claws, stood the detective no longer. In his place was the likeness of a huge vulpine. What I saw shocked me, but his soul song still rang true. Stronger and more dangerous—yes—but as reassuring as ever.

He bounded the stairs three steps at a time, myself tripping after, head reeling, following both songs with a sense of rising panic. I was even more sure now of what I suspected. I needed to stop this before things got bloody.

I was breathless by the time I hit the landing. Ahead, I could hear the unmistakable sound of wood breaking and splintering and that terrible music twisting, like a trapped snake.

I heard the call of a not-quite wolf, then silence.

When I reached the room, the fevered young man was by the bed, eyeing the detective warily. The detective's music was still steady, but I could feel the strain of those darker notes beneath, trying to break free. I didn't know how much longer he would be able to hold them back.

I followed the youth's eyes and, and—by the Lord—on the bed was the duke. In his coffin.

✗ ✗ ✗ ✗

I understood it all now. Though I didn't know the full story, I had enough. I could hear the young man's curse. The thing he was fighting. The thing that had wound itself around his soul so tightly it threatened to silence his music forever. And I could hear the detective's curse, too. Could hear how he had muffled its notes—confined them inside the metered song of his own soul. And it gave me hope.

"Detective, please listen to me," I said with slow deliberation. "There is only one victim here, and this young man is it. Right now, he fights for his soul just as you fight for yours."

The detective looked from me to the young man. I could see that my words had struck a chord, but I could see, too, how hard it was for him—for them both—to hold back the terrible demons which had them in their thrall.

The young man moved. Just a small shift but, in that instant, I thought it was all over. The detective roared and leapt forward. The two men clashed with a snarl, their music rising to a crescendo of fury. The young man retreated. His music demanded blood, but he held it back. Held himself back. The detective edged forward. His body tensed, readying itself to strike, his music throbbing and dark. I knew what I had to do.

I ran. I ran as if my life depended on it—as if three lives depended on it—and I placed myself exactly where I had promised I wouldn't. Directly in harm's way.

I stood between them, my voice calming. "Don't!" I said. "This boy is not the enemy. Come back to me!"

The detective took a series of deep breaths. One, two, his body shaking with effort. Three, four, a howl, a strangled half-human cry. The boy held himself steady, as one might when faced with a savage dog whose actions could erupt into ferocity at any moment.

Finally, the detective's silhouette began to shrink until I was once again looking at the face of my own dear Dougie Anderson.

When he spoke, it was with difficulty. He looked at the youngster, poised over the unconscious figure of the duke. "This beast and its kin have passed their curse to you, is that it?"

The boy nodded frantically.

"How was it done?"

"I can not tell," he answered, shaking with the effort of keeping his own monster at bay. "I danced for them. A private party. I remember how odd it was. They arrived in bathchairs, pushed by attendants, swaddled like old men. But my dancing somehow seemed to lift them. Feed them, almost. By the end they were dancing with me, laughing like drunkards although they hadn't touched any of the wine laid out. And, after, I was so dreadfully tired. I slept and slept. It was when I finally had my strength back that the nightmares started. They were calling me." He trailed off, looking lost, then continued with a shudder. "For months, I danced for them, and I slept. That was all. I knew that inch by inch, I was losing myself. That soon, I would be one with them. So I fought back. I thought that one death would be warning enough. That they would leave me alone. Release me from whatever compulsion they had lain on me. But they call to me still. The nightmare never ends...."

"Do you know what these beasts are?"

He shrugged, looking, even younger, even more helpless. "The gypsies who ply their trade in the Garden spin wild stories. There's a grain of truth in those, I hope."

"And it's release you're after?"

A nod.

"Is he the last one?"

Another nod.

"Then do what needs to be done. If their deaths will free you then, in conscience, I can not deny you what I myself have so longed for. Besides, tho' I'm an officer of the law, you can not murderer a dead man." He looked at me and I grimaced back in agreement. Whatever this thing in the coffin was, it was an affront against God Himself. We would be committing no crime by making an end to it.

⚔ ⚔ ⚔ ⚔

I heard it instantly. It was as though someone had taken the detective's soul song and stretched it thin. He gasped, staggering back, as the pale figure in the coffin rose, like a puppet on strings, surveying the room with a cold smile.

I could feel it. His emptiness. His hunger. There was death here. Not the duke's unnatural sleep, but true death: for the detective, for the boy. I could hear their soul music slowing, evaporating. Even the dancer's whirring, twisting tune began to falter.

I did not know if I was immune, or the monster simply hadn't seen me, but I did know what I had to do. The detective's pistol was still in my hand. A strange thing, with a short, rounded barrel. I aimed and pulled the trigger. The barrel spun, the pistol flared, and the room filled with the smell of powder.

He moved so impossibly quickly that I felt his touch before I saw him. I tried to pull away, but the duke's icy hands were on me—gripping my shoulders so tightly I could not escape. He was still smiling, his skin glowing with a strange opalescence, his eyes wide and unblinking.

I didn't know if the gun carried more than one shot, but I wound the little ratchet as far as it would go. At this distance, the barrel was practically touching the duke's belly. If it did fire, it could well explode and kill us both. I pulled the trigger anyway—and prayed.

There was a flash, the pistol bucked, a click-click sounded as its barrel spun. I carried on pulling the trigger until it clicked no more. The duke's grip never faltered, but my friend's soul song slowly returned to normal. And beside it came another song—no longer that sickening fairground parody—but light and joyous.

Finally, the terrible creature relaxed its grip, its eyes filmed over, and it toppled like a tree too old and rotten to stand any longer. I would like to have said that his face, in that final moment, carried some sign of release, of redemption, but it's not true.

Beside me the detective shuddered, brought his full six foot one inches upright and looked at me with a strained smile. "Well, Miss Kitty, I'm very glad you are not the sort of lady who takes orders." He stopped, then shook his head as if he were still fighting the fog in his mind created by his fearful symbiont. "And now you have the answer to your earlier question. I hope that it won't…. What I mean to say is that C-Division is grateful for your assistance and we—I—hope that this evening's events have not colored your perception…."

I stopped him with a raised hand. We had known each other such a short time, but I knew Dougie Anderson was my friend. Nothing would change that. The detective had said everyone had their own reasons for joining C-Division. He had his. And I knew that the thrill of the chase, and the warmth of his friendship, would provide me with mine.

Paula Hammond (@writer_paula) is a professional writer and artist based in Wales. She has been published by Abyss & Apex, Third Flatiron, and Air & Nothingness Press, amongst others. Her fiction has been nominated for the Eugie Award, the Pushcart Prize, and a BSFA award. Paula's new Sherlock Holmes collection, *Eliminate the Impossible*, is available from MX Publishing and all good bookshops.

MINERVA JAMES AND THE GODS OF SLEEP AND DEATH
Mark Bruce

I stared at the woman. I didn't mean to be rude. But she was supposed to be dead.

She didn't notice me. She sat at the café table with a handsome young man, laughing and giving him fetching looks which probably made him shiver. Her heart-shaped face, her sleepy but clear blue eyes, her button nose, her rosy cheeks—she was a woman for whom you would conquer empires. Or, at least, hold down a steady job and support a brood of kids.

The man's face was young and rugged, a manly face with a muscular body. He reacted to her enthusiastically, his eyes gleaming at the lovely creature in front of him.

We sat two tables away from them. It was August 1963. We were in a small diner off Fulton in Sacramento. My boss, the attorney Minerva James, had me working on a murder case in which our client, Jack Mason, was accused of killing Virginia Chandler, his mistress. Mason's wife Inga, a strident blond Valkyrie, had already forgiven him.

"There was no reason to kill her," she told me in an interview. "I already knew he had strayed. All I asked was that he break it off with her. And he did."

"How do you know?" I asked.

"Because I went with him to do it," she said smugly.

But an eyewitness saw our client throttle the woman with a rope and toss her from the Tower Bridge into the Sacramento River. The river gave up her body within days. Jack Mason sat in jail with no bail.

The woman in the autopsy photos sat laughing and drinking two tables away from me. The dead mistress and the live diner had the same dark mole to the left of her red-lipsticked mouth.

The victim was an only child and her grieving parents had given an angry, bitter interview on KCRA, the local news channel everyone watched. *Our only little girl*, they said through tears, *no one can replace her.*

I stared because I wanted to make sure I wasn't seeing things. From time to time, you think you see someone in a place you don't expect, only to see them from another angle which reveals you've been mistaken.

"Are you okay?" my dinner companion, Arachne, asked. She was a wiry young woman with hair so red it looked like her skull was on fire. Minerva employed her as receptionist/bodyguard.

"Look over there," I said. Arachne casually turned and scanned the room. "Anyone look familiar?"

Arachne gave me a long-suffering look.

"Another one of your conquests out to drown her sorrows in the arms of another man?" she said sarcastically.

"Two tables to your left," I said. Arachne turned and flinched. She looked at me in astonishment.

"It can't be."

"It can't, can it?" I asked.

"What do you think we should do?" Arachne said.

"Go over and ask her?" I shrugged.

"Sure," she said, leaning back. "Let's just go over and say, *Hey, last time I saw you, you were dead. What happened?*"

"When you put it like that…."

The couple stood. The handsome man put a coat over the formerly dead woman. They continued to laugh as if their young lives stretched invitingly before them.

I pulled out my Canon SLR and snapped a quick shot at the departing couple. As an investigator, I was rarely without a camera and was smart enough to load it with ASA 400, which can take photos indoors without a flash.

"Did you get her?" Arachne said anxiously.

"We'll see when I develop this," I said.

"Won't Jack Mason be surprised to find out he didn't kill anyone after all?" Arachne mused.

⚔ ⚔ ⚔ ⚔

At the law office of Minerva James an hour later, the three of us stood in a spare bathroom which doubled as a darkroom. The pictures from my camera emerged with a puzzle that stumped even the most notorious lawyer in Sacramento.

"It certainly looks like her," the Boss said, holding the wet black and white photo over the finishing tray with both hands. In the red light of the darkroom, her curly black hair resembled a dark halo. Her long patrician nose and sternly beautiful face took on a weird patina.

"A dead ringer, if you'll pardon the pun," I said.

"It's a good thing Arachne was with you, Mr. Robinson," Minerva said. "You tend to go overboard sometimes, but Arachne is a hard-headed woman. Both of you agreeing that this mystery woman was identical to the victim, and this photo…well, it makes one think."

"Do you think we're being sold a bill of goods, and the mistress is not really dead?" I asked. Minerva sighed.

"The autopsy photos will argue against that."

"A Doppelganger?"

"It has been known to happen." Minerva looked again at the sleepy-eyed beauty in the photo. "Sleep and Death. In ancient Greece they were twin brothers. Hypnos and Thanatos."

"But the mistress had no twin, according to the parents," I said.

Minerva looked pensively at the photo.

"I need you to check some records, Mr. Robinson," she said.

✗   ✗   ✗   ✗

Two days later I slunk into Minerva's L Street office. She had given me a simple assignment. I couldn't get it done.

"The records are confidential," I said.

"Confidential? Are you sure?" Minerva asked from across her enormous black walnut desk. The papers on the desk ebbed and flowed like the Pacific Ocean. As always, *53 Cal Reports 2nd* sat on a corner of the desk, a black revolver place-marking a case.

"I was there a full day," I said. "I talked to supervisor after supervisor. The birth records for Virginia Chandler are confidential. Only the family can open them."

"And?" she said, arching an eyebrow at me.

"And the Chandlers are not cooperating. So. No records."

"Excellent," Minerva said, sitting back in her leather executive chair.

"Excellent?" I asked. "I ran into a dead end."

"I suspected as much. It makes this a bit clearer for me." She pulled out the Mason file from the tide of papers as if by magic. "I see we're going into preliminary hearing tomorrow. I will need you to come with me, Mr. Robinson."

"Always at your disposal, O Goddess," I said. "Can I ask why?"

"I think you will know when the prelim starts," she said.

✗   ✗   ✗   ✗

Dr. Albert Kahn, Sacramento County Coroner, was on the stand. He was a thin man with a wispy moustache and horn-rimmed glasses. He gave evidence that the victim bore the tell-tale signs of rope burns on her neck, which led to strangulation. He spared us the photos of the autopsy, as it was only a preliminary hearing.

Deputy D.A. Mark Case, an earnest young blond man with dark eyes, smiled in satisfaction as if he'd performed the autopsy himself. He sat at counsel table like the Cheshire Cat sat waiting for Alice in the tree. I was surprised he didn't disappear behind his smile.

Minerva, dressed in a pearl white skirt and jacket, blood-red blouse, and white scarf, arose slowly. She stood five foot eleven in her flats (she never wore high heels), and her slow rising reminded me of a goddess manifesting herself to a hapless mortal.

"Dr. Kahn," she said, "you've testified as to rope burns on the victim's throat."

"Consistent with being strangled by a garrote," he volunteered.

"That is not the only possibility," Minerva said.

Dr. Kahn looked at her in puzzlement.

"It is consistent with the statement of the eyewitness," he said.

Minerva smiled.

"Doctor, you and I know that a medical analysis is best not tainted by outside information unless absolutely necessary." Minerva had been an Army nurse during the Korean War.

"No," he said slowly. "True, it is the better practice not to base your opinion on something someone else says."

"And in truth, all you can reasonably state is that the strangulation was caused by a rope about the victim's neck," she said.

"I don't see the difference," Dr. Kahn said.

"There are other ways one can die with a rope around one's neck than by garrote," she said.

Dr. Kahn seemed to consider this.

"You are correct, madame," he said.

"And there was nothing in the rope burns that indicated that the injury had to be a garrote rather than another method," Minerva said.

"I agree, madame."

Minerva nodded.

"Dr. Kahn," she continued, "I'm curious about the mole on the victim's face."

"Yes, quite perplexing," Dr. Kahn said.

"Because?" Minerva said, with a tone that indicated she already knew the answer.

"Because it was artificial. It was one of those false beauty marks one can buy at a cosmetics counter. The victim had placed it on her face with glue."

"Ah," Minerva said. "So, the beauty mark was not natural."

"No. My guess is she placed it there to make herself look more alluring."

"Thank you, Doctor. No further questions."

⚹　⚹　⚹　⚹

The Boss' cross examination of the coroner didn't seem devastating. Sure, you could die a hundred other ways with a rope around your neck. Sure, Victoria Chandler was a vain woman who altered what nature gave her to look more alluring. But the D.A. had an eyewitness, as Dr. Kahn stated. Deputy D.A. Mark Case called that witness with the panache of a magician performing a new trick.

"The People call Harold Thomas," he said.

I turned to see the witness enter the courtroom and nearly fell out of my chair. Striding up the aisle was the handsome man who dined with the dead girl last night.

Minerva turned to me with a knowing look.

"I assume this gentleman looks familiar to you," she said. I nodded dumbly.

Harold Thomas raised his right hand and took the oath to tell the truth. His earnest dark eyes and hard jaw were convincing, even though I knew he was about to lie.

"Mr. Thomas, do you know the defendant?" Deputy D.A. Case said.

"I've only seen him once," Harold said.

"You don't socialize with him?"

"No. I only know his name because his picture has been in the papers."

"Can you tell the court about the first time you ever saw him?"

"It was on the Tower Bridge."

"When was this?"

"About a month ago. It was late at night."

"How late?"

"Two in the morning."

"Can you tell us what you saw?"

"I saw the defendant and a young lady. They appeared to be struggling. At first, I thought he had his hands around her neck. But then I saw the rope. He was strangling her with a rope! Then she sagged. I knew she was dead. He lifted her up and threw her into the river."

Harold paused. He put his face in his hands.

"And you're sure it was the defendant."

"Yes."

"Did you know the young lady he killed?"

"Objection," Minerva said. "Facts not in evidence as to 'killed'."

Deputy D.A. Case gave her a long-suffering look. But the judge sustained the objection.

"Did you know the young lady you saw him struggle with that night?" Deputy D.A. Case corrected himself.

"Not at the time. But I saw her picture in the paper when they took her out of the river. It was the same person."

Deputy D.A. Case walked up to Harold, a picture in his hand.

"Is this the young lady?"

Harold studied the photo, as if to be sure.

"Yes, that's her. She was quite pretty, wasn't she?"

"No further questions."

Minerva studied Harold a full minute before she began questioning him. I noticed she held the photo I took last night.

"It was two a.m.?" Minerva asked without preamble.

"I have insomnia. I often take walks at night. I live near the Tower Bridge."

Minerva nodded. His explanation was a bit too neat.

"And you saw a man struggling with a woman."

"Your client," he said.

"You didn't cry out or try to stop him?"

"It happened so fast. I wasn't sure of what I was seeing at first."

"Where were you?"

"I was on the other side of the bridge. About a hundred feet from them."

"In the dark."

"There are lights on the bridge."

"Foggy?"

Harold hesitated. Everyone in Sacramento knew that the river often raised fog early in the morning.

"I can't remember," he finally lied. You'd remember if it was foggy or not. It could easily be disproved by looking at the weather reports for that date.

But Minerva didn't call him on it. Instead, she stood and regarded him calmly.

"May I approach the witness?" she asked. "I would like to have this photo marked number one for the defense." She gave the photo to the clerk for marking.

"Proceed," the judge said. Minerva briefly showed the photo to Deputy D.A. Case, who looked at it in surprise.

"Your Honor, I haven't seen this before," he said.

"Impeachment," Minerva murmured.

"If it is for purposes of impeachment, she is not obligated to share it with you before prelim, under the court rules," the judge said. "Proceed, Miss James."

During this colloquy, Harold had been looking curiously at Minerva and Deputy D.A. Case. Case now glared at his witness. Even the most arrogant D.A. does not like to be duped.

"Mr. Thomas, I am going to show you a photograph." She placed it in front of him on the witness stand. "I wonder if you could confirm that you are the gentleman in the photo."

Harold looked curiously down at the picture, then flushed bright red. He looked at Minerva threateningly.

"You witch!" he said.

"I am often called *the Witch of L Street*," she said lightly. "However, the only magic here is the magic of photography. That is you in the photo, is it not?"

"Yes," he said begrudgingly.

"And the young lady in the photo?"

"A friend."

"Not merely a friend. I have a witness who will testify that you and the young lady are intimately acquainted. In fact, affianced. Correct?"

"How did you know that?" he said, rising with his fists balled.

"Sit down!" the judge bellowed. The bailiff had already jumped from his chair and charged toward the witness stand. He stopped when the judge raised his palm. Harold sat back down.

"And the mole on the young lady's face. It's real, is it not?"

"You know it is, you witch," he hissed.

"Unlike the unfortunate girl who came out of the river, whose mole was a fake beauty mark."

"I don't know how you did this," he growled.

Minerva turned to me.

"Mr. Robinson, Arachne is waiting outside with a witness I subpoenaed. I wonder if you could retrieve them for me?"

I walked to the rear of the courtroom and opened the door to find Arachne holding the arm of the dead girl. The dead girl didn't look too happy.

"Come on in," I said.

Arachne forcibly escorted the young lady into the room. Harold saw her and broke down weeping.

The judge jumped from his chair. Deputy D.A. Case yelped in surprise. Even the bailiff and clerk started.

"This," Minerva said to Harold, "is Virginia Chandler, correct?"

Harold, through his sobs, merely nodded. The court reporter was so stunned she didn't admonish him to make a verbal response.

"And the young woman who was found in the river was her twin, correct?"

He nodded again.

"What in the hell is going on?" the judge asked.

"For an explanation, I would ask the court to allow me to take a witness out of order."

✗ ✗ ✗ ✗

Virginia Chandler, very much alive, sat disconsolately in the witness box, frown lines on her lovely face, her eyes glowing with anger.

"You were adopted," Minerva said to Virginia.

"Yes."

"And you had a twin who was not adopted by the same parents."

"Yes."

"You found this out because you looked into your adoption, as you are allowed to do when you turn eighteen," Minerva said. "But you did not tell your adoptive parents."

"They didn't need to know. It was kind of exciting keeping this secret from them."

"But your twin—"

"Her name was Linda."

"Very well. Linda, she was not a happy person."

Virginia hung her head.

"No. I learned she suffered from severe depression. I had hoped that by reconnecting I could help her, but in the end it didn't matter."

"Linda hung herself."

"Yes. I'm told that people who are severely depressed will sometimes commit suicide."

"And she did this about the time that Mr. Mason and his wife confronted you and told you his affair with you was over."

Virginia's brow reddened and her mouth drew taut.

"It was humiliating. They treated me like I was a piece of meat, an insect."

"Yet you had been misleading Mr. Mason as to your own situation," Minerva said.

"Yes."

"You were going to marry Harold Thomas while you were carrying on the affair with Mr. Mason."

A small smile crept onto Virginia's face.

"Harold said that so long as Mason kept giving me expensive presents, why not?"

"So when the affair was terminated, you needed to punish Mr. Mason?"

Silence. She glared at Minerva.

"It was so humiliating," she repeated.

"You found your twin sister's body not long after the humiliating interview with Mr. Mason and his wife," Minerva said.

"Yes. A few days later."

"That's when you decided to put a fake mole on her face and dump her into the river."

She stared at her lap. "Yes. I am ashamed to say, that's how we treated my poor sister."

"And when the police didn't make the connection between the body and Mr. Mason, Mr. Thomas decided to prod them into that direction."

Virginia shook her head.

"I just wanted Jack to see her picture in the paper and feel awful thinking I'd killed myself over him. I didn't want him to face murder charges. But Howard…"

"Howard wanted to punish him further."

"I think he was jealous after all. Can you blame him?"

Minerva didn't answer that question.

✗　✗　✗　✗

"Birth certificates are only confidential if there's an adoption," Minerva said. She was sitting behind her enormous desk in the L Street office on the 10th floor.

"How did you know there were twins?"

"As your hero Sherlock Holmes said, when you eliminate the impossible, whatever is left, however improbable, is the truth," she replied. "One girl clearly had died. Another was clearly alive. The only explanation was twins."

"How did you know where to find the living girl?"

"Howard's address was in the police report. I assumed Virginia wouldn't go back home so long as everyone believed she was dead. Howard's apartment was the only place she would feel safe. Though they made a shocking error by going out to eat."

"It was just a coincidence that Arachne and I happened to be at the same café," I said.

"Like Sleep and Death, Coincidence and Fate also happen to be twins. And as difficult to tell apart."

She nodded to me in dismissal. Then the Goddess of Wisdom picked up the file of another unfortunate caught in the wheels of justice.

Mark Bruce is a Vietnam-Era Veteran (served in Turkey and Italy) who practices family and criminal law in San Bernardino, California. He won the 2018 Black Orchid Novella Award with Minerva James' first appearance in print, "Minerva James and the Goddess of Justice." Eleven Minerva stories have been published in magazines such as *Alfred Hitchcock's Mystery Magazine* and *Black Cat Mystery Magazine*.

THE SURGEON'S SWINDLE
Jeffrey A. Lockwood

The smell of frying rashers and eggs drifted up from Mrs Hudson's kitchen through our half-open door at the top of the stairs. Holmes was still in his dressing-gown and perusing the agony column of *The Times*. I set down my recent copy of *The Lancet* in which I'd been reading about the outbreak of plague in Bombay and recalling with some nostalgia my first medical posting with the 5th Northumberland Fusiliers in India. We'd pulled our armchairs close to the fire in an effort to stave off the damp chill of February while sleet pattered against the windowpanes of my old quarters on Baker Street.

Holmes sighed and tossed the newspaper onto a pile teetering in a corner of his sitting room. He looked longingly at the sideboard. Knowing my friend and sensing his ennui, as a student of deductive inference I surmised that he was trying to decide whether smoking his before-breakfast pipe or taking a hypo would be more conducive to alleviating the boredom of not having been drawn into an investigation in more than a fortnight. For my part, I'd been without my dear Mary for nearly as long, since she was caring for her mother who'd taken a nasty fall on icy pavement.

As Holmes impassively rose from his chair and reached out—I feared he had chosen the cocaine—there was sharp knock on the door downstairs, followed by a bit of commotion as Mrs Hudson engaged the visitor, and then the sound of heavy footsteps coming upstairs.

Holmes observed, "An urgent matter is coming our way, as the fellow took only twelve of the seventeen steps in his hurry to reach our door."

As if on cue, a tall, almost gaunt man of distinguished bearing appeared in the doorway, lightly brushing the sleet from the shoulders of his overcoat.

"I apologise for arriving unannounced and at such an early hour," he said.

"Come in, sir. You look half-frozen," replied my friend, directing the visitor to sit near the fire. "Who are you and what is your concern on this dreary morning?"

"I am Bartholomew Phillips, but that is of no matter. I am the porter at the Savoy. Mr Winfred Harris, the general manager of the hotel, sent me to solicit your services on what, I am afraid, is a most grave matter."

Holmes cocked an eyebrow, lit his clay pipe, and leaned back into his chair—all of which served to amplify, rather than diminish, the messenger's agitation. "And what can you tell me about this matter?" asked Holmes, puffing languidly.

"Mr Holmes, I am afraid I can say very little, as I have not been informed as to the details. All I know is that Mr Harris wanted me to bring you to the Savoy as swiftly as possible," the man said, wringing his hands. "And again, I deeply regret this intrusion, but the matter must be very serious for my employer to convey such unusual urgency." At this point, he lifted his chin slightly and added, "Our establishment is properly known as an establishment of cultivated restraint, if I might be allowed to say so."

I knew the Savoy as a place of exceptional cost and commensurate service, at least from what I'd been told. I had fleetingly considered it as a possibility for the first night of my honeymoon but decided that the funds would be better put toward new furnishings.

Holmes replied, "I have consulted for Mr Harris in the past, and he is a dependable and stable fellow with little propensity for alarm. I cannot commit to taking the case with so little information but am willing to look further into the matter. If you will give us a few minutes to dress, Dr Watson and I will join you downstairs."

"But of course," our visitor said bowing gracefully and making his exit.

Soon enough we were in the Savoy's landau, by which the hotel normally transported its most important guests from the train stations. On the way, Holmes explained that he'd solved the theft of an exquisite yellow sapphire from a wealthy Ceylonese tea merchant staying at The Langham, where Mr Harris had been previously employed as the manager. The case had turned on Holmes noticing that the thief left behind even more valuable gemstones and deduced that the culprit understood the great importance of the sapphire to Hindoo astrology. From this, Holmes surmised the thief sought the favour of a celebrated swami, living in London at the time. And this chain of deduction led Holmes to a small group of suspects who, upon clever questioning, were induced to identify the thief in their midst.

Holmes finished his story as the coach stopped at a discreet entrance at the back of the hotel, where we were met by Mr Harris, a portly and distinguished but plainly anxious gentleman in a dapper grey suit. He was accompanied by a man who introduced himself as Mr Chapman, the hotel detective. The physical opposite of the hotel manager, Chapman was clad in an understated heather tweed suit which hung loosely on his lanky frame.

The two men bowed obsequiously to guests as we passed through the lobby and hastened up a back stairwell. Harris and Chapman provided a hurried account of the crime scene. The unusual and disturbing details of bloodshed, a missing victim's strange instructions, and shattered insect specimens were entirely sufficient to pique Holmes's interest, and by the time we reached the third floor I had no doubt he'd take the case.

Mr Harris glanced in both directions down the hallway as Mr Chapman let us into an opulent suite with twelve-foot ceilings and gilded crown moulding in the foyer. I was admiring the crystal chandelier and marble floor when Holmes firmly directed us to wait while he inspected the bedroom. The hotel detective held out a pair of linen gloves to Holmes.

"No, thank you. I prefer to utilise all my senses," Holmes replied.

Chapman continued to hold out the gloves. "The occupant of this room left a message stating that the maid should use such gloves or wash afterwards with dilute carbolic acid. The hotel had a few gloves but no carbolic acid readily available. Shall I show you the note?"

"Not until I've made my observations," my friend answered. "I do not wish to form any premature theory. Unbiased observations are crucial to reliable deductive reasoning."

Chapman looked perplexed and shrugged.

With that, Holmes reluctantly tugged on the gloves and entered the room. From the doorway, I could see that beside an elegant writing desk lay a smashed insect display and the fragmented remains of a large butterfly. But the bed on the other side of the room riveted my attention. The pale blue silk sheets were soaked in blood, yet no body lay there.

While I contemplated the violence responsible for the grim scene, Holmes systematically examined the shattered insect display, taking careful measurements and placing the butterfly remains into one of the hotel's stationery envelopes from the desktop. Humming quietly, he then took a series of measurements of slight depressions in the carpet before working his way to the bed. I recognised the tune as Mendelssohn's Violin Concerto in E minor, which Holmes had played for me earlier in the week in recompense after I'd suffered through an hour of his trifling glumly on the fiddle thrown across his knee. Holmes dropped to all fours and crawled to the bathroom where he spent several minutes before striding slowly across the room and rejoining us in the entryway.

"Before we continue, I have two questions," he said.

"Please," said Harris with cultivated politeness.

"First, the obvious query. With such dreadful circumstances in one of your hotel rooms, why did you not call the police?"

"That would be the normal course of affairs," said Harris, "but in this case there were overriding considerations. In particular, the note to which Mr Chapman referred."

"Yes, of course. I would like to see that now." The hotel detective pulled an envelope from his inner coat pocket, removed the note written on the hotel's embossed stationery, and handed it to Holmes. I stood next to him and read along:

> *I apologise for the mess in room 307. Having been a regular guest, I hope you will understand my request for strict confidentiality. The blood is the consequence of a surgical procedure that required a private setting. I will pay for all damages, but I insist your staff wear gloves while cleaning or wash their hands with one-percent carbolic acid. Respectfully,*

The note was written in tiny, meticulous block lettering, except for the signature which was an odd scrawl.

"I suppose the illegible name of the guest is a confidential matter?" asked Holmes.

"For the moment," Harris nodded gravely.

"Well, no matter, I'm quite confident from what I have already learned that he's not the sort of fellow who would use his real name. And am I to understand you chose to believe the guest's explanation and honour his request for secrecy?"

"For the moment," Harris nodded again.

"So what service do you seek from me?" asked Holmes.

"Mr Holmes, the interests of the Savoy are complex, as I'm sure you understand. Of course, the safety, comfort, and privacy of our guests is paramount. But we also have a reputation to uphold, and we have certain insurance and business considerations. For example, we cannot allow criminal activity in our establishment, although these rules can be stretched at times. In short, we wish to know what happened in this room so we can position ourselves accordingly."

"That is what I suspected, Mr Harris. And now the other question, which is much simpler. Did anyone from the hotel staff enter this room before our arrival?"

"No, sir," answered Chapman. "Upon being given the note, I looked into the room from the doorway as we've done now. I left the scene undisturbed until I had spoken with Mr Harris and determined how to proceed. We decided to contact you because of your well-known investigatory skills."

"Well done," said my friend. "You have left intact important evidence which requires keen observational skills and analytical abilities to interpret. Now then, I know what happened in this room. Why it happened is a matter of conjecture which I am not sufficiently confident to share. However, I can reveal what I've concluded through logical synthesis, in light of the available evidence."

"Shall we move to the sitting room?" suggested Harris, gesturing across the entryway. Holmes took a velveteen wingback chair, Harris and Chapman shared a floral print couch, and I leaned against the doorframe, as my old bullet wound still bedeviled my leg when the weather was damp, and standing was oftentimes more agreeable than sitting.

"Let me begin with the shattered insect display case," said Holmes. "Its unusual qualities lead me to posit that the evidence is central to the violent event. I recovered the rather badly fragmented remains of two extraordinarily large butterflies."

"Two?" asked Harris.

"Indeed," replied Holmes. "I would surmise that the display held both a gorgeously coloured individual and a rather drab specimen. Having measured the remains, I would estimate each of the butterflies possessed a wingspan in excess of ten inches."

"That is extraordinary," I said. When I was stationed in India, the villagers outside Hyderabad would catch large colourful butterflies and sell them to wealthy British visitors. Upon returning home, travelers prized them as centerpieces in their curiosity cabinets. But even these exotic creatures didn't reach such proportions.

"While the butterflies are stunning," said Holmes, "what's strange is that the frame of the display case, based on the splintered remains, was only twelve inches wide. The two specimens could not have been mounted in that case."

"No collector would put one butterfly atop of another," I added.

"Precisely, my dear Watson. And while I can appreciate the loss of what were surely rare and valuable specimens, I shall move on to the banality of human violence."

"Yes, please do. From the perspective of the Savoy, this is what matters most," said Harris.

"Of course." Holmes nodded. "There were three men in the room—your guest and two visitors. I know this from the footprints left in the carpet. Your guest, as I presume you are aware, is five feet five inches in height with an average build."

"How did you know?" asked Chapman.

"All too simple, from the clothes in his wardrobe and his footprints. But you might not be aware that he has extraordinarily well-developed, fine motor skills. This is apparent from his flawless, miniscule handwriting, produced even under duress. Furthermore, he uses a straight razor while many have taken to safety razors. Perhaps most revealingly, on the bedside table are gum rubber balls and elastic bands for building hand strength and dexterity."

"Perhaps he is a surgeon?" asked Harris.

"A plausible hypothesis, given his conditioning and knowledge of aseptic practices. However, the evidence points to his having been the patient in this case," answered Holmes.

"Then the other two might have been a doctor and nurse?" tried Chapman.

"One should never let theorising race ahead of observations," said Holmes. "Allow me to walk you through my reasoned inferences."

Chapman gave a slight, apologetic shrug and Harris a distinguished nod.

"Based on the size and depth of the footprints and the stride lengths, one of the men was at least six feet tall and weighed nearly fourteen stone. The other visitor was unusually small, and I initially thought the individual was female, but the shape of the shoe and stride dimensions are consistent with a man standing five feet and weighing perhaps eight stone, eight pounds. It was this fellow who straddled your guest, based on the symmetrical smears of shoe polish on the bedsheets, while the larger individual restrained the unwilling patient."

"Can you be sure he was unwilling?"

"Yes, indeed. A dressing-gown tie bound his hands, and a saliva- and mucous-soaked sock was used as a gag. However, he did fight back, at least enough for his attacker to cut himself."

"How do you know that detail?" Mr Chapman asked, now more fascinated than skeptical.

"A piece of lavatory paper lay on the floor. The paper was twisted into the shape one would use to wrap a finger, and there was blood on the inside. Given the amount of blood from the victim, a wounded finger would be of no account, so the tissue must have been used by the assailant."

"Remarkable," Chapman murmured.

Holmes nodded.

"What procedure, if that's the right term, was performed?" Harris asked, his mouth twisted in a grimace of revulsion.

Holmes looked sympathetically at Mr Harris. "Based on the location of the blood smears relative to the likely position of the victim, I believe the site of the trauma was the man's—" He paused briefly, then continued. "—groin."

Harris blanched, and even Chapman winced.

"Castration?" I asked. The hotel manager swayed forward, his face ghastly pale.

"An interesting conjecture, Watson. But my observations are even more intriguing. The injury appears to have been to just one side, for blood only ran down the inside of the right leg. Such asymmetrical hemorrhaging would indicate the excision of one of the man's bollocks, if you'll pardon the impropriety."

"Should I get Mr Harris a drink of water?" I asked. I didn't want to disturb any evidence in the hotel room, but the poor fellow was breathing shallowly with his eyes closed. Holmes assented and I brought back a glass of water from the bathroom. Harris looked grateful, while Chapman gave just the slightest smile of superiority at his boss's condition.

"Now then Watson, what did you notice about the bathroom?"

"There was much blood on the floor," I offered.

"Well yes, but what about the flannels and bath towels?" he prompted. Holmes delighted in testing my observational skills, particularly in fraught moments.

"The towel rail was empty."

"Well, there you have it," said my friend. "Having done their job, the assailants untied the wounded man and left him on the bed. He made his way to the bathroom, stanched the blood flow with the flannels, wrapped his loins with a bath towel to keep the blood from seeping into his clothes, wrote the note which he left at the front desk, and had the porter secure a cab. From there, he either went home to await the arrival of a doctor or perhaps went directly to a private practice."

"Not a hospital, given the severity of the injury?" asked Harris.

"If he were headed to hospital, he could just as well have called for an ambulance."

"Fine," said Harris. "Well, not fine at all. What I mean is we have a brutal attack of a guest on our premises. Surely some sort of illicit activity was involved. And knowing what warranted this violence and concealment is important to the Savoy."

"I would judge, based on my years of experience in such cases, although few are quite as striking as the scene we have here, that the most promising clue is the damaged butterflies," said Holmes. "To be sure, there is a lucrative trade in exotic goods of all kinds, including biological specimens. I suspect that the motive for this attack and deception goes deeper than a simple yearning to acquire spectacular insects, although one should not underestimate the passion of curio collectors."

✗ ✗ ✗ ✗

From the Savoy, Holmes and I took a hansom to the Museum of Natural History. Although my feet were soon numb from the cold, we stayed reasonably dry behind a leather curtain drawn across the front of the cab. Holmes explained his good fortune in knowing the museum's Entomological Assistant. Theodore Johnson was a new member of the Diogenes Club, the gathering place for London's least sociable men seeking peace and quiet without having to notice one another, let alone converse (the latter being explicitly prohibited). However, to join this uncongenial group, one must suffer an interview with a member. Holmes had been assigned this task by his brother, one of the founders, to assess the suitability of the insect curator—and it became quickly apparent he was much more comfortable among lifeless, pinned specimens than living, breathing human beings.

We found our way to the second floor office of Mr Johnson. His desk was heaped with teetering columns of scientific journals and surrounded by worktables covered in various scientific instruments for preparing insect specimens. No doubt the atmosphere resonated with Holmes's domestic aesthetic of piles of papers and chemical apparatuses. Johnson was a cadaverous fellow with a sallow complexion and wiry, unkempt hair. He greeted Holmes awkwardly but warmly, displaying his lack of social skills. By way of introduction, Mr Johnson explained that he had been only recently appointed to his position, having replaced the previous assistant who "did not know the difference between a butterfly and a moth" but had been the nephew of the mistress of one of influential trustees of the museum. He chuckled softly at his predecessor's lack of qualifications.

"Now then, what can I do for you?" asked Johnson, fidgeting with his coat buttons.

Holmes gently pulled the envelope from his coat pocket and slid the contents onto the desk. Johnson looked at the fragmented butterfly wings and issued a low whistle.

"Gentlemen, these are the remains of a male and female Queen Alexandra's Birdwing, the largest butterfly in the world—and a very rare find," he said.

"What would a collector pay for such specimens?" asked Holmes.

"As much as £100. That is, if they were intact." Now it was my turn to issue a low whistle, as this sum was more than the annual salary of an average worker. "Might I ask where you acquired these?" asked Johnson.

"I am afraid that is a matter of the greatest confidentiality. But you can be of tremendous assistance if you have information about anyone with the desire to acquire such specimens," replied Holmes.

"A most interesting question." Johnson returned to fingering his buttons nervously. "I have heard that Mr Ito, a major collector of biological rarities, arrived from Japan a week ago."

"Any types in particular?" asked Holmes.

"If a specimen is somehow monstrous, he's especially interested. I know of Mr Ito because his passions include butterflies, which are my own specialty."

"What is his fascination with malformations?" I asked, drawn into this strange account.

"I met Mr Ito only once, but the man is somewhat aberrant himself. He's extremely short-sighted and wears thick glasses. In addition, he is a delicate fellow. Given his physical vulnerability, it is understandable that he travels with a former national jujutsu champion as his bodyguard."

Holmes nodded. As a practitioner of bartitsu, he understood the potency of the martial arts.

"But the real issue behind his affinity for oddities is not so apparent...." Johnson shifted uncomfortably in his chair.

"Please go on," encouraged Holmes.

"I apologise for introducing a subject abhorrent to polite company, but some say that Mr Ito is a hermaphrodite. That is, having both male and female body parts, so-named for the son of Hermes and Aphrodite—whose body was merged with the nymph Salmacis."

"In my studies of human anatomy at the University of London," I interjected, "we were introduced to such deformities. I might note that there appear to be no true human hermaphrodites, by which scientists mean organisms capable of producing both sperm and eggs. However, people may have external elements of both male and female, with rather tragic consequences. But I apologise for the interruption."

Holmes nodded. "A fascinating commentary, but please continue, Mr Johnson."

"Entomologists have long known that a similar condition is found in some insects. The first documented cases were in butterflies, where it is especially obvious due to the marked colour differences between the sexes. In a so-called gynandromorph, one half of the creature is male, and the other half is female."

"One can imagine that Mr Ito would be very much interested in such specimens," said Holmes.

"I have heard, on good authority, that Mr Ito pays more than a hundred times the prevailing price for a specimen if it is a gynandromorph."

"What if someone had a gynandromorph of a Queen Alexandra's Bird-wing?" I asked, anticipating where Holmes's ratiocination was heading. He gave the slightest smile of approval.

"That individual would possess the largest butterfly species in the world with the rarest of bodily deformities. If a matched pair would bring £100, the seller of a gynandromorph could demand at least £10,000. The chances of ever finding another such specimen would be nought."

"A butterfly valued at the cost of a fine house in the centre of London," said my friend, "might well be worth perpetrating violence to acquire."

"I imagine so. You have brought me what appear to be the fragments of such a creature, but I am most reluctant to make an identification given its condition. These scraps would not draw more than a couple of shillings from a collector," he said, nudging the remains back into the envelope.

"Indeed," murmured Holmes, pressing his fingertips together and staring at the ceiling.

* * * *

The next morning, after Holmes neglected a hearty breakfast from Mrs Hudson, as was his wont while engaged in a case, we returned to the Savoy. Heeding my friend's instructions, I remained in the growler, peering out the window and avoiding the bone-chilling drizzle. Holmes approached Mr Phillips, the hotel porter who had escorted us yesterday. Raising the collar of his pea-jacket against the cold, Holmes engaged the fellow under the awning of the hotel entrance. After a brief exchange, Holmes pulled a hipflask from his coat and passed it to the frigid fellow. They talked for a few minutes, shared another swallow, and shook hands, while Holmes subtly passed him a few coins. My friend then walked along the gravel drive in front of the hotel, where several cabs were queued, waiting for fares.

Holmes stopped at one and spoke to the driver, huddled beneath a woolen rug. The fellow stepped down and Holmes chatted with him for a few minutes, while passing the flask back and forth until the driver was finally rewarded with a last gulp and a gratuity.

Back in the growler, Holmes brushed the water from his coat, wiped the mouth of the flask on his sleeve, and smiled.

"Well?" I asked.

"Well, one can acquire the most useful information by rewarding people with a couple shillings and a spot of Dry Gin, although I much prefer a good French burgundy for warmth."

"And what did you learn from your manipulations?" I had no objections to Holmes's tactics when disreputable individuals were involved in one of his investigations, but the porter and cabbie were merely innocent fellows doing their largely unappreciated jobs.

"My dear Watson, I do not deserve such a cynical question." Holmes placed his hand over his heart, as if wounded. "I am entirely capable of chatting with the working man, as I honour the virtues of honest labour."

"Although largely avoiding it yourself," I said. Between the breakfast's black pudding sitting poorly in my stomach, the miserable weather, and the absence of my beloved, I was in a foul mood. "I apologise for my petulance," I hastily added. "I am feeling a bit unsettled this morning."

"A friend overlooks hasty words," said Holmes. "And while I value the work of navvies and rat catchers, I am singularly ill-suited for either line of work myself."

"The same could be said of me," I replied with a smile that seemed to set things right.

"Now then, I learned that our hemorrhaging guest took a cab yesterday morning. And the porter, being committed to the well-being of the hotel's guests—particularly those looking infirm, memorised and recalled the cab's appearance."

"And you found the driver waiting for a fare this morning?"

"Indeed, I did. And with a bit more chatter, a splash of gin, and a shilling for his time, he shared the address of where he took his fare."

"Are we to head there now?" I asked.

"I think not," said Holmes, "as I would like to conduct some further, discreet inquiries in our mysterious victim's neighbourhood."

We agreed to meet back at our Baker Street rooms at seven sharp. He remarked that I would be well advised to clean and load my army revolver as there "may be some little danger" in our evening's confrontation. I asked him if he'd be armed.

He smiled. "My dear Watson, I'm bringing you."

⤨   ⤨   ⤨   ⤨

On the way to a respectable terrace near the Paddington station, grey-yellow halos surrounded the gas lights. Holmes shared his day's findings amidst vaporous puffs in the dank cab. According to neighbours, our victim was a rather unpleasant man who kept to himself and seemed to suffer from some sort of chronic illness that accounted for his disposition. A spinster across the street, who kept track of happenings in all of prosperous, polite Tyburnia, reported that Dr Niles Abercrombie had been a surgeon at St. Mary's Hospital but abandoned his prestigious position when his own health failed. According to this informative busybody, Dr Abercrombie would occasionally disappear for days, after which he enjoyed financial windfalls, which she attributed to gambling or some other impropriety.

Holmes had the driver stop well before the appointed address, so that the sound of our cab would not warn Abercrombie of impending visitors. We needn't have worried. Holmes knocked softly, and when there was no reply, with increasing intensity. Finally, we heard a raspy voice. It grew in volume as the speaker approached. "What the bloody hell do you want?"

"Delivery from the Paracelsus Chemist Shoppe. Your doctor ordered a stronger pain medicine," said Holmes.

"All right then," the voice said. The door opened enough for Holmes to wedge his foot in the opening and throw his shoulder against the panelling. There was a string of curses as the fellow was knocked backward to the floor and we rushed inside. I had a hand on the pistol in my coat pocket, but our quarry was in no condition to resist.

"Apologies for our rudeness," Holmes said, bending to help the man to his feet.

"If I tore my sutures, I'll kill you. Speaking of which, who the hell are you?" Abercrombie stood barefoot, clad only in his dressing gown, and was hardly in a position to make meaningful threats.

"I am Mr Sherlock Holmes, and this is Dr Watson." My companion performed the introductions as if having just entered a social gathering. "You are Dr Abercrombie, I presume?"

"You can presume all you want. All I will tell you is that I am in pain and about to telephone the police," he said.

"But of course you don't wish the authorities to be involved, and you are in no condition to telephone if Dr Watson decides you should not do so. Now then, Watson, please escort our host to his bedroom and make him comfortable while I take a tour." I took Abercrombie's elbow and guided him down the hall. He walked with a bow-legged shuffle, no doubt accommodating the dressings of his wounds. He collapsed onto the bed and closed his eyes with a deep moan. I took a chair. Holmes puttered about, humming softly until he muttered to himself, "I say, this explains everything." After another several minutes of rustling, he entered the bedroom.

"Well, Dr Abercrombie, I found many interesting things in your rooms."

"Go to the Devil," sneered Abercrombie.

"Now then, aside from being coarse, which might be excused in light of your discomfort, it seems you have a most unusual hobby. Your other bedroom has been converted into an impressive laboratory, complete with a Zeiss dissecting microscope with Koehler illumination."

Despite my reservations about our host, I was impressed, having labored with a Crouch microscope through my medical training.

Holmes continued, "I was perplexed as to the purpose of such equipment, until I found glass chambers, the function of which I infer to have been the rehydration and softening of dried insects. And then I came across blades for a surgical scalpel. Would you concur, Dr Watson?" asked Holmes holding out a small wooden box.

I studied them for a moment and nodded. They were, indeed, the finest and sharpest blades that one would find in a surgery, the sort of instruments used on eyes and nerves.

"From the dozens of common butterflies bisected and then tossed into a rubbish bin it was a simple matter to deduce their purpose."

"He was cutting butterflies in half?"

"Not merely splitting them but repairing them as well. There were, by my count, no less than nine different adhesives on Dr Abercrombie's laboratory bench: everything from casein and fish glues to various pastes, to Brazilian carnauba and Mexican candelilla waxes, along with Chinese insect wax—an exotic and expensive product from the Szechwan province."

"But why were you cutting and gluing insects?" I asked Abercrombie, who simply sneered.

"A fine question, Watson. The answer became apparent when I opened one of the many wooden boxes used to store insect specimens. I was initially amazed to see a spectacular collection of gynandromorphs. Even using the doctor's microscope, I could barely make out the incision line that joined the bisected halves. A most impressive exhibition of fine motor skills."

"Yeah, I was a bloody brilliant butterfly surgeon," Abercrombie said with evident pride, lifting himself to a sitting position with a wince and a gasp. "Perfecting the cutting and repair methods took six months of practice before I had the courage to try the process on a pair of £100 specimens. Putting together a gynandromorph of Queen Alexandra's Birdwing had me on track for a £10,000 payday."

"But why did you abandon your medical career?" I asked.

His angry attitude dissipated as he lapsed into a melancholy account. He had been a doctor in the British army, serving in Valletta under surgeon captain David Bruce when a febrile illness swept through the troops. The men were stricken with debilitating muscular and joint pain along with foul-smelling night sweats. Malta fever killed one in fifty who contracted the disease and many of the survivors developed chronic pain and swelling of the joints, including the lumbar spine. This latter condition made it impossible for Abercrombie to continue his medical practice, and he was drawn into bouts of malaise alternating with mania. During the latter, he would swindle wealthy people out of their money using various fraudulent transactions. Most recently, he decided to dupe the Japanese collector, Mr Ito, into buying a fake specimen of staggering value.

"What went wrong?" I asked, fascinated by this tale of deception.

"I was counting on Mr Ito's near-sightedness, figuring that even with normal vision a person couldn't discern my handiwork. We met three days ago in a hotel room where I often conducted business, and Mr Ito examined the specimen using a magnifying lens."

"How much magnification would that have been?" I asked.

"No more than ten-fold. I'd used my dissecting scope for the work, and you couldn't see the joint at even fifty-fold magnification, so I figured to score. But the little bastard must have seen some anomaly because when he came to my hotel room, he brought a satchel of cash and a compound microscope with five-hundred-fold power. While he set it up, his bodyguard blocked the door."

"I gather your hoax was discovered and your customer greatly perturbed," said Holmes dryly.

"Exactly so. Ito smashed the butterfly display case while the big bloke gagged me, tied my hands, tore off my pants, and held me down on the bed. Then Ito pulled a slender knife out of a lacquered sheath…"

"Most likely a tantō blade, a shorter version of samurai swords, but please continue," offered my companion.

"He said he would teach me a lesson and send a message to anyone who tried to deceive him in the future. That since I'd created a half-male specimen, he'd turn me into a half-male. I fought back but there was no escape."

Scowling, Abercrombie reached over to his bedside table, shook a couple of silver-coated opium pills from a bottle and swallowed them. "I fainted from the pain. When I awoke, I invented a story for the hotel, wadded up some flannels to absorb the blood, and made it back here. Then I called a doctor I could trust to be discreet." He shifted uncomfortably in the bed. "So now what do you plan to do?"

"I will, of course, report my findings to the individual who solicited my investigation," said Holmes. "But that is the end of my obligation. As to whether that party pursues any criminal action, I cannot say."

"Right. I don't imagine that the Savoy will keep me on their 'most preferred' guest list," he said, easily guessing who had engaged Holmes. "That was a fine place to do business. Four pounds a night is worth an assurance of privacy when buying and selling things that aren't exchanged in the light of day. But I know the management. They won't notify the police and soil their reputation."

"As you did their silk sheets," Holmes quipped.

"No, but I might have the last laugh. You see, Ito knelt on my legs to do his dirty work, and when I thrashed around, Ito cut himself. He walked away with a valise of money—and a case of Malta fever. Dr Bruce has shown that the causative agent, a bacterium to be precise, is carried in the blood. I'm quite confident that sufficient blood was exchanged between his wound and my own, and Ito will soon be incapacitated with fever."

"That's why you warned the hotel staff to use gloves and wash with carbolic acid?" I asked.

"I may have become a swindler and a rogue, but my targets are moneyed fools. I mean no harm to hard-working commoners."

⚔ ⚔ ⚔ ⚔

Back in our sitting room with a fire warming our feet, Holmes sipped a glass of port and sighed. "I have occasionally worried that my work as a consulting detective would be eventually curtailed by a lack of challenging and novel crimes."

"Does this possibility still vex you?" I asked.

"I think not, my dear Watson, for it appears that while a genius for observation and deduction is strictly limited in the populace, the human capacity for creative villainy is unbounded."

Jeffrey Lockwood worked as faculty member in entomology at the University of Wyoming before metamorphosing into a Professor of Natural Sciences & Humanities in the departments of philosophy and creative writing. His Riley-the-Exterminator series features a cop-turned-exterminator who struggles with moral dilemmas while pursuing both two- and six-legged vermin.

HIDING
Jenna Weart

The Weltons' cottage would be homey if the attic and the stairs would stay quiet. On an October evening, Jill settled into an armchair near the fireplace where flames flickered on a crackling log, spreading warmth and a fragrance of burning cedar. She opened her handbag and pulled out a lavender library book with a silvery title, *All About Exorcisms*.

Charles, her husband, crossed the room, his footsteps muffled by a shaggy, cherry-red rug. His handsome, squarish face and his brisk stride suggested strength, but when he glanced at the beamed ceiling, his eyelid twitched. From a built-in bookcase, he took his new paperback, *How to Sell Your House Fast*. As he turned to sit, the attic floor creaked.

"Go away," Charles shouted toward the ceiling.

"Please, please go," Jill called.

The creaks came down the stairway, tread by tread. The Weltons stayed still, knowing what approached—a murderer's ghost.

I won't let it scare me, Jill thought. She turned to face a window, where twilight dimmed their lawn and the empty Old Carriage Road. Her stomach tensed. Finally, the footsteps returned to the attic.

She breathed out. "We should sue the man who sold us this house."

"We can't, because he had a witness that he warned us."

A real estate agent had accompanied the owner when he showed the cottage, which on a summer afternoon appeared charming, sunlit. When Charles asked about problems, the owner said there was "a ghost for a host" in a joking tone while touching a wine decanter. Charles said he didn't believe in ghosts.

The starter home was a startling house.

During their first hour after moving in, the Weltons thought that the creaks were caused by some structural defect. When they entered the attic, a hazy figure of a man, larger than Charles, loomed through piled cartons, scowling malevolently. The Weltons fled; they ventured up the next morning, glimpsed the ghost again, and decided to keep the staircase's upper and lower doors closed. During their two months in the cottage, they heard it every evening and night and saw it dimly through the dark door to the attic stairs a dozen times.

"I can't stand it anymore," Jill said. "I've been thinking, when my cousin Roland visits us this weekend, he should try an exorcism. He's studied the practices of shamans."

"We can ask him. He believes in some of that stuff."

"I hope it works."

On Saturday, Roland Conan, an anthropologist, visited during a stop-over on his roundabout route to Siberia. His lean body and black spectacles gave him a professorial look.

That afternoon in the sitting room, sunlight spread over cream walls, rosy pillows, and daffodil-patterned curtains. Over coffee and chocolate cookies, Charles described the haunting.

"What do you know about his history?" Roland asked.

"Our next-door neighbor told us he's a murderer," Charles said. "About ten years ago, Mr. Kreal—that's his name—he inherited this house from an uncle. His uncle died from a fall, headfirst, down the stairs. Kreal was visiting that evening, so the neighbors suspected that he shoved the old man. No other evidence, so it never went to trial. Soon after Kreal moved in, he died from a stroke on the same stairs."

"He's nasty," Jill said. "When he was alive, our nosey next-door neighbor was so afraid of him that she didn't even go outside until she heard him drive away. She thought he was too quiet and creepy."

Roland leaned back and steepled his fingers. "Maybe he's doing a penance in this location. He hasn't harmed you, has he?"

"Oh, he only startles us every evening," Charles said, "and makes us want to move out."

"We can't invite our friends to visit us. Sometimes he shows up there." Jill pointed toward the dark door to the attic stairs. "If we could get rid of him, this house would be cozy and what we need. We have nice, quiet neighbors except for the nosey one next door."

"You know about exorcisms, don't you?" Charles asked. "Have you ever watched any that worked?"

"Possibly one in a Tibetan village where the monks wore costumes and banged drums and gongs and—"

"No." Charles held up his hands. "We can't have a commotion. The neighbors would notice. We're thinking of selling the house without telling prospective buyers about the murderer in the attic. Legally, we don't have to confess anything that we don't know."

"But doesn't the woman next door know that you know?" Roland asked.

"We pretended that we didn't believe her." Charles leaned toward Roland. "Have you ever observed a quiet, private exorcism?"

"One in New Guinea was fundamentally like what a priest would do."

"Show us," Charles said. "You'd be the best person, actually the only person, to try an exorcism for us because we can trust you with a secret."

"No tribe would choose me for a ceremony."

Jill clasped her hands. "Please, please, this is the only help we've ever asked from you. You could at least try."

Roland shrugged and raised his hands toward the attic. "By holy powers, I drive you from us, you infernal invader, be gone and—" He leaned back and folded his arms. "I'm not the right person for this. I'm sorry, I can't. I suggest that you rent enough storage space so you don't need the attic, play soothing music, and sleep with earplugs. Maybe it'll suddenly be his time to go." He stood. "I have to prepare for my flight tomorrow. Good luck."

"Won't you stay for dinner?" Jill asked.

"I'd rather not be on the roads after dark."

After Roland departed, Charles sighed loudly. "I'll post it on the internet tonight, a charming cottage."

"I'll feel sorry for the buyers."

"They'll probably do the same as us," Charles said. "You know that we're more honest than most people. Listen, dear, everyone tries to make their house look perfect when they sell. Do you want to move or not?"

"Move."

"So we'll praise the cottage, and when buyers ask questions, I'll tell them they can get a maintenance report."

Jill tried to shrug off a feeling of unease. "We'll only sell to someone who's young and healthy enough to stand the shock."

"Sure, no one with a heart condition. Now's our opportunity while our chatterbox neighbor is away on a trip, and the night's not too early. Kreal's never come downstairs before dusk, so we could we take a chance with buyers arriving up till five."

Jill turned on a radio, and that night they slept with earplugs. The next morning, she cleared away clutter, dusted, polished, and scrubbed. At two o'clock the phone rang, and when she answered, a baritone voice said, "This is Will Lawan. A gentleman at the airport informed me that you wish to sell your house."

A buyer so soon! *Roland's trying to help us*, she thought. *I shouldn't sound desperate to sell.*

She waited until her breathing slowed and said, "Yes, you're welcome to come and see it."

"May I come at six o'clock today?" Will asked.

"I'm afraid that's too late. Could you come at four?"

"Sorry, no, because we have another appointment, and we're flying out tomorrow on an early flight, dreadfully early. We might manage a few minutes after five."

"Okay, but my husband and I have to go out at quarter to six."

After giving instructions about which roads to take, Jill hung up and called to Charles in the next room, "A possible buyer is coming around five o'clock. He can't come any other time."

"You're cutting it close."

"I know. We'll hurry them."

While Jill prepared a cake, cleaned the kitchen, and begged droopy geraniums to perk up, Charles mowed the lawn. Together they pushed their sofa to hide a line of cracked plaster in a wall. When daylight waned, lamps glowed, chrysanthemums filled vases, the kitchen surfaces shone, and a chocolate cake was baking fragrantly. Jill turned on band music, and then she stared at the road.

At quarter past five, a limo brought a couple who were movie-star gorgeous, and they looked rich enough to be not much troubled if they lost money on real estate. The woman wore diamond earrings and more makeup than her perfectly oval face required: swoopy fake lashes, kohl around her green eyes, and lavender sparkles over her eyelids. The man's perfectly tailored suit made his torso appear a vee. Smiling, flashing ultra-white teeth, they introduced themselves as Will and Lorna Lawan.

After exchanging greetings, Lorna said, "Could you please be a darling, and turn off that music."

Jill apprehensively obeyed and was glad they heard only the chirps outside. The Lawans lingered in each room, not speaking.

After returning to the living room, Will asked, "Is there anything unusual here?"

"Extraordinarily solid construction," Charles said.

"Flowers grow with amazingly little work because of the sunlight in the spring and summer," Jill said. "A lovely neighborhood."

"Is the house haunted?" Lorna's black-rimmed eyes widened.

Jill took a quick breath. "No."

Lorna's smile dropped. "I'm so sorry."

"You wanted that?" Jill asked, her hand going to her throat.

"I have a huge idea for our very own reality show." Lorna lowered her breathy voice to a confidential murmur. "*True Scares from Beyond*, for which we need at least one ghost that'll show up on TV. We'll keep the cameras running."

"She thinks the nastier, the better, for our purpose," her husband said glumly. "She wants to commercialize a spirit."

Lorna gave him a quick, little smile. "We'd get millions of people to watch it, especially if we can get one with a history of crime. Our producer would pay oodles of dollars for that."

Jill opened her mouth, but Charles spoke first.

"Actually, we did have one, of a murderer, in the attic," Charles said. "My wife thinks it might be gone because we asked for an exorcism yesterday, but as soon as it's dark outside, you'll hear it."

Will squinted upward. "So sorry that it's departed."

"Sometimes it appears there." Charles pointed toward the door to the stairs. "If it doesn't come down, we'll go up and find it."

Jill shuddered at the idea of entering the attic, and Charles, noticing her expression, shouted, "Mr. Kreal, come down or we'll go up."

"Will, let's stay a bit longer," said Lorna.

Her husband glanced at his gold-plated watch, frowned, and sat facing the dark door. Jill turned off the oven, scraped burnt edges off the almost-forgotten cake, and served it with coffee. They chatted about the Lawans' bit parts on TV, their plans for their own show, and the house's history.

At dusk Lorna cupped her purple-tipped fingers to her ears. "Let's be still, everyone, so we can hear it." There was no sound except the chirps and twitters outside and Will's sporadic tapping on the table.

After five minutes, he said, "Time for us to depart. Sorry."

"We'll have to go into the attic. Every time we went up there, we saw it." Charles strode to the stairway door and opened it.

"Oh, do let's see what's up there," Lorna said, rising. "Come on, Will, be a dear."

Charles turned on the staircase's light and climbed up, followed by the others, Jill last, goosebumps prickling her arms. Kreal's got to show himself, she thought. *I must not scream when I see him. I won't scream.*

They entered a chilly, musty space filled with trunks, piles of cartons, and a rack with dusty coats. Cobwebs festooned the clothes and a little window. The Lawans stared around, motionless. Breathing fast, Jill thought of suggesting crawling into the darkness under the eaves to hunt for Kreal, but the idea made her want to flee. Where was he?

"Come out," she snapped.

Silence.

Lorna sneezed, rubbed her arms, and said, "Let's go."

Before following the others downstairs, Jill pulled a cord to turn on a harsh overhead bulb. Maybe a light would get rid of Mr. Kreal.

At the front door, Will said, "Sorry it's not showing up. Lorna, I'm becoming more doubtful about this idea of yours. We need something reliable."

Lorna pouted. "We have other likely leads to follow."

The Lawans said good-bye and departed. The Weltons watched ruefully as the limo backed out of the driveway and accelerated into the night.

A minute later, the staircase creaked.

Jenna Weart's jobs have included reporting for the Westchester County newspaper chain, editing periodicals at Prentice-Hall, and teaching English at a high school on Manhattan's Lower East Side. When she was a teenager, she baby-sat in an old house that creaked ominously at night. That house changed owners more often than any other house she knew of. She's been published in *Woman's World, Mystery Weekly, Seventeen, Highlights for Children, saturdayeveningpost.com,* and several newspapers and other periodicals.

THE MONSTER'S BLOOD
David Afsharirad

I was working the night desk when Barbara Clayton came in, marked up worse than I'd ever seen her. One eye was swollen shut and the other was damn near. Her lip was split and her chin painted with dry blood. I put away the horror magazine I had open, embarrassed to be caught reading on the job.

"Sheriff in, Jimmy?" she asked. Her voice was strong, but I could tell it took effort for her to speak.

I looked at the clock above the door. It was nine-thirty. Sherriff Dixon had gone home long ago.

"Can I help?" I asked.

"I guess I need to—"

Her breath caught and she buried her face in her hands and let out a wail so mournful I had to choke back tears.

"Oh, Jimmy! Jimmy, it's...awful."

I came around the desk lightning-quick and put my arm around her. She was older than my nineteen years by a half dozen, but just then I felt paternal toward her. Her body heaved in wracking sobs that, after a time, slowly died away. When she was finished with her cry, I went and grabbed a box of tissues and handed them to her.

"I didn't know where else to go," she said, and I believed it. Once, Barbara Abbott had been the most popular girl in town, and was friends with just about everyone. But seven years married to Charles Clayton had whittled the beautiful, bright young woman into a twisted shape, and people had turned their backs on her, the way people will.

"I'll get Henry," I said, meaning Henry Jacobs, the senior deputy on duty.

Barbara nodded, but I could see she was kind of embarrassed about it. She and Henry had once been an item back when they'd been in high school. They'd played the leads in all the school plays and everyone thought they'd wind up married.

I asked Barbara if I could get her anything, a glass of water or cup of coffee maybe, and when she said no, I went to get Henry.

I found him in his office, filling out paperwork and listening to a static-y dance band program on the radio. When I told him Barbara Clayton was here, he shot up out of his chair and hurried past me, down the hall.

When I caught up to him, he was in the lobby, his arms around Barbara in a way that did not look at all paternal. I cleared my throat, and he broke the embrace.

"Come on and tell me all about it," he said, guiding her to his office.

I sat back down and got out my magazine, but I didn't feel like reading. I hoped Henry would do more for Barbara than Sherriff Dixon ever did. She'd been in the station before, complaining of the abuse she suffered at the hands of her alcoholic husband. This was in 1968, and the women's movement was underway, but in Marble Falls, Texas, how a man treated his wife was his own business and what happened behind closed doors was expected to stay there. I got my hair buzzed every other Thursday at Ray's Barbershop on Onion Street, but I guess I was the town's resident long-haired hippie because I thought Charles Clayton ought to be dragged out of that broken-down farmhouse of his and hauled off to jail for what he'd done.

Fifteen minutes passed, and Henry came out of his office. He was alone.

"Come on," he said, his voice uneasy. He settled his hat on his head. I pushed back from the desk.

"Guess you better ought to take your gun."

It chilled my blood to hear him say it. It must have showed on my face because he looked at me, level, and nodded.

I unlocked the bottom desk drawer, took out my service revolver, and trailed Henry out the front door, fastening the holster to my Sam Browne belt as we went. The gun rode heavy on my hip.

Henry didn't say anything as we drove west past the city limits. He didn't have to. I knew where we were going. I looked in the rearview and watched as the town lights diminished behind us. It made me melancholy to see that.

"You a religious man?" Henry asked, his eyes fixed on the circle of road our headlights illuminated.

I thought of the Methodist Church I'd gone to as a boy and still attended most Sundays with my mother.

"No," I said, truthfully.

Henry nodded. "Probably for the best. This job, it has a way—there are things that you see, make you doubt that a good god could have created this world."

I didn't say anything because there wasn't anything to say.

"We're going up to the Clayton place," Henry said. "I'm sure you figured that. When we get there…"

His voice trailed off. The tires on the concrete and the soft fizzle of static on the police band radio were a roar in my ears.

"I don't know how to say this," Henry said.

I stole a glance at him out of the corner of my eye. The interior of the car was midnight-dark but in the faint illumination from the dashboard lights and the full moon up above, I could see that Henry was scared.

No, that was wrong. He was terrified. Like a man who has just looked in the mirror and seen an unfamiliar face staring back at him with malicious eyes.

"Jimmy, this is going to sound crazy, I know that. But I've known Barbara for years. And…well, I guess I believe her."

He paused again. Henry had a way of coming up on things from the side. It was best not to rush him.

"Aw, hell," he said. "Probably best just to tell you the way she told me." And so he did.

✗ ✗ ✗ ✗

The trouble had started a month ago, as best as Barbara could remember. Charles had been on a bender, and she hadn't seen him for two days. Likely he'd been sleeping in the barn, or in the back seat of the car—or in a gutter, for all she knew. There was a part of her that worried about what might happen to him. It was a part that she hated.

She was finishing up her dinner dishes when she heard the back door swing open and heavy footsteps stumble toward the kitchen. Charles filled the doorframe. He moved quickly for a man as drunk as he was, and Barbara instinctively stepped to get out of his way. He went to the sink and turned on the water. Steam rose, and Charles stuck his right hand under the faucet, cursing through gritted teeth as he did.

Barbara chanced getting closer to see what was going on. She came up on Charles's side and gasped.

"Don't be so damn dramatic."

"You're hurt."

Charles took his injured hand out from under the water. It looked like it had been caught in a fox trap. The puncture wounds were down to the bone in some places. Fat drops of bright red blood spattered the stained white porcelain. Charles put his hand back under the faucet.

Barbara went for the mercurochrome. When she returned, the water was off and Charles was seated at the table, a cup towel twisted around his fist and a pint bottle of cheap whiskey in his good hand. The towel was soaked through in a few places, but all in all, it looked like the bleeding had slowed.

"Here, let me help," Barbara said, unscrewing the cap on the disinfectant.

"It's fine." Charles took a long swallow of the whiskey.

"Just let me look." Barbara reached for his wounded hand and found herself slammed against the wall, her jaw snapping shut so hard that she saw blots of color dance before her eyes. Charles had backhanded her across the cheek, hard enough to set her stumbling. The mercurochrome bottle skittered across the floor, the red fluid seeping out of the bottle and into the carpet.

"It's fine, I said." Charles took a long drink. "Got bit by a damn dog, is all."

Experience had taught Barbara that it was unwise say anything, but she couldn't help herself. If a dog had done that to Charles's hand, it could get infected. Gangrene could set in. There was even the possibility, however small, that the dog had been rabid.

"What kind of a dog?" she asked.

Charles shrugged. "Big one. I don't know." He let out a short, humorless bark of a laugh. "The dead kind, now."

He pulled out the pocketknife he always carried with him, the one he'd once held to her throat. It was caked in tacky blood. Charles unfolded it, smeared it across the leg of his pants.

"Damn thing wouldn't let go," he said.

"Where?" Barbara asked, her voice not more than a whisper. "Where did this happen?"

"What the hell difference does it make? Out back. Was going to get something out of the barn and it come up on me."

The "something" from the barn being the whiskey he was now drinking. She'd found his stash out there long ago but was too scared to dispose of it.

"Damn thing up and went for my throat. If I hadn't got my hand up…" Another long swig from the bottle. The way he was going at it, he'd be passed out drunk soon, but not before he turned even more violent.

Barbara smoothed her hands over her apron. "Well, if there's nothing else that you need," she said, "I think I'll go on to bed."

As she turned to go down the hall, she heard the pint bottle shatter on the wall next to her head. Tiny shards of glass peppered her hair and crunched beneath the soles of her shoes, but she didn't so much as break her stride.

⚔   ⚔   ⚔   ⚔

She found Charles the next morning, passed out of the couch. Two more pint bottles, both empty, littred the floor and his injured hand had seeped blood into the rug. She'd have to clean that up later. She couldn't risk waking him. The mercurochrome in the dining room and the broken glass she could take care of now.

It was while taking out the trash that she saw the body. At first she didn't register what it was. She had forgotten all about the dog, had forgotten that its body would likely still be laying where it had fallen, Charles having first been too injured and then too drunk to dispose of it.

But this was much too big to be a dog. It was—something else.

As she crept closer, dawning awareness wormed its way through her body, starting with the tingling tips of her fingers and working its way through her core and up her spine until it spilled out of her mouth in the form of a primal groan.

"Oh, Charles," she said. "What *happened*?"

There was no need to get any closer. She could see the man's face clearly from where she stood. And she could see the knife wound in his throat and the spilled blood that pooled in the dirt.

He was a young black man, maybe seventeen or eighteen. And he was stark naked.

Henry paused in his story and looked over at me.

"So it's murder," I said.

Henry nodded. "Sounds that way. I always knew Charles was capable of it, but I guess we all are. You push a man hard enough and there's no telling what he's liable to do."

I wondered if that was true. I shifted in my seat, felt the gun stab into my side.

"You okay?" Henry asked.

I nodded.

"Because it gets worse."

"We're going up there," I said, "so I guess you better tell me."

✗ ✗ ✗ ✗

Barbara was scared enough that she shook Charles awake, getting a hard slap across the face for her troubles. She didn't so much as feel it.

"Charles," she said. "Charles, what did you do last night?"

Charles sat up on the couch, kicked at the empty bottles with his still-booted feet. There was hate in his eyes, but Barbara ignored it.

"You said it was a dog, Charles. You said it was a *dog*."

"What are you yakking about?" Charles cradled his head in his hands and managed to get to his feet.

"That did this to you." She grabbed Charles's injured hand and held it up in front of his face. The cup towel had worked its way loose at some point in the night and was now draped over the hand like a shroud. Barbara stripped it off and felt her mind slip a gear.

Aside from the fact that the hand was covered in dried blood, there was nothing wrong with it. The deep puncture wounds were gone, healed over, leaving not so much as a trace of scar tissue.

Barbara let go of the hand, and stumbled back, stifling a scream that threatened to spill out of her mouth. If she screamed, she thought, she'd just keep on screaming and wouldn't stop. Not ever.

Charles held his hand in front of his face. There was a look in his eye that said he thought perhaps the years on the sauce had finally taken their toll. He flexed his fingers, made a fist, and released it.

"It's not possible," Barbara said. "I saw—"

The look of amazed shock vanished from Charles's face, replaced by a scowl.

"You don't know what you saw," he said. "It was just a scratch, anyways."

"But the blood. Where did all the blood come from?"

Charles thought on it for a moment. "The dog," he said. "Must be dog's blood."

"Charles," she said, "that wasn't a dog."

"What the hell are you talking about?"

She left him standing in the living room and went out the back door. Charles followed. Once outside, they stood, shoulder to shoulder, staring down at the dead body.

"What is this?" Charles said.

"It's the dog you killed last night."

"Ridiculous."

"Charles, how drunk were you?"

The question got her a sock on the shoulder hard enough to make her arm numb.

"Not so drunk I don't know a dog from a nigger." But the fire had gone out of his voice and Barbara could see that he was scared.

"Then where's the dog, Charles? You killed a dog that attacked you last night, where is it?"

"How do I know?"

"Where's the dog, Charles?"

The punch in the stomach doubled her over and the backhand across the cheek sent her sprawling in the dirt, skinning her left knee.

"Would you shut your mouth for one damn minute and let me think!"

Charles began pacing frantically, weaving from residual drunkenness, running his hands through his greasy hair so that it looked like he was trying to pull it out by the roots.

Barbara lay where she'd fallen and tried to make herself invisible. It didn't work.

Charles turned and faced her, pointed an accusatory finger like a judge passing sentence.

"You're behind this," he said. "You and that man you been cheating on me with. Trying to set me up."

"Charles," Barbara said, gentle, like the cowboys in movies talked to wild horses to calm them. "I'm not—"

"Don't you dare deny it!"

She gathered herself and stood, never letting her eyes leave Charles's heavy hands or booted feet, ready to skirt out of the way if he struck out at her again. But his attention had left her for the time being. He was pacing again, his eyes fixed on the dead body.

"It was dark," he said. "I could have sworn. He must have been crazy to bite at me like that." He turned to Barbara. "You saw the hand. I didn't have any choice. It was self-defense. I swear it." There was now a pleading look in his eyes. "Barbara, honey, you've got to believe me. I didn't know. It was dark." He seemed to collapse in on himself. He hung his head, and Barbara wondered if he might cry.

She went to him now, put an arm around his shoulder.

"I'll call the police," Barbara said.

Charles batted the arm away. "You'll do no such thing."

"But if it was like you said… If it was self-defense…"

"You think I want Wally Dixon sticking his fat nose in my business? You think I want him draggin' me into town to answer his inane questions?"

"Charles, you've got—"

"And yeah, it's just some nigger kid. But Jesus God, with all this civil rights nonsense these days. They're like to have a protest rally on our front lawn, they find out about it. No, Barbara. No one finds out about his, you understand. No one."

"A man—*a teenage boy*—is dead, Charles, you think no one's gonna notice?"

Charles went over to the body, which was lying prone in the dirt. He wedged a toe under the boy's shoulder and turned him on his back and peered down into the face. Barbara looked away but not before she saw the dead white eyes staring at her.

"Never seen him before," Charles said. "Probably some drifter. No one'll miss him. I'll take him out into the field. Bury him."

"Charles, I can't."

"Can't what? All you got to do is keep your mouth shut."

"*I can't.*"

"You'll do it, or I'll see to it you wind up like him."

Barbara backed away. She could feel the rage coming off him like a high fever.

"They'd know it was you that did it," she said. "People know how you treat me."

"And that's why they'll believe me when I say you up and left in the middle of the night. You left a note saying you were going somewhere I'd never find you."

"No." She knew it was the truth.

"I mean it now, Barbara. You're going to help me deal with this situation here or you won't live to regret it."

As if to underline his point, he kicked out at the body of the dead boy, his boot connecting with his leg with a sickening snap.

✗　✗　✗　✗

"Since we're just now hearing about all this," I said. "I guess that she did what Clayton wanted."

Henry nodded. "Can't blame her. You should have seen her tonight. I had to just about pry it out of her she was so scared."

We were coming up on the farm now. I noticed that Henry had eased off of the gas a while back and that the speedometer read just over thirty. Whether he'd slowed in order to have enough time to fill me in or to keep away from the Clayton place as long as possible, I couldn't say.

"Like I said, that was about a month ago." Henry absently flexed his hands on the wheel. "Charles buried the colored boy, or Barbara says she guessed he did. Told her he did anyway, and when he came back into the house, his feet were caked in dirt and his shirt was painted with sweat, despite the cooler weather.

"'We have an understanding?' Charles said, and Barbara nodded. They didn't talk about it after that.

"Barbara had just about convinced herself that nothing had happened. After all, what proof did she have? The body was gone, and Charles's hand was healed up so it looked fresh as the day he was born. It was two weeks later, when she was going through the laundry and found the cup towel—the one soaked in blood—that it all came flooding back to her and she collapsed on the floor, sobbing.

"Bastard gave her a beating for that, you can bet."

Henry's jaw tightened and he pressed down harder on the accelerator. It made me sick to hear about how Clayton beat up on his wife, but Henry, he seemed to have an almost visceral reaction to it.

Still, I couldn't understand what he was so afraid of. I was scared, sure. But I was new to the job and hadn't dealt with anything more dangerous than a routine traffic stop. Henry had seen his fair share of action. I couldn't believe he'd get so worked up over a mean old drunk, even one who had no compunction about beating on his wife or covering up a murder.

I waited for him to continue his story and when he didn't, I said, "What aren't you telling me?"

Henry glanced over at me and pinned me to my seat with the heat of his gaze.

"What are you saying?"

"I'm saying that what you've told me so far is awful. No denying that. But there's something else going on, Henry. What is it? I'm going in there with you, so I guess I have a right to know." I hoped my voice sounded more assured than I felt.

Henry chewed on that for a while. He sighed, theatrically.

"Sure you won't just trust me on this one?"

I shook my head. "Not if I'm laying it on the line. Sorry."

"It's going to sound crazy."

"This whole thing sounds crazy," I said, not knowing if I meant his story or the world we lived in.

"All right then," Henry said. "You're right. You need to know." He let out a short, humorless chuckle. "Just don't call the looney bin when you hear it, okay?"

⚹　⚹　⚹　⚹

Charles roughed Barbara up some over the next three weeks—like when she'd broken down after finding the cup towel—but all in all, it was a quiet time. He lay off the booze, though of course he didn't quit. For Charles Clayton, stone cold sober meant he'd only had a few beers.

But about a week ago, something had changed. He wasn't drinking more heavily, at least not that Barbara could tell, but he was just...meaner. And hyper-sensitive. He's snap at her for the slightest thing, like setting a coffee cup down too hard on the table or scraping her knife too loudly when she was slicing vegetables. In the years they'd been married she'd learned how best to stay out of Charles's way when he got in one of his moods, but this was different. Short of wrapping herself in cotton, she didn't know what she could do to appease him.

She'd told Henry that it was worse at night, then paused.

"That's not right," she'd said. "It wasn't worse at night. It was *only* at night."

Sure, he was bad enough during the day, but not more than he usually was. It was only after the sun had set that he became intolerable. And it was getting worse.

Last night, he'd gone on such a rampage that Barbara had locked herself in the bathroom. She huddled on the floor, hysterical and bleeding, while Charles pounded and clawed at the door, screaming near-unintelligible obscenities about what he was going to do to her before and after he killed her.

After what seemed like hours, he finally tired out. When Barbara came out of the bathroom the next morning, aching from a night on the hard tile, she found him in bed, his clothes still on, his fingers torn bloody from scraping at the door, which looked like a wild animal had been at it.

✗ ✗ ✗ ✗

"When he started in again after dark this evening, she knew she had to get out of there," Henry said. "That if she stuck around, this would be her last night on Earth."

We turned down a gravel drive, past a shotgun-blasted mailbox that had the name Clayton written on it in faded black letters. If the full moon hadn't been so bright, I never would have seen the turn, overgrown as it was. Scrub brush scraped at the sides of the patrol car as we wound our way toward the house, like skeletal fingers reaching.

"She had to be plenty careful, though. She'd wanted to leave before it got dark, but Charles must have sensed something was up and he stayed on her heels all afternoon and evening, even roughed her up pretty good, as you saw. Finally, she made some excuse about needing to get something out of the garage and made a run for it. She'd had the spare keys to the truck hidden away in her brassiere all day. She didn't even have time to get the truck unlocked before he came barreling out of the house like a madman, screaming all the while about how he was going to kill her for trying to run off."

The scrub brush opened up and ahead the Clayton farmhouse hove into view. It was faded gray, but in the moonlight, it looked the color of bleached bone.

"She almost didn't make it," Henry said. "Charles was a good hundred feet away, but when he stepped off the front porch and onto the lawn, something happened."

The air in the patrol car took on an electric charge and I felt every hair on my body stand on end. It was something out of a bad movie, or one of the horror stories I was always reading, but it was true.

We were crawling along the path now, our tires crunching softly on the gravel. Henry's eyes were darting around, looking out for Clayton.

"When he stepped off that porch, out from under the awning and into the moonlight, Charles Clayton *changed*."

"What do you mean?" I said, though by now I had an idea, much as I didn't want to admit it to myself.

Henry swallowed so hard I could hear it. "He started writhing, like he was having some kind of a fit. At first Barbara thought that's what it was, and she nearly ran to help him. If she had, her good-heartedness would have gotten her killed. Charles's face distorted. His eyes glowed red. His teeth lengthened so they were the size of steak knives. He was covered in hair, and his hands looked like claws.

"His ranting became impossible to understand until it was just a wordless growl. Barbara jumped in the truck and high-tailed it out of there. She said he chased her all the way down the path, so close to the truck's rear bumper that she was afraid he'd be able to reach out and grab ahold of it, even though she was doing better than twenty miles an hour."

Henry stopped the car and turned to me. "I know this sounds crazy, Jimmy. I know it does. But there are things—things we can't understand."

But I understood all too well.

"Maybe Barbara was just out of her mind," Henry said. "You get beat up on that much, bound to make you a little punch-drunk. But I don't think so. I think we're gonna find something here that neither of us is ready for."

With that, he opened the door and stepped out into the night, fast, like he didn't want to see my reaction. Like he was embarrassed.

He shouldn't have been. Sure, the story sounded crazy, but there was something in his voice that made me believe. Not just believe that he believed. I knew it sure as he did.

I got out of the car, hitching up my Sam Browne and removing my service revolver from its holster. Like most kids who grew up in a small Texas town back then, I'd been shooting all my life, and no one on the force qualified better at the range. But just then, the gun felt like an alien thing in my hand.

The gravel crunched under my shoes as I followed Henry up toward the house.

"I'll knock on the front door," he said. "We don't get along too good, but I've known Charles for years. Maybe he'll talk to me."

His face said he knew otherwise. He didn't have his gun out—probably didn't want to provoke Clayton—but his hand was poised near it, and I could see his trigger finger twitch.

"Where you want me?"

Procedure said I should be just behind Henry and to his right, that way I'd have a clear shot if something went wrong.

"You go around back," Henry said. "Case he runs for it."

The idea didn't thrill me, but I could see the wisdom in it. I did as Henry asked.

It was darker around back of the house. The fields were behind me, stretching out toward the horizon, the unmowed hay swaying in the breeze like waves on a dark ocean. Off to the left, the barn loomed, and a rusted-out tractor sat hunched like the skeleton of some ancient mechanical beast. I stood a good distance from the door and held my gun at my side.

I heard Henry knock and call out to Clayton. He wasn't even through with his sentence before the back door exploded outward, the frame splintering to matchwood. A hulking shape blotted out the rectangle of yellow light streaming from the interior of the house. The creature let out a primal scream and charged down the steps toward me. It was a blur of black, matted hair and razor teeth.

It was almost at my throat by the time I got the gun up. I squeezed the trigger three times, sure that it wouldn't work because the bullets were lead and not silver. The shots were a roar in my ears, drowning out the world. Hot blood spattered across my face and hands.

The monster's blood.

The shape fell to the ground at my feet, dead.

I stood over the body of Charles Clayton and looked down into the face of the man—not a supernatural creature at all, just a man—crazed out of his mind from years of drink. His hair was long and stringy, and a growth of dark beard covered his face.

But he was human and nothing more. Always had been.

My fevered mind, hopped up on too many horror magazines and Henry's story, had made me see what was not there at all.

What felt like an eternity passed, and Henry came bolting around the house. He crouched low and did what I was afraid to. He took Clayton's pulse.

"Dead?" I asked.

Henry nodded.

I went to throw up.

✗   ✗   ✗   ✗

There was paperwork to fill out. Mountains of it. And there was a grand jury. Henry testified that I didn't have a choice but to open fire and I said much the same. I guessed it was probably true, though Charles had been unarmed when I shot him, but that it was the truth didn't make me feel much better. There was no mention of Charles's hand being mangled and miraculously healed, nor was the subject of werewolves ever broached. I certainly wasn't going to be the one to bring it up.

In the end, I got a commendation for bravery.

They never did find the body of the teenager Barbara said Charles had killed. They looked, but the Clayton farm covered a lot of ground, and Barbara said Charles never told her where he'd buried it. Personally, I doubt the boy ever existed. It was just another part of her and Henry's story, made up to strike fear into the heart of a nineteen-year-old deputy who'd read one too many scary stories. Then again, maybe he did exist. Maybe Charles murdering him had been the thing that had pushed Barbara over the edge, finally convinced her to do what Henry had been encouraging her to do, to find a way to leave Charles, once and for all.

The two of them got married two months after the grand jury let out. Ran off early one Friday morning after Henry's shift ended and never came back to Marble Falls. No one heard from them again. I wouldn't even have known about the marriage if I hadn't done some digging into state records. All these years later, I don't know if they're still together, but I hope so. They did what they thought they had to in order to be together, and God knows Barbara deserved better than Charles Clayton.

But their happiness came at a price, and I'd be lying if I said I felt good about being the one stuck paying it.

Charles Clayton was no supernatural creature, but he was a monster just the same. I have no doubts on that point. But his blood is on my hands. And monster's blood or not, it's a stain that won't ever wash clean.

David Afsharirad is Senior Editor at Ark Press. His short stories have appeared in various magazines and anthologies. He lives in Austin, Texas with his family.

"THE ONE I LEFT BEHIND"
Hal Charles

Kelly Locke was ebullient as she walked into city hall an hour after her Thursday telecast finished. The local second-quarter ratings book was just out, and her *The Six O'Clock News with Kelly Locke* had trounced the nearest competitor by a 2:1 margin. On top of that item, rumors were buzzing like a hive of happy bees that the network was going to promote her to lead anchor of their national nightly news report in order to bolster its sagging ratings and send her to New York. To celebrate, she used her reporter's connections to secure two VIP tickets to the upcoming Big Hair Reunion Fair of '80s bands, and she was going to surprise her father, Matt, as her plus-one.

After being checked through the security gate, she rode the elevator to the eighth floor and strolled down to the office bearing the title CHIEF OF DETECTIVES. As Caroline, her father's administrative assistant, was long gone for the day, she walked into his outer office and knocked on his door. No answer, so she knocked louder.

"Come in," boomed the larger-than-life voice of her father.

She found him pensively pacing as he usually did when presented with an overwhelming problem.

"Kelly," he said. "How nice of you to drop by and see your tired old father. What's up, or is it wazzup?"

And suddenly she couldn't tell him, tell the man who had raised her after her mother died when she was just a young girl, tell him that she might soon be leaving, tell him that she was deserting him when he was thinking of retiring. "Nothing," she said. "I just wanted to see you."

"And I'm glad you did. I'm not good at keeping secrets, so I'm just going to come out with it. I have a surprise for you," he said, making her feel worse. "Who's my all-time favorite rocker?"

"Growing up, I would have guessed Jon Bon Jovi or even Meatloaf, but there was this one female singer whose records and tapes you kept buying. A one-namer like Cher. What was it? Oh, yeah. Mandi."

"I'll bet you didn't know that Mandi is headlining the Big Hair Reunion Fair down at the arena tomorrow night. The old man has scored two front-row seats and, just as important, two backstage passes for after the show to meet Mandi."

"Dad, how could you—"

"Did I ever tell you it's not what you know, but whom you know?" he said proudly.

She gave him her *Six O'Clock News* smile. Now definitely wasn't the best time to talk to him about her potential triumph.

At that moment the phone on his desk rang.

"Chief Locke here," he said into the receiver. "What? Oh, no! I'll be right there."

"What happened, Dad?" she said.

"There's been an accident down at the arena where the bands were rehearsing for tomorrow night, and someone may be dead."

✗   ✗   ✗   ✗

Chief of Detectives Matt Locke had long since given up opening the passenger-side door for his daughter, but as he activated the flashing lights and siren to his unit, he couldn't help taking a fast look at her before he pulled out of the downtown parking garage. As the city lights twinkled by, he was pulled back to a night like this one over thirty-five years ago.

Right after being promoted to detective, Locke found himself assigned to the last unit on his "wish list," Narco. He and his short-timer partner, Buckshot Blattner, caught a case in the seedy side of town, River Run. Undercover for over two months, Locke followed the food chain to a major supplier named Underwood. When he heard Underwood on the phone talking about a major delivery taking place, he found a pay phone and alerted his partner. Blattner arrived while the deal was going down, and, not wanting to take a chance on anything ruining his upcoming retirement party, pulled a semi-auto out of the trunk.

"What are you doing?" Locke argued.

"Gonna light up all of them," said Blattner.

"But the supplier might take us one more step up the food chain."

"Not my problem. In fact, my only problem is making it till next Friday when Julie and I drive the U-Haul to our new condo in Fort Myers."

"Our orders are to take as many as we can alive."

"Exactly. 'As we can.' We can't."

With that, Blattner laid down a burst, dropping five guys to the asphalt. The supplier, seeing he couldn't make it into his truck, broke for the tenement behind and disappeared.

"Well, college-boy," said Blattner, "you got your wish. Now we've got to go room-to-room."

Calling for back-up, Locke ran around to the front of the building and stood absolutely quiet. Above him, he heard somebody crying. Somebody playing an acoustic guitar. Someone ran up some stairs. Second floor. A door slammed. The guitar stopped. Bingo. Locke took the stairs quickly and quietly. Two doors loomed on the left. One had at least four locks on it. Locke chose the next apartment. Almost prone, he reached up and opened the door. Two bullets thudded past where his head had just been.

Locke scrambled through the door, throwing himself behind a couch. The supplier was "shielded up," standing behind a girl in a halter top. The guitar lay on the floor.

"She's too small to protect you," Locke called. "I can put four slugs in you without hurting her."

The supplier tossed his gun toward Locke and stood up with his arms raised.

Blattner came through the door and fired the semi-auto.

The supplier went down, ripped apart.

"You're next, honey," said Blattner. "Can't have no witnesses."

Locke kneed his partner in the groin, catching the rifle as he dropped it. "Girl is so zoned out on drugs she probably thinks she's watching an episode of *Hill Street Blues*."

Blattner never said another word to him until his U-Haul left town.

"Earth to Dad," said Kelly. "You OK?"

"No problem. It's been a rough week."

But it was rougher back then. When the dust cleared and the investigators left the scene after getting not one word from the girl, Locke drove her to the doctor's office, where his wife was a nurse. The doctor came in, took one look into her eyes, and recommended a good rehab clinic he knew of. Locke left her there, offering to pay the bills. When he went by to see her a week later, she was gone.

Chief Locke cut through the River Run district, the back way to the arena.

"You seem strange tonight," said Kelly.

"'Life is infinitely stranger than anything which the mind of man could invent,'" he replied cryptically.

Two years later, Locke recalled, he saw the young girl again and learned her name was Mandi. He went to see a Poison or Guns N' Roses concert—no, it was Porch Rocket—and the opening act was a new group called Mandi-Lynn. Fleshed out and with make-up, she seemed a different woman. As she came off the stage, she saw him in the wings, his favorite position because it was free, and recognized him from his help earlier. She apologized to him for fleeing rehab, but this opportunity had come up when Lynn Michaels invited her to join the band. And she said, pointing to her baby bump, more good news—she was pregnant. They exchanged hugs and phone numbers, and Locke was certain he'd never see Mandi again.

"'A Case of Identity,'" interrupted Kelly. "I've been wracking my mind to try to figure out what Holmes mystery that quote came from. Am I right?"

"Always, my dear," he responded before diving back into the past.

The last time he saw Mandi was during the winter half a year later. His wife had been off work for over a week trying to adjust to the fertility drugs. Just before lunch he received a call from Mandi asking him to meet her in room 535 of the Staley Hotel. When he arrived, she greeted him at the door. Her face was lean, her eyes vacant, and he couldn't help but notice the tracks on her arms.

"I managed to stay clean for my entire pregnancy," she explained, "but it's no use. I am an addict. I will always be an addict. Which is why I can't be a mother."

She led him over to a port-a-crib on the bed, and Matt Locke looked in to see the most beautiful little girl he had ever laid eyes on.

"I can't name her," said Mandi, "because she was never meant to be mine."

"And the father? What does he think?"

"Who knows? Like the song says, 'I've had so many men in oh so many ways.' It's usually hard to see their faces through the fog of pills or Mary Jane."

Then she burrowed into him and began bawling. Involuntarily he held her. When the crying stopped, she said, "I'm not fit to be a mother. I've tried. And the road isn't any place for a beautiful little girl."

"I know three excellent adoption agencies," Locke said.

"She's too good for some adoption agency. Besides, I haven't got the time to check out everyone who would apply." She sat on the bed beside her child. "In my entire, whole life, only one person has ever shown me kindness without wanting something. You."

"I'm flattered, but—"

"Take her." She handed him a card. "Send me the adoption papers here, and I'll sign them all legal." She stood up and placed the port-a-crib in Locke's hand. "Now go. I've got a powerful urge to shoot up, and I never want to see either of you again."

Before Locke could protest, he was herded out the hotel room door.

He had not seen Mandi since that night. He brought Mandi's child home to his bed-ridden wife and explained the situation. The doctor for whom his wife worked was helping her with the fertility problem, and, being quite sympathetic, certified he had delivered the little girl in an at-home birth. Locke notified Mandi, but she never replied. For all intents and purposes, the baby they named Kelly after Locke's mother was their natural daughter. Now, only two people knew the truth, as both his wife and the doctor died years earlier.

"'I have trained myself to see what others overlook,'" interrupted Kelly again. "That's something else Sherlock Holmes says in 'A Case of Identity,' and I can see that something is really troubling you."

Locke hesitated, then told the truth, or part of it. "I have this terrible foreboding. Years ago I knew Mandi before she became as famous as Adele, and I'm worried something truly bad has happened to her. I know personally she has a history of drug use."

"So do a lot of rockers," said Kelly, "but that doesn't mean she Kurt Co-bained or Whitney Houstoned."

"I hope you're right, honey."

Locke pulled into the back of the arena, where all the acts entered. A uniform let them in the back door, and they headed to the stage that had been erected on the basketball floor/hockey rink. As they came onto the stage,

Kelly noticed a blanket had been thrown over a body next to a microphone stand.

Even though he knew the uniform by the body and the staff of the arena, Locke flashed his badge for the others to see. Slipping on a pair of plastic gloves, he took a deep breath and pulled back the blanket.

Immediately he rose and turned his head away from the crowd.

"What is it, Chief?" said Kelly, deliberately using his professional appellation around others.

"What I feared. Mandi."

"I don't think I've ever seen you so emotional around a victim," she said softly.

"I don't think you've ever seen me around a victim I knew." He turned to the uniform. "Anybody notify the coroner, Sanders?"

"Not yet, sir."

Locke pulled out his cellphone, knowing that any time he called after work hours Solomon was glued to the Golf Channel or on the course. "Solly," he said when he heard a "hello," "sorry to interrupt the drive of the year, but it is what it is. If you picked up the victim right now and started work on her arrival, it wouldn't be soon enough…. No, this one is personal, very personal, and I'm not going to bring up what you owe me from our little head-to-head last weekend on the Champions course…. I know you will. I'll be by early tomorrow morning."

Kelly always marveled at how her father took charge at a crime scene. His next move was to secure the building and assign interrogation teams to the bands in the arena. He took Mandi's group. Kelly busied herself by looking around the immediate environs of the body.

"'It has long been an axiom of mine that the little things are infinitely the most important,'" Chief Locke said.

"'I have trained myself to see what others overlook,'" she repeated, making him certain she understood the reference to "A Case of Identity."

Her father was supervising the assistant coroner as he placed the body on a stretcher when Kelly yelled from the empty orchestra pit. Sitting on the floor was a metallic refillable water bottle. No sooner had she yelled, "Detective Locke," than one of his men appeared. After placing a yellow plastic tent with the number seven on it beside the bottle, he snapped a picture of the bottle in its original site, picked it up with a pair of tongs, dropped it into a plastic bag, and labelled it with a Sharpie.

Before questioning his first person of interest, Matt Locke walked into the wings, which he recognized ironically as the same place he and Mandi had once exchanged hugs. He wouldn't let himself cry. That would come later. Now he tried to compose himself, recalling every word from last night's phone call.

"I've changed my mind, Matt," Mandi had said, "and I would like to see you again and that amazing daughter you've raised, Kelly. I'm clean and have been for two years."

"Are you saying that after all this time that you want to tell her the truth?"

"Only if it's all right with you. I've followed you two, the cases you've worked, and I just finished watching her newscast. She's good, very good. Also, I know your wife died, so I guess the greatest emotional toll on my meeting her for the first time as an adult would be on you."

"And her. I really don't want to rock her world."

"Especially since she's climbed so high," said Mandi. "Tell you what. I'll leave two tickets and backstage passes at the arena's will-call. If you decide it's best to tell Kelly the truth, that's terrific. If you don't show after the concert, I'll understand."

Mandi hung up before he could decide, something he still hadn't done.

Seeing how troubled her father was, Kelly gave him ample space, not joining him until they started interviewing the band members.

✗ ✗ ✗ ✗

After the interviews, Kelly and Matt Locke pooled their notes:

- Philip Justice. The promoter of the Big Hair Reunion Fair looked a lot like David Crosby. Shortly after Mandi joined the band, Lynn Michaels was killed in a car accident. Justice took over as frontman and lead guitar. The Louisianan managed to write five top-ten charting songs before his creativity ran out and the band broke up. Justice claimed Mandi had written a new song she was going to debut at the BHRF. He was standing in the wings talking to Hank Burns when Mandi keeled over.

- Ginger Raines. A Darryl Hannah look-alike who was once rumored to be Lynn Michaels' girlfriend. When Mandi left the remnants of Mandi-Lynn, Ginger tried to take over the lead female vocals, but lacked Mandi's range. She claimed she was "messing around" with Ray Farmer, Mandi's long-time manager, when Mandi collapsed.

- Hank Burns, the drummer, verified Justice's story and his whereabouts when Mandi went down at the mic. Known as "Firestorm" for his hot temper, he admitted at one time or another he had threatened to kill each member of the band. He was so drunk that verifying anything he said was going to be difficult.

- Ray Farmer, Mandi's manager, who admitted he had been sued by the band for non-payment of concert funds. Since he also kept the books, he was able to demonstrate considerable expenses, especially when trying to publicize a reunion of "has-been hair."

✗ ✗ ✗ ✗

After searching Mandi's dressing room and finding nothing but an old issue of *Billboard*, the Lockes wanted to check Mandi's hotel room, but no one had the slightest idea where she was staying. The Chief of Detectives went with a hunch. The entire ride downtown he was silent, and Kelly decided not to press the issue.

Matt Locke pulled into the Staley Hotel, flashed his badge, and asked if Mandi was staying in room 535. A bellboy with a key card rode up the elevator with them.

"How did you know she was here, Dad?" inquired Kelly. "I observed every piece of information you did, and I'd have bet the ranch she was staying at the arena hotel with the other rockers."

"To quote the Great Detective, 'You did not know where to look, and so you missed all that was important.'"

The bellboy opened the door and left them alone. The maid service had already been by to turn down Mandi's bed and even leave a chocolate on the pillow.

"It'll take a court order to get this closet safe opened," said Locke after he had found the dial behind Mandi's hung-up clothes.

Kelly busied herself checking the clothes in the dresser and then proceeding to the bathroom. "What are we looking for exactly?" she said.

"It's like pornography," he replied. "We'll know it when we see it."

Fifteen minutes later they were sitting in chairs, defeated.

"Should we start removing electrical outlet plates?" said Kelly.

"What did we overlook, Sherlock?" said her father. "Did you check the nightstands?"

"Blank notepad and a Gideon Bible." When she heard herself say it, she hurried over to the right nightstand and opened the drawer. She retrieved the Gideon Bible and thumbed through it. "It's really an address book wrapped with a Gideon cover," she explained.

"Let me see," said Locke, fearful his phone number was included. He fanned through the pages, but his name did not appear. She must have memorized his number.

Kelly took the address book and slowly and systematically pored through it. "Look at this. Mandi wasn't a resident of our fair city, but she's got a local post office box listed."

"I'll get a court order and meet you at the central P.O. tomorrow when it opens at 8:30," said Locke.

✗ ✗ ✗ ✗

The postmaster showed the Lockes a printout that detailed how the box had been purchased in the mid-'80s and paid for every year by money order. "Looks like Ms. Whitcomb had a real connection to this city," he said. Then he pulled out the mail in the box, noting that her instructions had been to throw out all circulars, and handed what remained to the Chief of Detectives. A single large envelope.

Kelly slipped on a pair of latex gloves and began to examine the envelope. "The letter's ancient, Dad," she said. "Look at the postmark."

"1986," he said.

"And the return address has the initials M.W."

"Mandi Whitcomb," he said.

"Why would a woman," Kelly said, thinking out loud, "send herself a letter to a distant post-office box?"

"The same reason writers used to mail themselves copies of stories they wrote," surmised Locke. "As long as the letter was unopened, they had proof of copyright."

"I think we need to open this letter in the presence of an impartial authority such as the postmaster," said Kelly. "It could be important."

"Agreed," said her father.

In the postmaster's office, they slowly ripped open the envelope and pulled out napkins, hotel stationery, torn notebook pages, and odd scraps of paper.

"There are poems written on the papers," said Kelly.

"More like song lyrics with crude musical notes. Look, each one has a date," said her father, "and Lynn Michaels' signature."

"'This Feeling Won't Stop,' 'You Got Me in Deep,' 'Shot with Your Love,' 'Where You Go, I Go,' and 'Forever in Love with You,'" Kelly said, reading the titles.

"All top-ten hits for Mandi-Lynn in the period after Lynn Michaels died and before Mandi struck out on her own."

"Did you ever consider you were too deep in the rock scene?" asked Kelly.

"I never felt I had to drag you to any of the hundred concerts you attended as a kid," said Locke with a smile.

"There's somebody we need to re-interview," said Kelly.

"And since no good rocker wakes till noon, I think we know where to find him, so that gives us time to make another stop first."

⚸　⚸　⚸　⚸

The medical examiner's office was in the basement of the city hall annex. They found Solly Weintraub in the "cold room" wearing an unbuttoned lab coat over his golfing outfit—patched madras shorts, high black socks, and a Champions pima polo.

"Locke," said the M.E., covering the body in front of him with a rubber sheet, "the club charged me to change today's tee-time, so I put it on your tab. L-72, isn't it?"

"You've been looking at too many bar tabs, Solly," said the Chief of Detectives, "but this time I won't charge you with identity theft."

"You find anything to help us, Dr. Weintraub?" said Kelly.

"First, I checked that metallic water bottle your assistant brought over. Only thing on it were the prints of the vic, Mandi Whitcomb."

"You check for residue inside?" said the Chief of Detectives, remembering how Mandi had told him she was clean. If she had been telling the truth, the only thing that made sense was that someone else had slipped something deadly into her bottle.

"Aye, there's the rub," said the M.E. "Did you know 'rub' means difficulty or an impediment? How appropriate. That bottle contained Pepsi as well as an opioid laced with fentanyl. A Mexican synth, I'd guess, fifty to one-hundred times more powerful than morphine."

"So with the Pepsi, the victim might not taste what was being ingested?" concluded Kelly.

"That drive is perfectly down the middle of the fairway, Kelly," said Weintraub, "and here's the kicker. I discovered traces of the exact same poly-drug in your vic."

✗   ✗   ✗   ✗

With the help of the "house dick," a former cop who had once worked as a detective for Matt Locke, they found the arena hotel room they needed. The ink-marked, 50-ish rocker was still in bed, his right arm and leg draped over a girl whom Kelly pegged as fifteen at most. Atop the nightstand were several bottles of vodka, a vial of pills, and a marijuana bong. One way or another, the rocker was going down today.

"Philip Justice," said her father loudly, "it's wakey, wakey time."

The right eyelid of the aging rocker opened like a reluctant blind. "Who dat?" he said in a distinct Cajun accent.

"Two fans of Mandi," said the Chief of Detectives. "Hank Burns claims he saw you give Mandi the water bottle right after she finished rehearsing her new song yesterday," Locke lied.

"Might've been me," said Justice, trying to sit up while the girl dozed on. "Last fifteen years or so, dey been mostly one big blur."

"Do you remember what you put in her water bottle?" Kelly tried.

"Water?"

"Think again," said Matt Locke. "At a minimum you've got a rape charge with Miss Teen-Bait here that's going to put you in prison long past your first eligibility to collect Social Security."

"Rape? Lila… Lola dere was willing. We just passing a good time."

"And when we find drugs and alcohol in her system," said Kelly, "you'll be lucky if you ever do anything but make license plates the rest of your natural life."

"So let's cut a big, big deal," said Justice, seeming to wake up from his drug stupor.

Kelly said, "I'm guessing you OD-ed Mandi because she knew you didn't write those five hit songs after Lynn Michaels' death."

Justice stared blankly without a word.

Matt Locke grabbed the rocker by his salt-and-pepper beard and screamed in his face. "I am losing what little patience I have with a scumbag like you."

Justice's face wrenched in pain.

Kelly had never seen her father anger so quickly.

The teenage girl began to snore.

"Now dat you mention it," said Justice haltingly, "I just mighta crushed some of dose Mighty O pills that Carlos got for me and added them to Mandi's soda pop. Just to relax her a tad, you understand?"

"When Mandi told you she knew you had plagiarized those five hit songs," said Kelly, "you wanted to 'relax' her for good."

"Did you two know that on de strength of dose five tunes, I'm being inducted into the Rock & Roll Hall of Fame next month? Can you imagine dis little nobody from Bayou LaFitte making the big time? Mandi said I had to tell dem it be Lynn Michaels who wrote those songs, not me."

"How did you know about those songs?" said Matt Locke.

"Lynn was always writing dings on scraps of paper, then putting dem into his notebook before he go to bed. When he died, I took his notebook."

"Did you know that Mandi kept the original paper the songs were on, complete with dates and Lynn Michaels' signatures?"

"She say so, but I couldn't find no paper nowheres, but she done told me that right after she rehearsed her new song she was calling the po-lice. I heard that damned song. I knows what it say. She no longer cared if I tell the world she been a drug addict."

Which, Kelly reasoned, explained why Mandi hadn't exposed his plagiarism years ago.

"And," said the Chief of Detectives, pulling out his handcuffs and Miranda card, "the po-lice are here."

By the time they led Justice out of the hotel room, the teenage girl's snore turned to a thunderous rumble.

⚡ ⚡ ⚡ ⚡

The rain stole in at the close of day and now sheeted down the windows of Kelly's top-floor condo. Her father told her a ticket for the Big Hair Reunion Fair awaited her at the will-call window of the arena, but for some reason she couldn't rationally explain, she chose to stay in that night.

The death of Mandi Whitcomb bothered her even though she was barely aware of the singer's existence. As Kelly stood looking at the rain, she decided that her father's intense interest in Mandi's death lay at the bed of her uneasiness. Her dad had known so much about the singer, especially her room in the Staley Hotel. What was the connection between them?

Kelly hated herself for her thoughts, but one possibility loomed large. At some time in the past, her father and the singer were close, maybe even having an affair. Had her mother still been alive then? Her dad had taken such good care of her mom that Kelly found it difficult to blame him even if there had been a close relationship.

Kelly walked over to her desk and picked up the jump drive her father had given her of Mandi's performance during her last rehearsal. He told her that the sound engineer made a copy of the song and passed it on to her father, who in turn made a copy for Kelly.

Kelly slid back in her favorite mid-century modern wooden chair, picked up her glass of port, and took a sip as "The One I Left Behind" flooded the living room. Solving this case with her father had convinced her their relationship was the one thing in life she enjoyed the most, and there was no way she was going to leave the man who had raised her alone in order to sit at a sterile anchor desk and read news far, far away.

✗ ✗ ✗ ✗

Matt Locke cried four times in his adult life. Once the first time he saw his daughter, Kelly, once when his son was nearly killed, once when his wife died, and tonight. The evening rain seemed a perfect mirror of his mood. He had passed the point of wondering what he would have done if Mandi had told Kelly the truth. He knew now that he never would. Nothing could be gained by the truth, a meaningless gesture that might weaken the father-daughter bond he had worked so hard to build.

Matt Locke knew now that yesterday's reference to Doyle's "A Case of Identity" crawling out of his subconscious had been no accident. But he saw the difference between his situation and the story clearly. In Doyle's story, the stepfather had plotted to further his own interest, while he as Kelly's stepfather had acted only in the best interests of Kelly, his wife, and Mandi.

Matt knew, too, that his only motive since meeting Mandi was trying to help another human being, a person who needed help. Never was there anything romantic or sexual about his relationship with Mandi.

He turned the thumb drive over in his hand for the hundredth time that night. He was convinced Mandi had left him a trail of breadcrumbs so as to make things right. Mandi knew him well, but he still couldn't bring himself to listen to her final words.

Finally, toward midnight he poured himself a glass of his best scotch and inserted the thumb drive. Then he sat down in his favorite leather recliner and let her voice wash over him.

The roaring of the crowd,
The spotlight that was mine.
I'd trade it all for you,
The one I left behind.
The time has come for truth
Before my soul is lost.
Give credit where it's due,
No matter what the cost.
My song is incomplete.
The one note I can't find,
The memories of you—
The one I left behind.

"Hal Charles" is the nom de plume Fred Dannay (one-half of Ellery Queen) gave to the writing team of Hal Blythe and Charlie Sweet. Retired professors of English at Eastern Kentucky University, they are well-versed in mysteries, having written for *Ellery Queen Mystery Magazine* and being the final ghost of Brett Halliday (Mike Shayne). They have published thirteen stories in the Kelly Locke series as well as nine novels.

THAT MEDIEVAL TOUCH
Pete Barnstrom

The bells rang noon and I was thinking about that place on the corner that has good mutton when the dame came into my office.

I say "dame." Turns out she was a duchess. Shows what I know from royalty.

What can tell you is she wore a cape and one of those big collars with all the stiff and fiddly folds that look like it'd be tough to buckle your shoes in. It's not every broad who can strut in with a scepter and make it look natural.

She left her retinue outside, a couple of big bruisers who were probably former condottieri. Looked like they only took off their armor so they could fit down the hallway. They gave me glares menacing enough to curl my beard, and I might have blubbered all over my jerkin had the woman not closed the door with them on the other side.

That's right, my office has a door, made of real wood. Guess you could say I'd come a long way from that Middle Ages private dick I always thought I was.

Funny, I didn't feel like a Renaissance Man. Maybe I hadn't come that far. Maybe my clients just came to me when they needed someone with that medieval touch.

She asked, "You are Filippo of Napoli?"

As she'd just come through the door with my name on it, and as we were in Naples, I figured she knew that much. These nobles, they expect a certain formality from their servants, so I struck a tone up front to let her know who's the lord and who's the vassal here.

"My friends call me Flip," I told her. "My clients call me when they need me. My ex-wife calls me when the florins run out. Which are you?" I crossed my fashionable knee-length boots on the top of my desk, casual-like. "Just so you know, I'm prepared to mark one of those options off the list right away."

"You have a reputation," she said. "Raphael speaks well of you." She didn't sit in my client chair. To be fair, in that outfit I'm not sure she could. "He says you are discreet."

"More than he is, I guess." You step on the toes of some angry husbands for one of the Old Masters and all of a sudden you've got a reputation. Not that I'm complaining, gets me a lot of work. But would it have killed the guy to paint my portrait? That's how you get a reputation that lasts.

"I understand you are a soldier," she said.

I told her I was once. "Not anymore. Didn't like the hours."

She didn't smile. She'd never been a soldier, that much was clear. "But you know how to behave as a military man?"

Where was this going? "I suppose I do. Those no-necks you left in the hall look like they've done a little time in the ranks. You looking to upgrade your protection?"

"Hardly," she said, and now she did smile, the slightest bend of her lips, and I can tell you, it did not endear her to me. "I simply wish to ascertain that you have the skills required for the task I wish to set before you."

It was just possible I'd had enough of this lady, nobility or not. "And what makes you think I want to do anything for you?"

She underhanded a sack onto my desk. It landed with a thump heavy enough that I wondered how she'd carried it.

I lifted my chin so that I could see what spilled out. Gold coins. Enough to scrub any scruples.

"And again as much," she promised, "after you complete your duties as assigned."

I gave it a moment's thought, but not as long a moment as I'd like to believe.

"So who do you want dead?" I asked.

✗   ✗   ✗   ✗

I'd been under the impression that I was joking. And the Duchess had assured me that no one needed murdering, purely a matter of applying a little pressure in the right place.

But she wasn't the one going to Venice with a dagger in her boot.

There was a girl—wasn't there always? Her name was Emilia, and she'd been married off to a soldier with no prospects. She was "favored," the Duchess said, by a scion of the Venetian court who wanted to see her advance.

I asked if this "scion" had a name, but got no response. No surprise. Was this Emilia his mistress? Illegitimate daughter? Not my business.

Her soldier husband had been passed over for a promotion, instead kept as an ensign to a general. I'd seen the type before; the faithful servant who thought he was positioning himself for the next step, but that wasn't happening. Once the officer decides he likes how you lay out his pantaloons, that'll be your job until you're mustered out. Better get used to it.

Unless, that is, your wife has a secret benefactor who is willing to pay to get your competition eliminated.

It was a young chump named Cassio who was in the desired lieutenant's slot. Remove him, the Duchess theorized, and the husband could be promoted from his position as the General's food-taster.

Didn't seem likely to me, but for the kind of gold she'd dropped on my desk, I promised to give it my best shot.

It's not hard to infiltrate an army the size of Venice's. It's so big, no one really knows who belongs and who doesn't. As long as you look the part and know what to say, you're in. If anyone asked, I told them I was transferred over from Palermo. All I needed to do was be gone before they checked with my former commanding officer in Palermo; I doubt he'd forgotten what I did to his nose.

Getting close to young Cassio was a little tougher. It required strategy. And while I may appear to be nothing more than muscle and devastating good looks, one of my secret weapons is cunning.

I was there less than a week before Cassio's horse threw him. The kid loved his horse, took special care to feed it properly and care for it, and it was unusual for it to react violently to him climbing into the saddle.

A few of his subordinates ran in with swords drawn, eager to be the one who would kill the animal for its effrontery to their boss. But I pushed them aside, took the reins, ran a calming hand over its snout.

"Things like this happen," I scolded them, loud enough for Cassio to hear. "There's no reason to do harm upon a faithful steed over it."

Cassio witnessed my level-headed response, and he admired me for it. What he didn't witness was me pulling the thorn-knot out from under the saddle where I'd placed it.

From there, it was easy to get into his circle. The kid was a good soldier, smart, but a little naive. He only kept counsel with his closest buddies, which now included me.

We took meals together, and we drank together. Too much, in Cassio's case, that was a habit he needed to learn to control. It was going to get him in trouble one day.

The one thing we didn't do was ride together. He rode up front with the officers, while I marched with the grunts. All the reasons I'd stopped being a soldier were coming back to me.

I only ever saw the General from a distance. A dark-skinned type who rode like an officer, brow patrician, head high, so that the enemy could see him and flee in fear. Unlike those of us in back, who marched with darting eyes, always prepared to run for cover.

I could see the three of them talking together as they rode, the General's dusky head bent toward Cassio now, and then to the ensign, the General's toadie, the one I was supposed to be there to help.

Only, I wasn't so sure I wanted to help him. I'd grown to like Cassio, and the other guy I could see through like watered-down wine.

He had that skill good schemers have, making himself into whatever the situation required. Ingratiating his way into friendships with the General, Cassio, whoever he needed to get past, and stomping on anyone he had to climb over.

Takes one to know one, I guess.

He had his own plans for moving up, and unless I missed my guess, it wasn't going to end well for Cassio. Not my problem, of course. And it would make my job easier.

But maybe I'd find a way to make it happen before then and keep Cassio alive in the process.

⚡ ⚡ ⚡ ⚡

It was in a tavern in Cyprus, where we'd come to repel a Turkish invasion that didn't happen, that I saw my chance.

The toadie was pouring Cassio's wine. It was clear he'd recognized the kid's flaw as well as I did and wanted to take advantage of it. I suspected he might have procured a poison tincture to slip into the wine, so I stepped in.

By which I mean I slapped Cassio across the chops and sent his goblet spiraling away through the air, wine sloshing across the table.

"Ruffio!" he shouted sloppily, and seeing as I'd told him that was my name, I knew he meant me. "What is the meaning of this?"

"How dare you impugn the name of the General's wife?" I demanded, taking care that everyone nearby could hear me, as if being spewed with Cassio's wine hadn't already gotten their attention. Brawling with a common soldier might not get him in too much trouble, but to a gent like the General, insulting his woman would put the offense over the edge. "I demand satisfaction!"

I was counting on the kid being drunk enough not to realize he hadn't insulted the woman, or at least not care if he had. And I was right.

He pulled his short sword, which one might have called unfair, seeing as I didn't have mine, but he didn't get a chance to use it as I broke an earthenware pitcher over his head and put him down for the night.

And that's when at least two dozen soldiers landed on me. I got out of it better than I might have, but I can't say I gave as good as I got.

Last thing I remember is seeing the toadie looking at me on the floor, his amphibian eyes glittering with something I interpreted as gratitude. It was warranted. If this didn't get him the position, it wouldn't be my fault.

✗ ✗ ✗ ✗

As I figured, Cassio was stripped of his rank, and I was drummed out of the army. Which spared me the trouble of deserting. I grabbed the first boat south.

The next time the Duchess came through my door, I stood like a gentleman. It took a little effort, as I still had some bruises, but I made like I was glad to see her.

She didn't seem as glad to see me.

"I suppose you heard of the affair?" she asked.

I smiled. "Heard of it? I was the cause of it." I waved her to my chair, but again she didn't take it. "Got the kid Cassio out of the way, and by now Emilia's husband will have stepped up. Or so I assume."

Her dead-eyed gaze did not radiate satisfaction. "Do you?"

I noted no satisfaction in her tone, either. "That's not how it worked out? Because I cleared the way for the toadie."

"Toadie?"

"Emilia's husband," I explained.

The Duchess flared her nostrils. Reminded me of Cassio's horse. "His name," she announced, "is Iago."

I nodded. Meant nothing to me. I guess I'd heard it at the time, but I always thought of him as the toadie. "So?"

"I take it you do not keep abreast of the news from Venice," she said.

"Venice? No." To tell the truth, I wasn't much on current events unless they involved sports. I always had a few florins down on the Calcio game.

"Iago did indeed 'step up,' as you so blithely put it," she said, her tone still as frigid as ever. "He somehow came up with the idea to convince General Othello that his wife, the good lady Desdemona, was unfaithful, and so to murder her."

I remembered my jibe at Cassio, making up that business about the General's wife. And the toadie had used it to put a worm in the big man's ear. I'd played him short, comparing his cunning to my own. He made me look like an amateur.

"And Iago then killed his own wife," she added, and waited for me to make the connection.

"Wait, Emilia?" The whole reason I'd gone there. Dead.

Her lip curled just a bit, as close as her face allowed emotion to be expressed. "That admirable Moorish general ended his own life soon after he realized he'd been duped by this...what was your word?" She peered at me through heavy-lidded eyes. "Toadie?"

Not often I'd put up with anyone giving me the business like this, but I figured I deserved it. "What about Cassio?"

"The young officer you so absurdly assaulted?" Guess she'd heard the details. Not from me. "He was appointed to the General's position. It is his duty now to punish Iago." She heaved a breath that strained her bodice. "One hopes mercy is not in his nature."

She threw something on my desk again. Another heavy pouch. I didn't look at it.

"You performed your duties as requested, Filippo of Napoli." She turned away from me and moved to my door. "I trust you will spend your reward in good health."

⚹   ⚹   ⚹   ⚹

I spent her gold on a boat. Rented, yes, but private.

For the second time, I was traveling to Venice with a dagger in my boot. Only this time, I planned to use it.

Lights on the shore, an inn with a pier. It had been a long journey, but I would not be stopping for the night.

Once I tied off the boat, I kept to the shadows as I worked my way up the hill to the base where the garrison slept, outside the Duke's palace.

I found the General's quarters. Unlike most of the others, light came from the window instead of snores. I chanced a look in, and I saw Cassio at a table. There was wine in front of him, but he wasn't drinking it.

Instead, he stared into his goblet, looking for something. Wisdom? Courage? I knew he had both of those. I also knew what he didn't have.

Unlike the Duchess, what I knew was that Cassio was too kind a soul to do what needed doing. Mercy wasn't just in his nature, it's who he was.

When what he needed was vindictiveness.

Good thing I carried a portion large enough for both of us.

The guardhouse wasn't far. It was a simple matter to let myself in. Their interest is more in keeping people from getting out.

I found him in a cell.

"Hello, toadie," I said.

He didn't get a chance to say anything.

Pete Barnstrom is an award-winning writer and filmmaker. His most recent worldwide release is the feature film *Satanic Hispanics*. He's shot documentaries in Greenland for the National Science Foundation, made movies with the Blair Witch guys (not that one), and seen one of his films screened at the Smithsonian. His fiction has appeared in such diverse publications as *Alfred Hitchcock Mystery Magazine*, *Leon Literary Review*, and *Strangely Funny*. He's on the socials as @Mistah Pete and he'd love to hear from you.

SNIFFING OUT THE PROBLEM
Laird Long

"Boys," Colonel Thaddeus Jackson drawled, "we've got ourselves an inventory shrinkage problem."

The ancient security guards (the three blind mice as some called them) stared blankly at the colonel.

"Plain truth is: someone is stealing from me, and I don't like it one bit."

Ben Harper, plant manager, nodded eagerly at the Colonel, then spoke in an authoritative business voice to the rheumatic security corps. "Tools—drills, rotors, planers; wood—planks, sheets, dowelling; and miscellaneous items such as glue, nails, and tacks have all gone missing over the last six months. And—"

"It's got to stop," the Colonel said bluntly. He surveyed the old guard mustered about the conference room table with a critical but sympathetic eye. "Any ideas, boys?"

Pepper Hawkins, day shift, former high school football teammate of the Colonel's, suggested security cameras. Sowell Jenders, night shift, former wildcat drilling partner of the Colonel's, suggested metal detectors and random pat-downs.

The Colonel frowned, pushed back his spotless, white office-Stetson, and shook his craggy head. "You boys know how I run my furniture business—with southern manners and northern know-how. We're a family here. Would you frisk your youngsters every time they left the house? Set up a camera in the family john? No, I don't think so."

Harper scoured the hairy bottom of his nostrils with a pale digit. He considered himself a twenty-first century businessman; the Colonel, a crumbling anachronism. "Maybe we just have to live with these immaterial—"

"Virgil'll stop 'em," Clay Friendly, afternoon shift, hunting buddy of the Colonel's, broke in.

"Virgil!?" Harper snapped. "Who the—"

"Now how is that old hound-dog of yours going to solve my thievery problem, Clay?" the Colonel asked.

And while Harper impatiently tattooed the table with his fingers, and the other watchmen struggled to keep their watery eyes open, Friendly laid out his plan.

⚹ ⚹ ⚹ ⚹

"This here is essence of dogwood!" Friendly croaked at the afternoon shift gathered around him on the plant floor. He held up an old-fashioned corn jug fitted with a spray cap. "It gives off a scent that can only be smelled by the best of tracking dogs—and not at all by humans. Sorta like a dog whistle for the nose."

The large crowd, many of whom were new to the country and the English language, stared intently at the jug, at the white-haired man in the dusty, blue uniform. Where a lot of them came from, the only thing respected more than age, was authority.

"And this here," Friendly gave Virgil's leash a tug, "is the best tracking dog around these parts."

Virgil raised his wrinkled head, gave the assemblage a baleful stare, then let the weight of his droopy ears drop his head back down again.

The workers glanced from the dog to the man to the jug, many of them amazed at the ways of Americans, others, locals like Ben Harper, less impressed.

"The plan," Friendly continued, "is for the shipper-receivers to spray every load of raw materials and tools coming into the plant with essence of dogwood—just a little squirt, mind you—for identification purposes. This here is powerful stuff—once the scent is in there, you can't get it out again. Kinda like skunk spray. When a shift leaves for the day, everyone stows their smelly overalls, gloves, and boots in their lockers, and then drives nice and slow out of the parking lot. Virgil will be stationed at the guard shack to give a quick whiff to every car. He'll sniff out anyone leaving with things that don't belong to them."

Excited chatter filled the plant floor until the Colonel raised his hand. "When one man steals from his employer, he steals from all his fellow employees," he said, and the southern-tried security system went into effect.

⚡   ⚡   ⚡   ⚡

A week later, as the office staff and afternoon shift slowly cruised out of the plant parking lot, Virgil started howling like possum hunting season and a full moon had arrived simultaneously. He dragged Friendly around Ben Harper's car, jumped on the trunk, and bayed at the sun.

Harper piled out of the shiny vehicle and gestured angrily at the red-coated, full-throated bloodhound. "What's wrong with that mutt!?"

"Mind if we take a look in your trunk?" Friendly asked, unfriendly-like, as Virgil clawed gold strips of paint off the car.

A crowd of onlookers quickly gathered around the car-dog pile-up, among them the Colonel.

"You want me to call my old army buddy, Chief Brubaker, and get him to pop your trunk, Ben?" the Colonel said.

Harper's face turned redder than a debutante dragging a train of toilet paper. "But, but…you now that dog can't smell anything…" he spluttered, then hung his head like a hound that's lost his way.

⚡   ⚡   ⚡   ⚡

"Old Virgil didn't really smell the company tools in Ben's car, did he?"

the Colonel asked Friendly, as the two men lounged in the Colonel's huge, oak and leather-heavy office.

Friendly pulled one of the Colonel's fat stogies out of his mouth and reached down and patted Virgil on the head. The dog took no notice; he was busy eyeing his twitching tail.

"No, sir, he didn't," Friendly admitted. "Essence of dogwood is nothing more than colored water and chicanery. But lots of your workers aren't exactly familiar with hunting dogs, hunting period, Colonel, so I thought they might fall for it."

"Hmm," the Colonel agreed. "So why was Virgil howling at Ben's car to the beat the devil?"

Friendly chuckled. "That was the five pounds of ground round I put in Harper's trunk last night, along with some tools with shaved-off serial numbers that I found at his big, new house in Sunny Hollows—that new suburb out in the middle of nowhere. I sniffed around and confirmed some suspicions I'd had for awhile."

The Colonel stopped puffing. "You broke into his home?"

Virgil staggered upright, plopped his head down in Friendly's lap.

"Like you always say, Colonel," Friendly replied, scratching behind the hound-dog's floppy ears, "southern manners..." He pulled a lock-pick set out of his shirt pocket and tossed it on the Colonel's desk. "...and northern know-how."

Laird Long pounds out fiction in all genres. Big guy, sense of humor. Writing credits include: *Blue Murder Magazine, Plots With Guns, Hardboiled, Thriller UK, Damnation Books, Bullet, Robot, Eternal Night, Another Realm, Ennea (9), The Dark Krypt, Albedo One, Baen's Universe, Sniplits, Woman's World, The Forensic Examiner, The Weekly News, that's life!, knowonder!,* and stories in the anthologies *Your Darkest Dreamspell, The Mammoth Book of New Comic Fantasy, The Mammoth Book of Jacobean Whodunits,* and *The Mammoth Book of Perfect Crimes and Impossible Mysteries.*

X MARKS THE SPOT
Josh Pachter

It had been one hell of a shift.

Del Marlowe beat up on his wife Dot again and had to be cuffed and dragged out to the patrol car after she managed to lock herself in the bathroom with her cell phone and dial 911. A free-for-all at the Brazen Bull took him, Sergeant Al Penny, and both of the WaKeeney PD's patrolmen to break up. And as if that wasn't enough for a Wednesday evening, he'd had to run out to Ogallah to chase a lead that promised to help him bust a fentanyl ring but turned out to be a false alarm.

By the time Chief B. Jefferson Warren parked his cruiser behind his wife's twelve-year-old pale-blue Honda Fit at ten that evening and opened the front door of their modest two-bedroom ranch house on the north edge of WaKeeney, just before the town petered out into farmland, he was whipped.

"Shellie?" he called in the direction of the kitchen. "I'm home!"

There was no response.

"Shel?"

Nothing. And that was odd: it was too late for her to be out on a weeknight, too early for her to be in bed.

He looked around the foyer, confused, and spotted a square white envelope, flap side up, on the narrow console table where they kept their keys and sunglasses and the mail. He picked it up and turned it over:

The hug and kiss were scrawled across the front of the envelope in dark brown lipstick, and Jeff Warren was about to smile when he realized he'd never seen anything *close* to that color on Shellie's lips in all the years they'd been together.

He scratched one of the letters with a fingernail, and—instead of smearing—bits of color flaked off the paper.

That's not lipstick, he thought, and a cold fist closed around his heart and squeezed. *That there's blood.*

He flipped over the envelope and tore it open. Inside he found a plain white sheet of paper. He unfolded it and read, in Times New Roman capitals that could have been typed on any computer in the world and printed out on any printer:

I HAVE HER. I HAVEN'T HURT HER—YET. GATHER $10,000
IN UNMARKED BILLS, NOTHING BIGGER THAN A 20, AND

DON'T DO ANYTHING STUPID. FURTHER INSTRUCTIONS
WILL FOLLOW.

He ran the back of his hand across his dry lips and swore.

✗   ✗   ✗   ✗

"Where the *hell* am I supposed to get ten thousand dollars, Howard? I've
got maybe four hundred bucks in my checking account, and the last time I
had any savings it was dimes in a piggy bank my folks gave me for my seventh birthday."

Howard Findlay, president of the Solutions Bank on North Main, leaned
back in his swivel chair and rubbed his gut with the fingers of both hands. "I
don't know what to tell you, B.J.," he said. "I—"

"Jeezus, Howard, I *wish* you wouldn't call me that. You know I hate it."

The banker sat up straight, loosened his necktie, unbuttoned the top button of his pale-yellow dress shirt. "Sorry, Jeff," he said sheepishly. "Blame
your parents for saddling you with those initials. I—"

"The money," Chief Warren cut him off. "Can you lend me the money?
You know I'm good for it."

"I would if I could," Findlay said, frowning. "But you already got a second mortgage on the house, and I—"

"Dammit, Howie, this son of a bitch has got my *wife*, and I think he's
already cut her. Look at this." He showed his friend the brown X O on the
front of the white envelope. "I figure that's blood, probably Shellie's blood.
I overnighted some scrapings to the KBI's Forensic Science Lab in Topeka,
but what are they going to tell me? Either it *is* blood or it ain't, and either
way the guy has her. Next time, he might send a finger or an ear. I need this
money, Howard, and I need it ASAP."

Findlay sighed and reached for his phone. "Let me call the home office,"
he said. "See what I can do."

✗   ✗   ✗   ✗

The cruiser's tires spat gravel as Warren spun off Fourth Street into his
driveway. He slammed the gear shift into park, snapped off the engine and
jumped out of the car.

There was a white envelope sitting face up on the raffia welcome mat
outside his front door.

Once again, an X and an O had been drawn on the front in what seemed
to be blood. This time, though, there was a second X placed about an inch
below the O, a hug and two kisses:

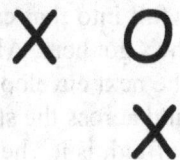

Warren got a pair of disposable blue nitrile gloves from the cruiser's trunk and put them on. It was unlikely there would be prints on the envelope or its contents, but better safe than sorry was his motto. He opened the flap and slid out a folded sheet of white printer paper and read the words that had been typed on it:

HAVE YOU GOT THE MONEY YET, CHIEF? I WON'T HURT HER UNLESS I HAVE TO. FURTHER INSTRUCTIONS WILL FOLLOW.

✗ ✗ ✗ ✗

"No prints," Al Penny said, disgusted, "not even a partial. This asshole's a cautious mother, whoever he is."

"Why doesn't he say what to do with the ransom money, though?" Warren prowled back and forth across the hardwood floor of his office. "What's he waiting for?"

The sergeant shrugged. "I ain't the brains of this outfit, Chief. Figuring stuff out is your department."

Warren parted with a grunt. "Well, I got nothing, Al. All I know is he's holding Shellie somewhere, and *sooner* or later he's going to tell me how to deliver ten thousand dollars I don't have and don't have any way to get."

Penny looked up at him shyly. "I've got a thousand bucks I been saving for a down payment on a new truck," he said. "It's yours, boss, if it'll help."

The chief stopped pacing and studied his deputy as if he'd never really seen the man before. Man? Penny was young, little more than a kid, really, less than eight months out of the academy. He had a shock of hair bleached blond by the Kansas summer sun—and freckles, for Pete's sake, *freckles* sprinkled across the bridge of a pug nose that made him look like Opie Taylor. But with Assistant Chief Lester Jackson out on medical leave for at least six weeks recovering from a knee replacement, that made Al Penny the department's temporary second-in-command.

Warren eased himself down into his chair and folded his arms on his desktop and leaned forward. "That is a very generous offer, Al, and if I had the other nine grand I might take you up on it. But I'm not even close. Whenever he gives me these 'further instructions' he promises, I honestly don't know *what* I'm going to do."

"You sure you don't want to bring in the Feds? Kidnapping's pretty much their jam, ain't it?"

Warren shook his head. "First note said don't do anything stupid. I figure calling in the Fibbies would fall into that category, and I'm not gonna take the chance. This is my *wife* he's got here, Al."

"So we sit and wait for the next envelope, is that it?"

Jeff Warren washed a hand across the stubble that was beginning to appear on his chin. "That, I'm afraid, is it," he said.

✗　✗　✗　✗

The chief's eyes widened at the sight of the pile of well-worn currency on Howard Findlay's desk. "They approved it?"

The banker gritted his teeth and shook his balding head. "Turned it down flat," he said. "Your house is underwater, Jeff, and with two mortgages on it already, they say there's no way they can take the risk."

"I don't understand," Warren said, narrowing his eyes at the stack of bills. "If they won't—"

"This is my own money, buddy. Thirty-eight hundred dollars. If I could raise more, you could have that, too, but this is all I can put my hands on right now."

The chief pulled in a deep breath and sighed it out. "This—this is above and beyond, Howie. I can't take your personal savings."

"It's a loan," Findlay said, "not a gift. You can pay me back—with interest, if that'll make you feel better—but—"

"You don't get it," Warren cut him off, and there was a blend of sadness and bitterness in his voice. "If it was ten K, I would snatch it right up. But thirty-eight hundred dollars doesn't do me any good. The guy wants ten thousand, and I don't get the sense he's likely to negotiate. He's already cut Shellie—if I can't come up with the full ten thou by the time he tells me what to do with it, I'm afraid he might kill her."

✗　✗　✗　✗

Both of the WaKeeney PD's patrolmen were putting in unpaid overtime knocking on doors, searching for a witness who'd seen someone leave the Warrens' house with Michelle Warren in tow or spotted her in the passenger seat of a car whose make and model and plate number they might possibly have noticed and remembered.

They weren't doing it because their boss was the great grandson of Albert Warren, who together with James Keeney had founded the town back in 1879 and named it after themselves.

They weren't even doing it because Jeff Warren was a good boss, a man who saw them not just as employees or public servants but as colleagues and friends.

They were doing it because, in a little place like WaKeeney—population growing slowly but still under two thousand—everyone knew pretty much everyone, and Shellie Warren was one of the best-liked folks in town. She remembered every officer's and Trego County sheriff's deputy's birthday and anniversary with a card and a thoughtful little gift, was always one of the first to stock up on Do-si-dos and Samoas during Girl Scout cookie season, could be counted on to whip up a couple batches of lemon bars for every charity bake sale. And of course it was *her* influence that had matured Jeff Warren from—if truth be told—the arrogant swaggering kid he'd been in high school to a mature and responsible adult.

They were doing it because they knew her and *liked* her, and like her husband they were terrified that something awful might happen to her if they couldn't find her in time.

They were knocking on doors and talking with every member of the community they could get to—but they were drawing blanks. No one had seen a thing. No one had a clue who might want to kidnap Shellie Warren and hold her for ransom.

The hours ticked by very slowly.

✗　✗　✗　✗

The chief heaved a sigh of relief and cradled the phone.

"Good news?" asked Sergeant Al Penny hopefully.

Warren nodded. "That was the KBI. The brown stuff on the first envelope *is* blood, but it's chicken blood, not human. I expect it's chicken blood on the others, too."

It was Friday morning, and Shellie had been missing for at least thirty-six hours, depending on what time Wednesday she had been taken.

Warren and Penny were in the chief's office, and there were *three* white envelopes on the desk between them. Penny had found the third one slipped under the PD's front door when he'd come to work early that morning. This time, a dark brown O had been added an inch to the left of the second X, so the letters now read:

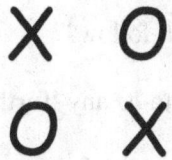

Inside was the usual folded sheet of plain white paper:

PUT THE MONEY IN A GROCERY BAG AND DELIVER IT
TO THE INDICATED SPOT. YOUR WIFE IS STILL UNHURT.
THERE WILL BE NO FURTHER INSTRUCTIONS.

"He's been saying all along he hasn't done anything to her," Penny pointed out. "Said so right there in the first note."

Warren slid the original message out of its envelope. "I haven't hurt her," he read aloud. "Yet."

"We should of figured ourselves that wasn't Mrs. Warren's blood on the envelopes," said Penny.

The chief looked across the desk at him, his face devoid of expression. "Because why would a fella who would kidnap my wife tell a *lie*?" he said drily.

The sergeant swallowed. "Anyway, good news from the lab."

"Yeah. But even if I *had* the money, Al, which I don't, where the hell is the *indicated spot*? Did we miss an envelope?"

Penny considered the question. "I don't think so," he said at last, "unless it was before the first one, maybe with just one X on the front, and we never found it. Then the X O one would be the *second* one, and—"

Warren shook off the suggestion. "No, the first one has to be the first one. 'I have her,' he wrote. That's got to be his first message."

"But this third one says 'the indicated spot,' like you're supposed to know where that is. And then 'there will be no further instructions.' That seems pretty clear, Chief. He thinks you—"

And then Jeff Warren stared down at the third envelope, and his mouth dropped open.

"You got an idea?"

Warren's tongue pushed absently against the achy tooth he'd been meaning to get filled. "Maybe I do," he said, reaching for the chipped coffee cup in which he kept his pens. "There was no real reason for the guy who's got Shellie to send me his second and third notes, was there? I mean, he doesn't really *say* anything in them he didn't already say in the first one."

"No, sir." The sergeant nodded eagerly. "And he was taking a hell of a risk dropping them off like he done, at your house and here at the station. What if somebody spotted him?"

Warren chewed on his lower lip. "The first two times," he mused, "he ended the notes the same way."

"Further information will follow?"

"Yeah."

"But there doesn't seem to *be* any 'further information' in the second or third note."

"Doesn't *seem* to be," the chief repeated. "But what if there is? What if the information isn't in the notes themselves but in those chicken-blood scratches on the envelopes?"

Penny looked puzzled. "The exes and ohs?"

Warren clicked a pen and drew a horizontal line beneath the upper X O on the third envelope, starting half an inch to the left of the X and ending an inch and a half to the right of the O.

"You think that first hug and kiss is the most important part of the—?"

"I don't think they're supposed to be hugs and kisses," the chief said. "Watch." He drew an identical line beneath the lower O X.

The sergeant scratched his head. "I don't get it, Chief. What's your—?"

Warren touched the point of his pen to a spot between the upper X and O and about half an inch above the tops of the letters and drew a vertical line downward, ending an inch and a half below the second O:

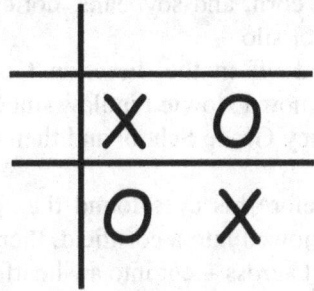

"No way," Al Penny said. "You mean—?"

The chief touched the point of his pen to a spot half an inch to the right and half an inch above the upper O and drew a second downward vertical line, ending an inch and a half below the second X:

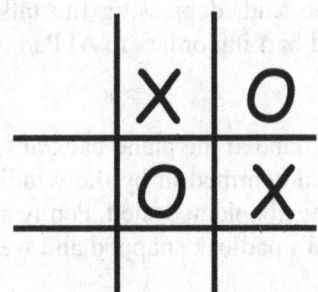

"He's playing *tic-tac-toe*?" the sergeant said in disbelief.

Warren nodded. "Further information will follow," he said again. "He's been giving us *clues*, Al. And this third one shows us where he's holding my wife."

"Who in the Lord's name does this joker think he is?" demanded Penny.

"Close," the chief mused, "but not the Joker." In the empty space at the bottom right of his diagram, he drew a capital X.

"Right show, wrong villain!" the sergeant shouted. "He thinks he's the *Riddler*!"

"Maybe so," Jeff Warren said. "That might just be *exactly* what he thinks. And if he does, I guess that must make *me* the Batman."

"There!" Jill Gomez shouted above the roar of the crop duster's single engine. She lifted her left hand from the throttle and pointed down and to the west.

They were two thousand feet above central Kansas in Gomez's Piper PA-36 Pawnee Brave, sweeping back and forth across a green-and-tan patchwork of fields of wheat, corn, and soybeans, dotted here and there with a lonely farmhouse, barn, or silo.

Chief Warren looked off in the direction Gomez indicated. He had known Jill, like he had known Howie Findlay, since the three of them were kids together at WaKeeney Grade School and then through junior high and high school.

It took a moment before his eyes found the spot, but then he saw it: like a Halloween maze mowed into a cornfield, there was a giant tic-tac-toe board—a good thirty feet across—cut into a wheatfield tucked inside a bend of the Saline River. A big X had been scythed into the board's upper-left corner and another in the central square, with an O above the central X and another one to the left of it.

In the lower-right corner of the makeshift board, a crude X had been painted onto the roof of a sagging shed that had once upon a time perhaps been used to store farm implements but that he could see as they approached it was now abandoned.

"X marks the spot," he said, depressing the talk button on Gomez's handheld aviation radio and barking orders to Al Penny on the ground.

✗   ✗   ✗   ✗

By the time Jill Gomez landed the plane back at Galloway Airport and Warren found the wheatfield hemmed in by the winding river and beat his way through the wheat to the dilapidated shed, Penny and the two patrolmen were already there, the shed's padlock snapped and weathered wooden door hanging askew on one hinge.

As he emerged from the wheat, he heard the most beautiful sound he had ever heard in his life: "Jeff!" his wife screamed, and she raced across the twenty feet that separated them and flung herself into his arms. She was dressed in black yoga pants and one of his old Wildcats sweatshirts, her usual evening-at-home attire, and she was weeping.

"I'm here," he reassured her, holding her tightly and stroking the disheveled brunette hair at back of her neck. "I'm right here, Shel, honey."

He found Al Penny's eyes and mouthed a question: *Did you get him?*

The sergeant shook his head. *Nobody else here,* he mouthed.

Later, when Shellie was calm enough to talk, Warren sat her beside him in the front of the cruiser and asked for a description of the man who had taken her.

"I never saw his face or heard his voice," she said. "When I opened the door, he was standing there on the mat wearing some kind of stupid green mask, and before I knew what was happening, he—"

"I'll be damned," Penny said from the back seat. "It *was* the Riddler."

✗ ✗ ✗ ✗ ✗

The bell over the door of Queen City Comics jingled as Jeff Warren and Al Penny stepped into the shop, which occupied a storefront on Russell Avenue, around the corner from the building shared by the Trego County Sheriff's Office and the WaKeeney PD. Warren had passed the place a thousand times, but though he had watched his share of superhero movies and TV shows he hadn't really gotten into the comic books and had never ventured inside, though he and Howie and Jill had all gone through school with Frank Gorman, the owner.

The store's walls were lined with shelving packed with *hundreds* of titles: Batman and Superman and Spider-Man and the Justice League and the X-Men, sure, but also books whose brightly colored covers suggested there was much more to the world of comics than the chief had suspected, much more than a cornucopia of heroes and villains, much more than DC and Marvel. He spotted a Nazi swastika and a couple of kneeling rodents on a graphic novel called Maus, and a whole line of lurid books featuring lifelike representations of Elvira, Mistress of the Dark, who he remembered as the host of some long-ago horror-movie show. There were romance comics and war comics and children's comics and foreign comics—including dozens of Japanese-looking titles in a big section labeled "Anime/Manga."

And then there were the posters hanging above the shelves, and the display cases filled with action figures and trading cards and expensive models of science-fictional beings he couldn't have named if his life depended on it.

Along the shop's back wall was a long glass counter, and behind it, sitting on a stool at the cash register, was Frank Gorman, flipping the pages of an oversized paperback. When he looked up at the sound of the bell and saw Warren and Penny coming into the store, he closed the volume and stashed it away below the counter.

"Well, well, well," he called, "if it isn't the Lone Ranger and his faithful Indian companion. To what do I owe this honor, gentlemen?"

"Like to talk with you, Frank," Warren said.

"Really? You never had time to talk to me back in school, *Jefferson*. I was just one of the nerds, and you were king of the hill. I—"

"Is that why you did it?" asked Al Penny, practically dripping with disbelief. "You were *jealous*?"

Gorman sat up straighter, his dignity offended. "I have no *idea* what you're talking about, Officer."

Jeff Warren sighed. "I think you do, Frank. But whether you do or not"—he fished an official document from his back pocket and held it out—"I've got a warrant here to search your shop, your home, and your vehicle. You want to call a lawyer, we can—"

"Search for *what*?" the man said. "You think you're gonna find coke or meth or something in my car?"

"I think we're gonna find a green mask and the keys to a padlock and a leg shackle," Warren said evenly—and Frank Gorman deflated like a cartoon balloon whose air had escaped in a *whoosh*.

"I didn't hurt her," he said quickly, his voice half an octave higher. "She'll tell you I didn't hurt her. I left her plenty of food and water, and I was fixing to let her go in a day or two. I didn't want your damn money, Jeff. I just wanted to put a scare into you, show you how *I* felt back in school, when you and the rest of the jocks treated me like less than a piece of shit."

"You want me to hook him up, Chief?" Al Penny asked, reaching behind his back for his handcuffs.

"I don't think there's any need for that, Al." Jeff Warren turned his attention back to Frank Gorman. "I am truly sorry for what we put you through in high school, Frank. But twenty years is a *long* time to carry a grudge, and taking it out on my wife wasn't cool." He grinned and waved Gorman up from his perch. "Come on, now. You and me are gonna take a ride around the corner in my Batmobile, and while the county attorney figures out what all to charge you with, I'll set you up with a nice place to sleep in the Batcave."

Josh Pachter was the 2020 recipient of the Short Mystery Fiction Society's Golden Derringer for Lifetime Achievement. He is the award-winning author of more than 120 short stories, the novel *Dutch Threat*, and the YA book *First Week Free at the Roomy Toilet*, the editor of some two dozen anthologies, and the translator of fiction and nonfiction from Dutch to English.

DANCE OF THE MAENADS
Richard Zwicker

This is the city-state, Athens. The jewel of Greece, the fruit of Athena, the birthplace of democracy, or the stillbirth if one is a slave or a woman. When things don't go as planned, I come in. My name's Phokus. I wear a tunic.

It was midsummer. The sun hung high, but morale was low. Athenians trudged listlessly past the tents of the marketplace, in search of food, information, and shade. It was so dry that the grass snapped under their sandals. My assistant Alastor and I sat at our stand, trying to drum up some business, but no one was moving to our beat. To pass the time, we argued about Plato's "Apology." I maintained the title referred to Socrates's defense of his unorthodox teachings. Alastor thought Plato was apologizing for writing the dialogue.

"Why would he apologize for writing the dialogue by writing the dialogue?" I asked.

He shrugged. "Some people just can't help themselves."

That was why I teamed with Alastor. No false airs, so average, so comfortable in his own dark bowl haircut and young, muscular body I couldn't imagine him ever leaving it. Whenever I got pretentious, Alastor brought me back to reality. I was about to thank him when a large, ponytailed man approached us. He could have rented out his full beard to a nesting phoenix.

"Which of you is Phokus?" he asked. His right cheek was slightly swollen and his eye twitched like a lizard's tail.

"I am he. This is my assistant, Alastor. What can we do for you?"

He hesitated. "I've never been to a detective before."

Hardly anyone had lately, which was why we had only this primitive stand. He continued, "My name is Bendis. I believe my daughter Natassa is being held against her will by Maenads."

Alastor's eyes lit up. Everyone knew about the Maenads, wild women famed for drunkenness, wanton sexual behavior, and tearing animals into little pieces. A group of them practiced in the woods on the northern edge of the city.

"You believe or you know?" I asked.

"I believe. Natassa has a rebellious streak and has often praised this group of crazed women. I think she ran away to join them, and now they won't let her go."

"How long has she been missing?" I asked.

The visible part of his face blanched. "About a month."

"Why did you wait so long?" Alastor asked.

"I'm a banker and very busy. I also spend much time in the citizen's assembly."

I tried to look impressed.

"Could you describe your relationship with her?" I asked.

He grimaced. "There was friction. I believe a strict upbringing is essential for the wellbeing of young girls. Natassa insisted the only place she can be herself is with the Maenads."

"And you have been in contact with them," I said.

He hesitated. "How did you know that?"

I pointed to his swollen cheek. "You didn't get that at the citizen's assembly."

His nose sank so low into his beard, I feared he'd suffocate. When he looked up, his face was a mix of embarrassment and anger. He reached into his cloak and pulled out a panel painting of a serious-looking girl with piercing eyes beneath curly hair cut short. "She's only fifteen. Please, get her back home. I have money."

That was something I didn't have, so I took the case. Bendis's joy was muted, however, when I said I wanted to hear his wife's side of the story. He maintained she lacked social skills, but I insisted. We agreed to meet at his home in an hour. After he left, I asked Alastor for his thoughts.

He shrugged. "If she'd been missing for a few days, I'd say she ran off with a friend, but a month is a long time to stay hidden, unless she were with the Maenads."

"And it could be against her will. As Bendis's face attests, the Maenads are not known for being understanding. It confounds me why anyone would choose that kind of life."

But maybe I didn't want to understand. Three years ago, my wife left me for a Spartan. At the time I thought, why would anyone choose to live in that cultural wasteland? I came to the conclusion, however, that despite listening to my wife's daily complaints, I'd never really heard her. Though their interests were limited, Spartans—and Maenads—gave women a voice.

I noticed Alastor had a faraway look. "What's with you?"

"I have a soft spot for uncontrollable women," he said.

"You might have a bunch of sore ones before we're done."

✗   ✗   ✗   ✗

Bendis's two-story mud-brick house stood proudly on a dead-end road in a wealthy part of the city. A sullen Thracian slave opened the door and led us to an inner courtyard, empty except for a couple of vined plants and a blank-faced statue of Hestia. Alastor took the slave's silence as a challenge and attempted conversation. This earned him a mute glare. After the slave departed, Alastor muttered, "Thracians have no sense of humor. You lost. Get over it."

I was about to reply when our host appeared and embraced us as if we were long-lost uncles. He then left to go to the gynaikon section of the house, where his wife wove and spun. I thought he was going to bring her down, but instead, he shouted, "Ask her whatever you want."

After a pause, I yelled, "I was hoping to speak to her directly."

"She'd like to," Bendis said, "but she's at a critical point in a robe. It's all right. She has excellent hearing."

So did I, but there was nothing to hear. With Bendis as translator, his wife's responses were identical to his own. When I asked for her name, I got the answer, "Bendis," before her husband added, "I mean Agape." Being an only child, Natassa did have a small room of her own, and Bendis let us see that. It was just a bed and blank walls, however, revealing nothing but loneliness.

"That was a waste of time," I said as we left.

"I feel sorry for Agape," Alastor said. "I believe a wife should be allowed to do whatever she wants."

"As long as she cooks your meals, services you regularly, and bears you eight children."

He gave me a skeptical look. "Well, of course."

We asked the neighbors if they ever saw Natassa outside of her home, but none had. I thought maybe Bendis had brought her to the marketplace once in a while, but the slave did all the shopping. If Natassa had joined the Maenads to escape the iron bonds of her father, she'd done so with little knowledge of the outside world. Our next step was to attend a Maenad festival and learn more than Bendis had.

✗ ✗ ✗ ✗

Neither Alastor nor I had ever been in the northern woods at night, as we had no wish for our limited wealth to be redistributed by thieves. Armed with knives, we walked cautiously out of the city. The sky was awash in constellations, and a half-moon shone on the looming pillars of the Parthenon to our west.

Resolutely, we entered the woods, our eyes glued to the narrow path. We heard more howling as we wound our way up a hill, then around a corner to a small open field, ringed by flickering torches. A group of about thirty Maenads moaned and lurched in front of a statue of Dionysus. Despite his intemperate habits, the god looked svelte, with rippling muscles and a raised cup of wine. In the flickering light he appeared to be moving. In the throes of their freeform dance, the Maenads resembled victims of falling sickness. Each wore an amalgam of animal skins, vines, and snakes, with their private parts often exposed. Each woman shook a thyrsus—a leaf-covered staff—in threatening or erotic motions. Some of them rapped on makeshift drums, which sounded more like a hail of stones than a recognizable rhythm.

We sat against two tree trunks and watched. I've never understood the appeal of dancing. It leaves me breathless and dizzy, and I don't know where to place my feet. When I shared this observation with Alastor, he said, "You just go with it."

But a detective can't just "go with it." What made these women abandon structure, calm, and moderation—for this? If I could understand, I'd have a better idea of who Natassa was.

"We'll get nothing out of them now," I said. "Let's wait until they've spent themselves. In the meantime, keep your eyes open for Natassa."

But we didn't see her. A few hours from sunrise, we flexed our legs and crept from the trees. The torches had gone out, and the Maenads lay on the ground, the only music their wheezing snores. We chose one of the smaller, less imposing women, without a snake in her hair. Sleep had transformed her to a docile child, more in tune with the nocturnal flora and fauna than the raving dancers we'd seen earlier.

I knelt and gently nudged the woman's shoulder, flinching at the touch of her leopard skin. I increased my rustling, to no effect. She lay as if dead, making me wonder what these women imbibed to achieve their frenzied states.

"I've had nights like that," Alastor said. He grabbed her thyrsus out of her clenched hands and whacked her over the head. I protested, but he insisted you don't treat a plague with tea leaves. The woman moaned, then laid her hand across her forehead. Her eyes widened as she saw us.

"Get away from me," she hissed.

"We need information, then you can rejoin Morpheus," I said. I noted lines under her eyes. She looked at least two decades older than Natassa, though I didn't imagine Maenads aged gracefully.

She moaned again. "I feel like I head-butted the Minotaur. Ask and be gone."

"We're looking for a girl named Natassa, daughter of Bendis the banker."

Despite the glaze, her eyes showed recognition and disapproval.

"She was here, but Athens wasn't big enough for her."

"Explain."

"She wanted to go to the source. For Maenads, that's Thebes. She talked this other girl, Chloris, into accompanying her."

"Two women traveling alone to Thebes. That's crazy," Alastor said.

"That's Natassa. They're both probably dead by now."

Thebes being a rival city-state, we Athenians automatically hated it, but there were more logical reasons. It was a plague magnet, as well as a nesting place for sphinxes.

"When did Natassa and her friend leave?"

She shrugged. "About ten days ago."

I wasn't crazy about walking to Thebes, but at least we'd done it before. Years ago we'd done a favor for Cadmus, its king. I turned to Alastor. "You up for a trip?" What I really meant was, *will your wife let you go?*

He snorted. "When duty calls, Alastor answers."

We thanked the woman—for a Maenad she was quite rational—then let her get back to sleep. We returned to our homes to do the same. We had a long trip ahead of us, assuming Bendis signed off on this. I almost hoped he wouldn't.

He did.

⚔ ⚔ ⚔ ⚔

"So everything's all right with Io?" I asked Alastor as I picked him up at his modest home the next morning. Io was still a good-looking woman, though gone were the days when Alastor nicknamed her I-opener.

He waved his hand dismissively. "Of course."

"She doesn't mind you spending a couple of weeks with Maenads?"

"I left that part out. I didn't want her to worry."

"Right."

Thebes was a three-day walk; less if you got killed along the way. Legend has it that Theseus cut down all the bandits between Trozen and Athens. More likely, they moved north between Athens and Thebes.

On the first day we met a guy who thought he was Charybdis, the creature that swallowed large portions of the sea. Boy, was he lost. He told us to turn around or he'd swallow us. We would have been fine doubling back if Alastor hadn't retorted, "Eat me!" We compromised, surrendering a half loaf of bread for access to the path.

The next day we encountered a small band of radical Cynics. I'd seen a few of these people on the streets of Athens, preaching their philosophy of clarity through a disdain of wealth, power, and fame. As we tried to pass, they started barking like dogs, demanding we embrace their philosophy and hand over our possessions. It took a lot of petting, but we convinced them that we needed to save someone from the Maenads, a group they diametrically opposed.

The third morning I woke up to find an elflike creature tugging at my sandals. Another was rifling through my backpack. A third already had Alastor's on his back.

"Hey!" I yelled, rousing my assistant and causing the children to drop our belongings. They giggled nervously, and by their rugged faces I saw they were not children at all but Kobaloi, the mischievous dwarves associated with Dionysus. They could lead us right to him. As they scampered away, we quickly gathered our gear and followed, but then lost them in the thick woods.

That afternoon we reached Thebes. When I inquired about King Cadmus, a farmer said he'd died months ago and been replaced by his grandson Pentheus. I cursed the slow dissemination of news, then approached two guards and insisted I was a friend of the deceased king.

The larger one sneered. "Maybe you should spend more time with him."

"You're the one who'll be spending more time with him after Pentheus finds out you insulted me," I said.

The guard looked me over. I stood my ground. He shrugged and led us to the new king.

Unlike his grandfather, who shunned ostentation because he had little to show off, Pentheus dressed to impress. His tunic, dazzling white with purple-dyed edges, hung loosely over his broad shoulders. A black sash wound around his slim waist. His forehead sported a wreath of laurel leaves. Two dark-skinned slaves flanked him.

"Why are you disturbing me?" he asked our two-guard escort.

"These Athenians say they knew your grandfather," one said.

He sized us up. "I hate Athenians. How did you know Cadmus?"

"He hired us to protect your Aunt Semele," I said.

He grimaced. I didn't blame him. Under our protection, Semele ended up getting fried by one of Zeus's lightning bolts.

"Why are you here now?"

"Another job. We've traced my client's daughter to Thebes. We believe Maenads are holding her hostage."

At the mention of the wild women, Pentheus's eyes roiled. "Do you know their leader, Dionysus?"

"No, but we were hoping to talk to him."

Pentheus chuckled mirthlessly. "Luck is with you. I recently banned the Maenads' rites. In retaliation, they seduced my mother and two aunts into joining their mad cult. All three refuse to return, so when Dionysus foolishly walked the roads of Thebes, I arrested him. Would you like to see what happens to those who defy me?"

I thought, *you arrested a god? Why don't you just call Ares a coward or Aphrodite a whore and kiss your posterior goodbye?* Not wanting to get on the wrong side of a lunatic, however, I said, "I'm sure we'd find it instructive."

Pentheus led us to a small room that reeked of urine and feces. A tiny window allowed a sliver of light. Dionysus sat in the center, his legs crossed, his tunic torn. Vines wove through his curly, dark hair. With barely enough room for Pentheus, Alastor, and myself, the king bade his two guards to stand outside the doorway.

"You have two visitors from Athens," Pentheus announced to Dionysus, then turned to me. "Ask your questions."

"Is there a young woman named Natassa in your group?" I asked.

Dionysus's battered face showed no emotion. "Names are but labels given by others. True names come from actions," he answered. I showed him the drawing, but Dionysus remained obscure. "I encourage my followers to liberate the infinite power from within. I don't always notice what lies without."

Pentheus grabbed his captive by the shoulders. "You noticed my mother and aunts though, didn't you, mystery boy? And I'll make sure you notice me. Until you tell those women you're a fraud and that their revels are against the law, you'll celebrate nature inside this room. And if you think

Persephone has a long wait in the underworld, you've seen nothing yet." He glanced at us. "Perhaps after more interaction with my guards, he will be more concise in his answers."

More likely he would turn them all into gnats and step on them. I had more questions, but Pentheus signaled our audience had ended. It being late afternoon, we repaired to the Tavern Inn. Our room was small and dark, and the owner had forgotten to empty the chamber pot, but we were tired. There was plenty I didn't understand. Why was Dionysus allowing himself to be held prisoner? Why hadn't the Maenads stormed the prison and rescued him? Was Pentheus's ego so large that he thought he could hold a god, or did he truly believe Dionysus was a fraud? After a good night's sleep, we'd ascend Mount Cithaeron, the Theban home of the Maenads, in search of answers.

✗   ✗   ✗   ✗

The next morning as we loaded up on nuts and fruits, Dionysus was the talk of the marketplace. Pentheus and two guards had kicked the four humors out of him in the evening. Hours later, Dionysus, using one of the vines in his hair, strangled the dozing guard. He then fled his cell, leaving a message in grape juice on the wall that said, "Even with my godhood tied behind my back, I can escape Pentheus." Discovering the empty cell early the next morning, the furious king announced he couldn't trust anyone and marched to Mount Cithaeron himself, alone except for his pride.

"If you hurry, you might catch up to him," the pomegranate salesman told us.

Someone as out of control as Pentheus could only muddy the waters, but one must drink what the gods serve. Perhaps we could use the confusion to our advantage.

Alastor and I puffed like Aeolus the god of wind as we hauled ourselves up Mount Cithaeron. When I asked if he was all right, Alastor gasped that we needed more coastal clients. At mid-afternoon we reached the tableland near the top where the Maenads lived. With trees and bushes stunted by high altitude, it seemed an odd choice for nature-lovers. On the other hand, the changeable weather undoubtedly appealed to the wild women's impulsive tendencies.

I had hoped to arrive before the Maenads went into action, but already a hundred fur-clad women danced in a circle to their own music. Some wore masks, some wore almost nothing. They snarled, howled, contorted, and shook. We still didn't see Natassa, but we had no trouble spotting the defiant Pentheus, who stood center stage in heated but drowned-out argument with Dionysus. The god stood aloof as a vine, in sharp contrast to the surrounding anarchy. Three women undulated in front of a small stone temple. Without warning, Dionysus rushed at them and ripped off their masks. Without their disguises, they appeared at least ten years older than most of the women. What happened next froze my blood.

I guessed these were the kidnapped mother and aunts. But while Pentheus recognized them, they seemed to have no idea who he was. He tried to pull them away from the dancing mass, but they resisted. Pentheus slapped one of the women. She howled in pain, and then, like a pack of wolves setting on a wounded deer, a circle of women attacked the Theban king.

We rushed onto the scene, but the women closed around Pentheus, blocking our way. We suffered bites, kicks, and hair pulls but were able to retreat. When the circle opened, Pentheus lay in a sprawl of bloody body parts, while the mad dance of death continued.

"This is your idea of freedom?" I screamed at Dionysus. "You could have stopped this."

"Freedom and stopping are incompatible," he said matter-of-factly. "The Dionysian way is like boarding Helios's sun chariot, cutting the reins and using them to whip the horses. The destination matters less than the ride."

"You don't seem to be on that ride right now," said Alastor.

"Someone must facilitate and provide the forum."

"And be worshipped," I said in disgust, ignoring Alastor's attempts to restrain me. "Why did you allow Pentheus to hold you? Why didn't you just kill him yourself?"

He shook his head, and in his eyes I thought I saw evidence of the gods' burden, boredom. "Too easy. I wanted to see what would happen if I held back."

It was all a game. The gods indulged themselves while humans paid the price. But that was a larger problem than I'd been hired to solve.

"Where is Natassa?" I demanded.

He met my eyes. "Here," and he motioned at the chaos.

I took another glance at the pieces of Pentheus, then turned back to Dionysus.

"Could you be more specific?"

"You must find her yourself, though I warn you, she will not cooperate."

As the dancers jumped and jerked, Alastor and I continued our search for Natassa, but whenever we got close to a woman, we received a whirling kick in the groin. In a high-pitched voice I told Alastor we again had no choice but to wait out the Maenads. My head still reels from the hours of discordant, grating noise. For a while Dionysus joined his gyrating acolytes. Was he for real or just acting? Could anything be real to an immortal?

I must have fallen asleep because the next thing I knew, most of the Maenads had dropped to the ground. The music had stopped, but a few dancers continued to lurch back and forth like irregular pendulums. I saw no sign of Alastor or Dionysus. I went from woman to woman, flashing Natassa's picture, saying her name, but I got only hisses, snores, or silence. Had Dionysus lied about Natassa being here, had she changed beyond recognition in a month, or was the panel painting a poor likeness?

I was about to give up when I heard heavy breathing just outside the clearing. Looking for the source, I tripped over what could have been the most frightening sight yet: a Maenad and a half-undressed Alastor groping each other.

"Do you have a death wish or something?" I asked, incredulous.

He released the Maenad, who fell breathless on her back. "Just doing research."

"Is that her name?"

"Huh? No, she didn't say her name, but she told me where Natassa was."

"Where?"

His hair flared out like the arms of a fisherman showing the width of his catch. His tunic hung at half-mast.

"Natassa is Dionysus's main woman right now. Last I saw, he vanished into the temple."

"All right. Come on," I said.

The temple had only one room, no windows, and barely enough ventilation to keep the raised torch in the center lit. In the far corner, Dionysus and Natassa lay in a bed asleep.

"What do we do?" Alastor whispered.

"Try to reason with the god of chaos." Technically, Eris was the goddess of chaos, but close enough.

I rustled Dionysus, while Alastor tried to rouse Natassa. The god woke first, his eyes wild, then focused on us. Natassa squinted through a cave of dark hair, then turned onto her belly.

"Nice temple," I said. "How did you get the stones up the mountain?"

He grunted. "It's amazing what humans can do under my influence."

I motioned to Natassa. "We're taking this one home."

"Home?" He sniffed and gave her a tender look. "Natassa, these men wish to take you back to your father."

Natassa groaned. "Go away."

I studied Dionysus, who possessed more power in his fingertip than I had in my entire body. "What if we take her by force?"

"I will offer no resistance, but do you really think she's better off in her father's home, to be made a prisoner of a husband chosen for her?"

"It's better than being a prisoner here."

"She can leave anytime."

But at her age was she capable of making that decision?

"Do you love her?" I asked.

"Often," he said, smiling.

Alastor glanced at me. "I don't have a good feeling about this, boss."

I nodded.

It was ugly, but Alastor and I wrestled Natassa back to the Tavern Inn, where the chamber pot still hadn't been emptied.

I urged Alastor to get some sleep while I kept an eye on Natassa, but we both just watched her pace the room, lurching like a long, flickering flame.

"You might want to rest in a bed while you can. It's a long walk back to Athens," I said.

"I know how long it is," she snarled. That reminded me of something.

"Didn't you travel with another woman?"

"Chloris," she said. "No cares about her."

"Is she here?"

"No. On the second day out of Athens we got attacked by a crazy man." Her voice was flat. "I got away. She didn't."

Crazy men, crazy women, amoral gods.

"We'll make sure nothing happens to you on the way back," said Alastor.

She stopped pacing and glared at us. "I would rather die than go back to Athens."

"How can you say that? Athens has so much. There's…" And I was going to say arts, sports, intellectual discussions, and everything else she was barred from. "Maenads don't live very long," I said, finally.

Her eyes smoldered. "But before they die, they live. My place—my only place—is with them. Did my father tell you I was kidnapped? The kidnappers are you!"

I chewed on that until my jaws got sore. Under different circumstances, my wife and I might have had a daughter like Natassa. At her age I hungered for knowledge and got it at the Lyceum, leading me to my career. Natassa had probably been instructed by her mother to serve her father, and eventually, her husband. Now, we all had limited choices. My wife had made hers. I made mine.

In the morning Natassa was gone.

During the walk to Athens, Alastor and I talked about many things, all of them theoretical. Though I returned the fee minus expenses to Bendis, he was purple with anger.

"You fool, I'll ruin your reputation! How could you leave her there? She is my daughter!" he raged.

"Not anymore," I said, and walked away.

Richard Zwicker is a retired English teacher living in Vermont, USA, with his wife and beagle. His short stories have appeared in *Dragon Gems*, *On the Premises*, *Heroic Fantasy Quarterly*, and other semi-pro markets. *Walden Planet and other stories*, *The Reopened Cask and other stories*, and *The Sum of Its Parts* (forthcoming) are three book collections of his short fiction. In addition to writing and reading, he plays the piano, jogs, and fights the good fight against what he used to call middle age. His website is at https://rzwicker56.wixsite.com/my-site-1.

THE KEEPER'S DROWNING SECRET
Kelly A. Harmon

December 1900

Strange—the tall, rocky island of Eilean Mor looks deserted, First Mate Olson thought, steaming the *Vesta* toward the lighthouse for the ship's weekly visit and drop-off. But the day had been all rough water and high wind, so he wasn't surprised that the yellow re-provisioning flag was absent from the pole on the ocean-side docks.

Still, it filled him with unease. There was always work to be done on the island, and three men to be doing it, so where was everyone?

He steamed around the imposing island toward the shallow bay where the second set of docks nestled in that small protected strip. Heading into the wind, Olson gave the ship a little more steam, the bow of the *Vesta* rising and falling sharply on the choppy water.

The severe weather they'd had for the last six days had finally subsided, but the wind was still pushing the waves up and rocking the boat more than Olson liked for an unloading. The small bay would provide some relative shelter from the wind and the largest of the waves, but they'd have to use the launch to get supplies to the docks. That always felt like double work to him. He much preferred unloading on the ocean-side, where the deeper water allowed him to steam the *Vesta* right up to the island.

Double work or not, he was looking forward to jawing with the lighthouse keepers this week, and even had a spot of gossip for Thomas Marshall, who was always keen to hear an amusing story. Marshall could spin a few tales of his own, though—mostly old mariner yarns of mermaids, selkies, and sea serpents. Olson had always thought that unusual subject matter for a lighthouse keeper—a true land-lubber—even if he made his home by the sea. Olson smiled, thinking of the story he had to tell of the foolish men he'd seen brought to fisticuffs in the Delaware port—over a fancy-colored seabird that had stowed away on a liner. He knew Marshall would appreciate it—and Marshall would have plenty of time to wring every last detail from him.

They would drop off supplies, as well as James Moore—the keeper who had been on relief this week—and take back Marshall, who was rotating out to the mainland, leaving them plenty of time to gossip.

But as Olson eased into the bay, no one stood at the dock to greet the *Vesta*, and the western flagstaff was also empty. Olson's smile faltered when he saw that the large, wooden provisioning boxes had not been left on the dock for re-stocking. Marshall was absent, as well as his small brown valise.

There was no sign of the men at all.

Were they ill? Why was there no one to meet the steamer?

The gray stone island looked utterly abandoned. Even the rocks were empty of resting shore birds, and curiously absent was the family of seals he usually saw gamboling and sunning near the rocks.

It was a gray day, but the first clear one in nearly a week, which had brought nothing but wind and freezing rain for most of the trip. But the relief he'd felt about steaming across calmer waters disappeared with the strangeness of the scene on the docks. The grayness only made him feel worse. Something odd was in the wind.

Olson turned to the ship's boy, who'd been cleaning salt spray from the wind screen—a never-ending job aboard the steamer. "Get the captain, boy."

"Aye, Mate." Ducking his head, the youngster tucked the rag into his pocket and ran for the captain.

Olson slowed the tender and stared at the empty stone hillock. Eilean Mor had never been a hospitable place with its craggy, granite cliffs that seemed to explode out of the sea. No trees dotted the landscape, no greenery of any kind, in fact. But for the presence of the beacon, its warm light and gentle rumbling of the horn—and the men who kept her lit—there would be nothing to recommend it.

"What's going on, Olson?" The captain stepped onto the bridge and doffed his hat. He scrubbed his face with the back of his hand, tucked the hat into the open vee of his coat, and looked to the first mate with tired eyes.

"Sorry to disturb your rest, Captain. Something's not right on shore. No boxes, no men." Olson nodded toward the docks. "The flagstaff is empty."

"Mighty peculiar, but I suppose they could have forgotten it's loading day—unless they're on the other side of the rock?"

"I didn't see a flag as we came around, and it doesn't seem likely, Captain. Wind's blowing in fierce from that side, definitely more sheltered here." He supposed there could be something wrong with the docks themselves, keeping them from docking even a small boat. He lifted a glass to look. "The docks look fine—nothing preventing us from landing."

"Let's blow the whistle, then, and see if that doesn't rouse them."

Olson nodded and pulled the rope. A deep, resonant tone sounded from the throat of the steamship and echoed off the granite rocks. Olson and the captain waited for some response from the island—shouts, waving... anything. Per protocol, when none came after ten minutes, the captain fired a flare gun.

As they waited for any response, the wind picked up, and Olson was forced to keep them from running atop the rocks by reversing the engines and pulling away. The captain continued to scan the shore, looking for life.

Long moments passed before the captain heaved a sigh. "How is your wireless telegraphy, Olson?"

"Fair to middlin'."

The captain nodded. "Probably better than mine. See if you can raise the Lighthouse Board." He turned to the cabin boy. "Get the relief keeper."

"Aye, Captain."

The boy respectfully ducked his head and flew off.

Olson made several attempts to raise the Lighthouse Board, but no one answered. A few moments later, James Moore appeared on the bridge, hatless, and seemingly impervious to the wind. Olson always thought his close-cropped, steel-colored hair and large, bushy mustache made him look like one of the gray seals which frequented the lighthouse rocks.

"You wanted to see me, Captain?"

"Yes, Moore. When you rotated out on relief this week, were there any problems at the lighthouse? Anything that might cause the others to go missing?"

"Missing?" When the captain didn't explain, Moore shoved his hands into his pockets and said, "Nothing more than usual, sir. With three of us alone for long periods—sometimes we get into a tangle—an argument here and there. It's good that one man rotates out every few weeks—I can't imagine all four of us in that tiny space. But the winter months can be... trying. We're inside together a lot."

Captain Harvey nodded. "Well, let's see what you find when you go ashore." He turned to Olson. "Prepare the launch. You and Mr. Moore will go ashore to investigate. I'll take the helm and resume trying to reach the Lighthouse Board. While you're inspecting the living quarters and the lighthouse, we'll work our way around the island, take a look at the docks on the other side, see if we spot anything on the trip around. Let's meet back here in—" He checked the chronometer on the instrument panel, "—ninety minutes."

"Aye, Captain."

✗   ✗   ✗   ✗

Olson handed Moore a life jacket and secured his own, gazing at the deserted shoreline, dreading what they would find there. He hoped the men were simply too sick to meet them at the docks. He didn't like to wish anyone ill, but the alternative was unthinkable.

"Is it possible the men have just abandoned their posts?" Olson asked Moore as he ferried the boat toward shore.

They passed through a high swell, and the bow of the small boat dipped quickly. Moore reached for the gunwale for support. "I suppose anything's likely," he said, keeping his eyes on the dock.

Olson thought he looked a little green. Moore might keep a lighthouse, but he didn't have any sea legs on rough seas.

The keeper gripped the gunwale more tightly, saying. "McArthur wouldn't abandon his post, for certain. He's meticulous with order and duty. And the others follow him well enough."

Olson nodded, pulling the small boat closer, and Moore jumped out and tied it off. He took a few deep breaths, probably to tamp down the sea sickness, but straightened resolutely once Olson joined him on the dock. Quickly, they walked the steep rocky hill and through the gated paddock of the lighthouse.

"Ducat! Marshall!" Moore called to his fellow keepers. "McArthur!" None answered. Moore continued calling their names, pushing through the closed—but unlocked—door of the keepers' quarters attached to the tall lighthouse.

The first floor was divided into two rooms, a living area with comfortable chairs, a small shelf with several well-read books. A small table with a backgammon board and deck of cards was situated near the large fireplace. A kitchen could be seen through the doorway in the rear.

"No fire in the hearth," Olson said, moving closer. "The ashes have been swept out. It's laid for the evening."

Moore nodded toward the mantel over the fireplace. "The clock has stopped. No one's been here to wind it—in what? Three days, at least?"

Both men faced each other, taking in the eerie silence.

"At least," Moore said. He called for the other keepers again. "McArthur!"

Olson joined in. "Ducat! Marshall!"

No one answered.

Olson felt a churning in his gut. "Maybe they're sick abed," he suggested. The thought he'd tried to avoid thinking rang clearly in his head. *Maybe they're dead.* Moore gave him a sharp look. *Had the man picked up on the unbidden thought?*

Instead, the relief-keeper nodded, not seeming to catch the seaman's morbid imagining.

"This way."

Olson breathed a sigh of relief and followed Moore to a steep, narrow stairway at the back. Upstairs, there was a single, large room. Inside, the beds were made and the room was neat, as though the men had straightened it up before starting their duties for the day. Olson was breathing a sigh of relief when Moore gasped.

He looked to where Moore's gaze was focused. On the floor in front of each bed was a small seal rug, the short fur fluffy and white, almost glowing in the dim, gray light of the bedroom. "You object to the fur?"

"I objected to them killing the seals—and babes, no less. I knew they'd caught one before I left." Moore swallowed hard. "But I hadn't realized they'd managed to poach all three—"

"All three?" Olson asked. It seemed a curious way to refer to the seals.

"Brothers. Brother seals. I used to watch the mam and her three while I polished the brass at the top of the light."

"But how could you know these skins belong to three *brother* seals?"

The question hung in the air a few moments, and then Moore shrugged, pushing his hands into his pockets. "They always played together. I just assumed. Perhaps I'm mistaken."

There was more going on here, Olson thought, but was it connected to the men's disappearance? He couldn't say. "Let's check the kitchen."

Olson followed Moore down the stairs and into the kitchen. It was smaller than the living room, but still contained a small table and three chairs. One was overturned, laying on its back away from the table, as though someone jumped up in hurry and the chair fell back. But everything else in the room was neat and tidy. A slate and chalk lay on the table.

Moore bent to right the chair.

"Don't," Olson said. "We should leave things the way we found them. At least for now."

Moore nodded and leaned over the slate, carefully studying the markings.

"What's that?" Olson peered over his shoulder.

"Donald's notes," Moore said. "Donald McArthur. He was in charge—and meticulous about keeping records, as he was required to do. During the day he made notes on the slate: when the light was extinguished, when the wicks were trimmed, how much oil was carried to the top of the lighthouse." Moore turned to Olson. "In the afternoon, when all the work was done and everything prepped for the evening, he would copy all the notes into the logbook."

"We have to find that."

"It should be in his cubby," Moore said, motioning to the far wall. He set down the slate and walked to the first open locker. Then he pushed aside a towel hanging on a hook and withdrew the book from a narrow shelf in the back, and handed it to Olson.

Olson flipped to a marked page. "The last entry was for December 14—"

"The slate is dated the fifteenth," Moore supplied. "Nine a.m. was the last entry."

Olson tucked the book under his arm and looked in the other cubbies. "Oil skins and boots are missing from McArthur's cubby, and from the third—"

"That's Thomas Marshall's cubby," Moore supplied, "but Ducat's oil-skins are still here." He fished around in the bottom of the cubby. "Wellington's, too."

Olson looked around the room, thinking. "Waterproof coat and shoes missing for two, but not for the third man. Overturned chair. Records kept through the morning..." His voice trailed off as he went over what they'd learned. They were pieces to a puzzle, but he couldn't quite fathom it out. Something was missing.

Moore said, "We only wear our wellies and our oilskins to the jetties on the east side."

Olson went to the eastern-facing window, directly across from the overturned chair. "The crane ropes are all tangled and wrapped around the bucket," he said. "Wasn't there a tool shed on this side?"

Moore's eyes widened, and he rushed to the window. "It's gone," he said, quietly.

"We need to check the lighthouse," Olson said, "and then we can get help from the *Vesta* to search for the tool shed."

"I can check the lighthouse," Moore said. "It's a long way up if you're not used to it. Why don't you alert Captain Harvey about the damage on the east?"

Could Moore be trying to hide something? No—he seemed genuinely surprised that the tool shed was missing. Olson shook his head. "What if there's been an accident at the top? You might need my help."

"Suit yourself."

Olson returned the logbook to McArthur's cubby and pulled up the collar on his coat. He wrapped his scarf around the collar to keep it close and pulled heavy oiled gloves from his pockets. Moore seemed impervious to the wind, only pulling his hat down harder when they left the keepers' quarters and shoving his hands into his coat pockets.

The door to the lighthouse was closed but unlocked. Olson followed Moore inside, then shut the door behind him. Immediately, they were plunged into darkness. Moore mumbled a curse, then there was the flare of a match, and he lit a small lantern hanging on a nail by the door. "Always close the door *after* I light the lantern," Moore said. "Easier that way."

"Sorry."

Moore nodded. "You couldn't know." He looked at the narrow staircase spiraling up the center of the brick and stone structure. "McArthur!" he shouted, his words echoing up the shaft.

"Ducat!" Moore joined in.

"Marshall!"

When the brief echoes of their calls died away, all was quiet, almost tomb-like, in the stone structure.

Olson shivered. The silence seemed even creepier in the lighthouse than it did in the keepers' quarters. There you could hear the ocean and the occasional call of a seabird. Inside the shaft of the windowless lighthouse the stone blocked the comforting sound of the waves, leaving only a pervading silence. He could almost hear his heart pound.

"Up we go," Moore said, holding the lamp higher and reaching for the railing. Olson followed him up the staircase.

"How far does the tower rise?" Olson asked, after he'd counted thirty paces. He was already getting winded.

"Only seventy-five feet, but it's over one-hundred and fifty steps to reach the top." Moore stopped, and he looked over his shoulder to make eye contact with Olson. "Do you want to stay down here? I can shout down from the top if I need your assistance."

Olson shook his head. "No, let's keep going." Moore turned back and started walking again. Olson couldn't see his face, but he was certain Moore was enjoying his discomfort.

"You should try this while carrying two gallons of whale oil," he said. "Twice or more."

Olson couldn't imagine taking these stairs more than once in a day, but it seemed that the keepers did it multiple times. Why hadn't they installed some kind of pulley system to lift the oil that powered the lamp? As they trudged up and the lighthouse narrowed, he could see where that wouldn't be feasible. There was no getting a bucket over the edge of the staircase when they reached the landing.

At the top of the lighthouse, it was still dim, but not as dark as the bottom. Moore hung the lamp on a hook and pulled back the curtains preventing the tall, floor-to-ceiling windows from letting in daylight.

"The curtain's been pulled." He walked to the center of the room and pulled the protective dust bags from the lamp itself. "Wick's been trimmed, weights are coiled."

"Why would anyone draw curtains around a lighthouse?" Olson asked.

"The lens is delicate," Moore said, returning the dust bags to their place. "Sunlight can discolor the prisms which magnify the light, and we'd lose distance on the beam at nighttime if that happened. Also, sunlight gets magnified coming through all that glass. You wouldn't want to catch the lighthouse on fire in the middle of the day."

"And the weights?"

"The weights are drawn up and locked into position in the morning when the light is extinguished. Once the wick is lit at sundown, they're unlocked and allowed to drop. As they fall to the base of the lighthouse, they rotate the lens and cause the beam to turn."

Olson was nodding, looking at the squared-away machinery, at the polished brass, and bagged prisms. "So, the light was snuffed at sunrise, and all morning duties were taken care of?"

"Seems like," Moore replied. He toed two buckets sitting against the wall. "Even the oil was brought up to re-light the lamp at sunset."

"So, whatever happened to the men, happened sometime after sunrise."

Moore pulled the curtain back around the large lens and lifted the small lantern from its nail. "After nine a.m., according to McArthur's slate. He'd made an entry about a fishing boat passing the lighthouse a little after nine on the fifteenth." Moore stepped down onto the staircase.

"But the weather—" Olson said, running the information through his head.

"Was clear on the fifteenth, according to McArthur's records."

Olson stopped. "But if the weather was clear, what happened to the men?"

✗   ✗   ✗   ✗

Moore and Olson were surprised to find the captain waiting on the dock when they arrived. Beside him stood an unknown man huddled in a wool overcoat, a scarf pulled up to his eyes, hands tucked deep into the overcoat pockets. The man carried a leather folder tucked under one arm.

"We're in luck," the captain said, greeting Olson and Moore as they approached. "When I telegraphed the Lighthouse Board, they told me that an inspector was already headed this way. This is Mr. Tully. We concluded our inspection around the island together."

Tully nodded and held out his hand. He shook first with Olson, then Moore, and asked, "Any sign of the men?"

"None," Olson responded.

"I was afraid of that," Tully said. The wind suddenly gusted, lifting his hat, and he grabbed for it quickly. "Can we move this discussion inside?" Without waiting for an answer, he strode toward the keepers' house, hand on his hat.

When they were all inside, Tully said, "Gentlemen, let's see if we can reconstruct what happened here." He doffed his hat, unwound his scarf, and sat in the chair nearest the door. He opened the leather folder in his lap. "I have a report received by the National Lighthouse Board, and my own notes taken with the captain while we inspected the shore from the *Vesta*."

He looked at Moore and Olson. "Why don't you tell me what you found here?"

Moore explained, and Tully made notes on his paper, occasionally addressing something in the margin of the pages. "Is that all?" He addressed his question to Olson, who had remained silent while Moore reported.

Olson nodded. "He's left nothing out."

"Thank you, gentlemen. Here's what we learned from our own inspection: The east landing appears to have been hit by bad weather. The iron railing is bent, and one of the marker stones high above has become dislodged."

Moore gasped. "Those stones weight over a ton each."

"I know," Tully said. "Seems improbable they could move at all, no matter the weather. A lifebuoy has been ripped from its mountings, as well. It's nowhere to be seen."

"And the tool shed by the crane?" Olson asked.

"Yes—we noticed that, also. I've sent two men 'round to look for it."

Tully turned to Moore. "The lamp has been out for at least six days—since you were rotated out last week. A ship bound for Philadelphia reported the light out when they passed by on the fifteenth, but the weather has been so bad the Lighthouse Board hasn't been able to get anyone out here until now." He referred to his notes, then glared at Moore. "You also failed to report the outage this week while you were on relief."

Moore frowned. "I didn't see the outage. I was visiting family farther inland and only returned to town this morning," Moore said. "I don't like what you're implying here, Mr. Tully."

"I'm not implying anything, Moore. Simply trying to ascertain all the facts. One fact is that while you're on relief, you're still obligated to report to the Lighthouse Board if you see anything usual about the lighthouse. No light is definitely unusual."

"I've already explained that I was out of town."

The door opened and Tully's men appeared, their faces reddened by the wind, stocking caps pulled down tightly over their ears.

"Anything?" Tully asked them.

"Ropes tangled haphazardly over the crane, as we could see from the boat. No sign of the tool shed at all, probably washed into the sea."

"Any sign of foul play?"

The second man shook his head. "Nothing."

Tully nodded. "Gentlemen, here is my timeline: the last records we have are Keeper McArthur's slate dated the fifteenth when the light went out—but not for lack of oil. The light was extinguished manually, the wicks were trimmed, everything was polished and ready for the evening's lighting, which never occurred. The hearth in this room was tidied. The kitchen was clean, everything put away, with only an overturned chair amiss. Two sets of oils and wellingtons are missing. The eastern docks have been damaged: bent railings, ropes tangled on the crane above, the tool shed missing, presumably swept into the sea." He looked around the room. "Do I have it right so far?"

Olson and Moore nodded.

Tully cleared his throat. "Then, I think I can honestly say what happened here. It's a shame, a damned fluke, but I believe we have nothing but the weather to blame for this tragedy."

"How so?" Moore asked.

"Isn't it obvious?" Tully said. He read from his notes. "The fifteenth dawned bright and clear. The men extinguished the lamp and went about their business of preparing it for the evening re-lighting. They did their chores, had breakfast, cleaned the kitchen." He looked up to see if he had their attention. "But as the morning passed, the foul weather rolled in. You know how bad it's been all week. Marshall and McArthur donned their oil skins and wellies to check on the crane. With the wind and the rain, the seas were getting choppier. Ducat, still in the kitchen, watched the weather from the window. He must have spied something life-threatening, for he jumped up—overturning the chair—and ignoring his coat and boots in favor of expediency, he ran to alert McArthur and Marshall. Whatever he saw that endangered their lives, must have taken his, too—along with the tool shed. I suspect a giant wave crashed over them from the sea, washing them all away."

He sat back in his chair, capping his pen, and closed the leather folder.

But Olson couldn't get his earlier conversation with Moore out of his mind. "But the weather was clear on the fifteenth, according to McArthur's slate. Waves as high as you're saying wouldn't have been possible that night."

Tully shook his head and stood. "McArthur probably mis-wrote the date. Gentlemen—" He offered his hand again. "Moore, I guess this puts you in charge until we hire new keepers."

✗ ✗ ✗ ✗

Wrong again, Moore thought, shaking his head. "I won't be staying."

Tully seemed surprised. "That's highly irregular. Someone must man the lighthouse—at least give us a proper notice. A month should be long enough to fill the positions."

Moore shook his head again. "With three missing men, I'm too spooked to stay. Captain, may I ride with you back to the mainland?"

Captain Harvey raised a loose fist to his lips and coughed discreetly. "I—"

Tully interrupted before he could respond. "Captain, if you help this man in the dereliction of his duties, I'm certain the Lighthouse Board can find another company to fulfill their relief contract." Captain Harvey closed his mouth, offering Moore an apologetic shrug. Tully smiled at Harvey. "I knew you would see it my way."

"It's okay, Captain," Moore said. He was only keeping up appearances anyway. Tully couldn't keep him here, even if he had convinced the captain it was in his best interest not to help him. "Mr. Tully, I suggest you remain yourself, to light the lamp tonight. I'm sure Captain Harvey can telegraph to the Board that new keepers are needed, and that you'll be overseeing the lighthouse until they arrive."

"Impossible."

Moore shrugged. "I won't be lighting the lamp tonight."

"Then dereliction of duties will be the least of the charges brought against you in court—" The wind picked up, and a light rain started to patter against the windows, "—especially if an unlit lamp causes any ship to run against the rocks here."

"As I've given notice, it's no longer my problem," Moore said. "I need to collect my things." He took the stairs two at a time and reached the bedroom. There were only three things he wanted to retrieve—the rest could be swept out to sea, for all he cared.

Moore knelt and tenderly lifted each sealskin rug from the floor and cradled it gently against his chest. He lifted the fur against his face, sniffing for the comforting scent of his family. But it was gone, all gone, masked by the smells of whale oil and body odor. He allowed a single tear to fall before he wiped it away.

He stood, loosely rolling the furs into a bundle and carried them down the stairs.

"Furnishings remain with the lighthouse, Moore," Tully said.

"These are mine." He lifted stark eyes to the inspector, daring him to disagree.

Olson looked at him with wide eyes, realization dawning. "I can attest that they belong to him, sir."

Tully seemed angry that Olson would take Moore's side. His words were clipped. "Take it, if it's yours. But good luck getting off the island."

Moore nodded and walked out the door, not overly bothered by the wind and the rain. He would be comfortable, if not *comforted*, in a matter of moments. And making his way off the island? It wouldn't be a problem.

He strode down the hill toward the docks, then veered sharply to the right where the seals sometimes gathered if the men kept their distance. The rocks couldn't be seen from the keepers' quarters.

Olson had asked him: *How could I know they were the three brothers?* He thought, *how could I not know they were my sons?*

Moore reached the rocky incline where it met a small span of sandy shore. He shed his clothing, leaving it behind, feeling the change in his body even before his toes touched the freezing ocean. Hands became flippers, toes became tail, and he skidded away into the deeper section of the water near the rocks.

He dove below, deeper and deeper and deeper, to where he found McArthur, Marshall, and Ducat, chained together in death to one of the marker stones he'd pushed down the cliff.

The missing tools shed? That had surprised him, yet he had lived around the sea long enough to know that freak storms and rogue waves sometimes come out of nowhere unannounced. But Tully had been right about one thing: Ducat had seen something strange from the kitchen window and rushed to help. He just didn't think it would get him bludgeoned to death along with McArthur and Marshall—just as they had bludgeoned his sons.

Kelly A. Harmon, MFA, is an award-winning journalist and author, a member of the Horror Writers Association and the Science Fiction & Fantasy Writers Association. A Baltimore native, she writes the *Charm City Darkness* series—a fantasy adventure set in contemporary Baltimore. Find her short fiction in many magazines and anthologies. Ms. Harmon writes non-fiction about libraries, writing and publishing, and productivity.

THE OLD PAYPHONE IN WEE GEORGIA
Eddie Generous

A solitary road butts up to a highway that nobody drives anymore. Lewis Tooney is on the road this evening, looking at the old highway that is fog gray and charcoal stains. The yellow paint is faded and flecking. Around him are the done-for buildings of his new, old neighborhood, leaning, sagging, rotting. It's a mundane spectacle and makes him wonder how he's ended up back where he'd started and years late for any kind of good life on offer.

Really, he knows why, but placing blame doesn't seem fair.

In 1989, Wee Georgia had fifty heads, give or take. The buildings remain, but only one home has any occupants.

Two years ago they'd tried to sell the musty old house his mother had died in, tried to sell it right up to the moment they could no longer afford the treatments as well as their apartment and had to move into the deserted hamlet.

Turning to glance over his shoulder, Lewis looks back and drinks in the gentle, distant glow of a burning porchlight. The only light aside from the moon. He wishes he were home, not at his mother's house, but home where he and Lena had lived before the medical bills ate their hope.

Lewis punches his leg just above the knee. To save a few bucks—and only for a temporary time, he and Lena had both argued the stern sensible side within themselves—they'd let their health insurance lapse because they hadn't needed it. A year came and a year went, and dammit, the money they saved paid for a trip to Orlando: saw the big mouse and the princesses, rode the coasters and drank beer from all over the world.

A week later, Lena found lumps.

They weren't done in yet, Lewis had been making more than minimum wage and Lena earned double what he had, but she left her job when the chemotherapy began and the factory downsized Lewis when the owner used a federal tax-cut to buy more efficient machines.

Lewis punches his leg again and starts across the highway. Thinking on those zeroes littering the medical bills, he can almost see Mitch McConnell's bugged eyes tearing up with happiness.

The old variety store has a wide front lot, paved over, but was once home to a gas pump. The big windows are boarded, and the roof is mossy. Next to the highway is an ancient Bell telephone booth. The glass is yellowed and cracked. The dark blue trim has faded to baby blue. The phone inside is dirty and all the stainless steel accents are gummy and scummy with mysterious residue.

Lewis stares at the telephone for twenty-nine seconds, looks to his left and then his right, before turning around and heading home.

He dreams of the old days, dreams of smoggy cars and cigarettes between a million fingers. He dreams he stands in the phone booth awaiting a call, and then the call comes.

✗　✗　✗　✗

"Did the doc call yet?" Lewis has come up from the basement, the sump-pump is on the fritz and a whopper of an afternoon rainstorm has the basement housing a kiddie pool.

Lena is on the couch, looking tired as she always looks lately. Remission is a cheat word, like dieting—riding high until you're crashing. Seeing her this way, Lewis knows, he *just* knows, the sickness is still in her, chowing down on her life.

"It's six." She yawns. "What doctor calls after three?"

"I need some air," he says. "Rain's quit. I need some air."

Lena says nothing, turns back to the TV.

✗　✗　✗　✗

The telephone booth is where he left it, *where else would it be?*

Instead of staring from afar, he crosses the highway and stands in the open doorway where the grass rises to his hip. The wet heads and stalks paint his pants with damp shadows.

The booth, old and grimy sure, looks as good as the last payphone he'd used. "When...?" His question drifts away on the cool evening air. It hits him: he'd gone to see Snoop Dogg and Dr. Dre and Eminem and Method Man and Redman and was too drunk to get in, too drunk to wait for the bus to take him home. He'd dialed his mom and she'd called him a dumbass and told him to use his thumb.

The memory makes him sneer.

He turns away from the phone, half expecting it to ring in his wake. Lena maybe. She'd tell him the doctor called and told her that she had breast cancer in her blood and breast cancer in her eyes and teeth and lungs.

It doesn't ring, of course.

✗　✗　✗　✗

"Maybe you should get a dog." Lena is up, washing dishes. They'd eaten Kraft Dinner and the kitchen smells like powdered cheese and boiled noodles. "You're already walking lots. Be almost like having a friend."

"I have friends... I have you, anyway."

Lena runs a cloth around the interior of the pot while Lewis sits at the same table he sat at growing up. She has nothing to say to his rebuttal. He has nothing to add on the subject.

"Did the doc call?"

Lena puts the pot on the draining rack, pulls a knife from the sudsy water and turns. "If you don't quit asking that, I'll cut your dink off." She grins, but more like an acquitted Lorena Bobbitt than a Cool Hand Paul Newman.

"Maybe I'll take a walk."

Lena spins on pivoting heels and begins washing anew—nothing to see here. "You need something to take your damned mind off the doctors. It's driving me crazy."

✗ ✗ ✗ ✗

"It's not fair. I know she's hurting and scared, but so am I. And the damned doctor's useless." Lewis speaks into the telephone receiver. No dial tone, no nothing. "Sometimes I wish it would get her, eat her up and have it done. You know?"

He waits for a voice and hangs up when all that comes back to him is the burning sensation of pressing the phone's receiver to his ear.

He steps out of the long grass in the booth, lets his feet take him to the shoulder, and stops when he hears the shrill ringing of a foregone tune. He turns and hurries back. A ball of panic lodges in his throat and he swallows the feeling of shattered glass six times before it disappears.

The receiver is still warm to the touch. "Hello?"

Nothing.

The ring goes off again and he recalls his cell; the ringer he assigned to one-eight-hundred numbers is a landline ring, to warn him. He shakes his head at the sound.

He fingers the steel change door and it doesn't move how it should, as if something's stuck in there. He envisions finding a rare coin, something valuable enough to pay off all the bills.

The phone rings a third and fourth time while he reefs on the slightly bent door—bets he's not the first to try to rip it out. On the fifth ring, the hinge's pin breaks and the door flies into the long grass.

Inside the slot, there is no money, but there is a piece of paper. He reads it and breaks into a run to get home and show Lena.

✗ ✗ ✗ ✗

She takes it after he says *look'it what I found in that old payphone* and she reads aloud, "I know you're all still looking for me, but you'll never find me and this is the only note I'll write. To my count, fourteen people live in Wee Georgia, fourteen plus the most recent whore I've put in the basement. If you count the bodies, it's many, many more. Wee Georgia is like a metropolis if bodies count. Okay, not quite, but none of that matters because Wee Georgia is a ghost town and you'll never find this note." She flips the page and looks at the crumpled backside. "Huh. Says it's from April, oh-two." She looks at her husband and smiles then. "April fools, my guess."

Lewis takes the note, hadn't thought of the April fools possibilities, though had considered it to be a phony note. But.

"Yeah, probably, but what if it's not fake?"

"Police are probably going to laugh. Someone is getting you a good seventeen years after the fact."

He spies the note and frowns with the left side of his mouth. "Yeah," he says and folds the page neatly.

⚓ ⚓ ⚓ ⚓

They're in bed and he leans over to run his hand over his wife's flat chest, trails it down to her bellybutton and stops when she doesn't say anything. They haven't had sex in months, but for some reason, Lewis is anxious to perform.

"If you need to, I've got lube." The way she says this, it is obvious that her eyes are closed.

He retracts his hand. He flings aside the blanket. He says, "No, I'm good."

In the living room, he considers watching porn, but doesn't, and begins searching out how many wanted and suspected serial killers live in his state. It's enough that thoughts of his failed attempt to entice his wife are washed away like so many nameless victims.

⚓ ⚓ ⚓ ⚓

After a long emptiness that seems to encompass his entire adulthood, a voice speaks, but it is quiet and muffled, coming at him like Ma Bell's ghost from the filthy, old telephone receiver.

"What?" Lewis holds the phone so hard to his face that he tastes the caller on the other side of oblivion.

"Sorry, wrong number."

"What?" Lewis looks at the receiver. "Hello? Hello?"

He hangs up.

The phone rings and he snatches it.

"Kill her, get it over with."

"What?"

"Sorry, wrong number."

The line dies. He hangs up, but does not cradle the receiver.

It rings. He lifts his fingers from the flipper.

"Cut out her soul!"

"But I love her."

"The doctor will just want more money."

Lewis scrunches his face. "What?"

The voice hisses, "Sorry, wrong number."

He lets go of the phone and runs so far and so fast that he's sweating when he awakes, looking at the living room ceiling from where he lies on the couch.

"Are you happy?" Lena is on the toilet, going with the door open so she can talk to Lewis.

He turns his head from the living room, inhales a rank whiff, and wonders when they reached the point of emptying bowels for an audience.

"What?"

"Sorry, wrong number."

He stiffens, jerking to his feet from where he sat on the couch. His eyes pinned on the light shining through the open door down the hall. "What did you say?"

"I said I'll be happier once I'm done with this cancer."

"Right. Me too. Hey, think it will be okay if I take the car out to Hamilton Sound tomorrow?" He turns and steps away, leans against the hallway wall. "You think the doctor will call and need to see you right away?"

"Jesus, Lewis, I've been telling you for weeks to get out more. The medicine makes me feel like crap, sure, but I don't need a full-time babysitter."

"Yeah, but—"

"But nothing. You're making me," she pauses, the toilet paper makes a rip sound, which is followed by the brushing sounds of wiping, "feel worse, moping around all day."

The toilet flushes.

"Okay." Lewis has already made it to the kitchen, getting away from the bathroom functions he doesn't really like to hear, thinking about microfiche.

"Wee Georgia never had a newspaper, but Hamilton Sound did. We have every issue, some in scrapbooks and some on the dinosaurs in the back." The librarian is a young-ish woman, probably around Lewis' age: thirty-four. "What years and months do you need?"

"I don't know. I was hoping to look into missing persons… maybe start with two thousand one and two?"

"I hope you're not inferring that you'd like my opinion because I'm not from here. I just know that Wee Georgia never had a newspaper and Hamilton Sound had one until oh-eight, when George W's recession hit." The librarian begins walking and Lewis follows. "Pick a machine and I'll get you the carousels."

Lewis crosses the carpeted room and sits at the middle machine of three, pondering whether or not to tell the woman he's local, knows about which papers existed… maybe not when the *Hamilton Sound Sentinel* went under, but he's local, he knows things.

Decides it's a waste of breath, she doesn't care.

The machine is big and tan colored. He hits the power button and a fan begins whirring. The screens lights up a half-second later. He waits, thinking about the note. An idea lands and he reaches into his pocket for his smartphone; he will cross-reference the missing names—if he finds any—with Google searches on his phone. That way he's not forever scrolling blindly through the old newspaper.

The librarian returns and Lewis watches her demonstrate loading the machine with the first of twenty-four carousels she'd lugged out in a dusty brown carton.

"Have fun," she says as she walks away.

✗ ✗ ✗ ✗

At two, he stopped for a coffee and a donut from Dunkin's, at four, he went to the can and sat for twenty minutes, texting Lena who'd spent the day feeling all right, but not yet hearing back from the doctor, at three minutes to five, the librarian comes up behind him at his chosen machine and says she's closing and he can come back tomorrow if he needs.

"See this?" He's pointing at the front page story from April 3, 2012. "Cassandra Wily considered officially missing. You ever hear of her?"

The librarian scrunches her face left to right and right to left. She casts her eyes to the dull gray of the early evening beyond the windows. It's obvious she's thinking. "Maybe. Something. She could be the one I heard about a couple years ago, was an out-of-towner and was only here for the summer or something... why anybody would've come *here* for the summer, I don't know. Someone was going to write the *My Favorite Murder* podcast, but they didn't have enough information. If I recall correctly."

Knowing he shouldn't wear out the welcome, Lewis stands and pulls the carousel from the machine and hits the power switch. "Was she ever found?" He's putting the carousel into its box as he says this—the information and the date are the most important bits, though he'd read the story through four times already.

The librarian accepts the full box and shakes her head gently. "No clue. Don't remember her being found, but I don't remember hearing her *not* being found either. Might've been a whole different woman I heard about."

✗ ✗ ✗ ✗

"There's like nothing on her."

Lena had fixed a packet of Sidekicks alfredo and a half of a chicken breast for Lewis. She'd eaten the other half-breast and two pieces of toast, was dabbing the last chunk of toast over the chicken leavings remaining on her plate. "That's something."

"I'm going to cross reference names I can find on Google. Maybe the library has old phone books or something, too." Lewis speaks around chewed noodles, excitement overriding manners. "Too bad I burned all the crap Mom left behind. I'm sure there were phonebooks. The library though, they'll have one, maybe. Then I can look at who was left living here in April oh-two."

"Lovely, but what if it's a gag?"

Lewis looks at Lena like he can't believe her. How could all this amount to a gag?

✗ ✗ ✗ ✗

"You're back." The librarian has warmed much to Lewis with this second visit. "Microfiche again?"

"No. Do you have any old phonebooks or records of who lived in Wee Georgia in thousand-two?"

The librarian scrunches her face same as the day before, but does not wiggle it. "No, we don't keep anything like that. The county office burned down six year ago too, they still have the digital records, but you can't just go in and look. They demand a written explanation and if they agree, you can request specific information about a property.... Some rancher burned it down last time, guess he sold everything and the buyer died and he tried to steal it back by burning the evidence of the sale."

"Wild.... So, you have any idea how I might find out who lived in Wee Georgia in two thousand two?" Lewis is slumped against front desk, crestfallen.

"You think someone from Wee Georgia abducted Cassandra Wily?"

"What? Oh, maybe, I don't have proof or anything, I was just thinking...." Lying was never Lewis' forte. "Like, the girl goes missing and there's this community that's almost empty, did they check everywhere? The cops I mean."

"But you didn't know before looking at the papers?"

"No, but, yeah, I knew generally and I'm out there and it's spooky and I was thinking, see..." He trails, uncertain of how to proceed without sounding like a nut.

"Thinking it would be a good place to stash a body?" She's nodding. "I was in Canada once, I know that feeling. Like you could put the body anywhere in Canada once you're out of the cities."

Lewis smiles at the librarian and then she makes an *aha!* face and points a finger gun at him. "Maude Brewer," she says.

✗ ✗ ✗ ✗

Lewis had studied the note for another ten minutes before heading inside Herbie's House of Coffee; the place is old and appears to function on a nostalgic level. The patrons are primarily gray haired and they don't seem opposed to the ripped vinyl seating or the cracked tile flooring. They drink from white ceramic mugs and eat deep-fried treats from red wicker baskets.

Lewis saddles up to the bar, stool wheezing gently beneath him. He orders a coffee from a waitress in a striped blue-and-white shirt and black slacks. Before he can take a sip, the door opens and a woman with bright pink hair steps inside, she's wearing a canary yellow pantsuit, Hollywood diva sunglasses that are almost comically large, and enough play jewelry to impress a troop of nine-year-old drama club girls.

"Come, sit at my booth." She waves her hand and Lewis then understands that this is Maude Brewer: gossip queen and lady in the know. "Ooh, but bring me a coffee and bear claw first, would you, dear?"

Lewis reaches the table with the two cups and the red wicker basket pinched between fingers. He hasn't yet decided if he'll show this woman the note or stick to the lie he told the librarian, he's leaning toward the lie.

"I know I shouldn't, but I can't help myself. Besides, I gave up smoking, what more can they want of me?" Maude takes a bite and fixes a euphoric expression on her face, which is surprisingly light on the makeup. Given the rest of her attire, he had clownish expectations. "Oh. My. Heavens. These are to die for." She rolls her eyes. "Why do I say such silly things, these are to live for."

Lewis takes a sip of coffee, imagining his entire day slip away to the women's eccentricities. So he says it simply, "Do you know who lived in Wee Georgia in April thousand-two?"

Her smile twists up. "April two thousand two, huh? Bad year. I know what you're thinking." She wags a frosting-speckled finger. "Poor, poor Cassandra Wily, or rather poor her parents. They had a website for a while, you know. Had kooks telling them they were a liberal hoax and if Cassandra carried an assault rifle she'd be with them today. People are horrible…. That's what you're asking about, right?"

Lewis takes a breath and spills the fabrication. That note, it belongs to him; hell, it might've been a mistake to show Lena even.

"I've always wondered. Anyway, here," Maude flips a paper Herbie's House of Coffee placemat over and withdraws a No. 2 pencil from her huge, red leather purse, "this is the highway and the convenience store." She continues talking as she draws. Lewis is awed silent by the display. He hadn't expected anything like what he sees. "That about sums it… I haven't been down these side streets in a few years, so it's possible those trees are gone."

Wee Georgia is essentially the two roads, but little veins peel off and between two and four homes remain down each, unoccupied.

Lewis is slack-jawed. "That's incredible. You're an amazing artist."

Maude snorts. "Artist. This is drafting, not art. Art takes effort. Just lucky it looks like much of anything without the right tools." She puts the pencil down and picks up the bear claw. She's eaten more than half already. "So, first we put your mother. I only met her once and it was in passing. She kept to herself better than most." Maude says this as if it's her nosiness against the world's privacy. She takes a big bite and chews, making a game of it with her shoulders dancing, eyebrows up as she looks at the ceiling. She swallows. "Okay and now here…." Maude gets into it then, pointing out homes and writing little notes and names.

Once finished, Lewis picks up the map and feels his chest rise and hope bubble. Maybe there is a reason he is back in Wee Georgia, maybe fate is a real thing.

x x x x

"Isn't it usually the antisocial one that's killing people?"

Lewis had hurried home, opened his notebook, unfolded the map Maude had drawn, he'd been reading the stats about the people living in the seven occupied Wee Georgia homes from 2002, now, he stares at Lena, curious about what she's getting at.

His expression conveys that far enough that she catches it where she sits in bed—a jammy day. "Okay, you've got three singles. One is a wheelchair-bound bachelor—now dead—and then your mother, and then one other. Doesn't that make your mother a prime suspect alongside this other guy?"

Lewis wrinkles his nose. "You kidding?"

"No, what about it? You look at every angle, what about it?"

Lewis throws a bunched up sock. "Screw off."

x x x x

Lewis rolls over and looks at the clock. It's four-thirty and he can't get his mother out of his head. Of the cast, she suddenly seems like the perfect suspect. Growing up she'd been a solitary woman. After his father left, his mother would leave him with the TV to take walks or to take extra shifts—back when the factory was in action, or, at least, that's what she'd said. But what if?

"What if?"

x x x x

The old phone booth is different at night. The moon is low and the sun isn't yet on the horizon. He lifts the receiver and imagines his mother's voice coming at him from across the cosmos or from the other side of the dirt. She's confessing to a series of murders, telling him he had sisters and that while she pretended to work, she was killing her children and the children of other young women, rich ones. That's how they lived and paid for things.

Stupid. He hangs up the phone and lifts it again. The grimy receiver helps him think. He fingers the vacant coin return, thinking he'll maybe look in the grass for the door he tore off. For the first time since falling into this investigation, he begins to ponder the existence of Cassandra Wily.

She'd been in Wee Georgia with her family, her parents eventually confessed to running from creditors and renting a slum house for the month while they tried to figure out life. People accused them of attempting insurance fraud, but they had no policy on their daughter. People accused them of killing her to save money, for sympathy assistance, but how could that be worth it? They were broken, on TV pleading—one of the videos was in VHS-scratchy on YouTube—Lewis couldn't believe they'd done it. People love to blame the victim, love to blame the victim's family because if there's nobody to blame, the trouble could come into their home, could make them victims too.

Above the phone is a cardstock advertisement bleached white. Lewis begins fiddling with it while he runs through the names: his mother, Sarah Tooney, Jennifer and Stewie Jones, Peter Ronson, Gayle Lindenschmidt and Johanna Summers, Trudy and Laurence LeFleur, Kendra Newton and her mentally disabled son Barry, and the wheelchair bound Harold Graham. The names go through in reverse like a memory game. The names float out of order. The names keeping coming and going and coming back anew while he reefs on the stupid card of paper stuck in the advertising window.

The plastic slips and the window frees. Three pieces of paper fall, two are bleached rectangles the same size as the window and the third is a business card, yellowed, the letters are gone, but Lewis runs his fingers over indents from the pressing. With his index, he begins spelling:

L
A
U
R
E
N
C
E
L
E
F

He stops and speaks, "Laurence LeFleur." His finger plays over the top portion, feeling for a header. There's nothing. The remaining letters, the ones below the name, are too small. He hangs up the phone and breaks for home, thinking about what Maude said... "Old Laurence had about fifty jobs, sold fish, sold encyclopaedias, you name it."

✗ ✗ ✗ ✗

"Maude? It's Lewis." He's a bit frantic, certain he's onto something, he explains.

"Sorry, doll, Laurence LaFleur's moved. I heard he's in Providence. Trudy died back, oh, about a year after the poor girl went missing. I suppose you could call his big sister. Penny don't like me, not one bit, and if I'm honest, I don't like her much either."

"Penny's his older sister? Where can I find her?"

"Call the cops during business hours. She's a detective, has to be close to retirement though... then again, ya never know these days. People aren't as old as they used to be at that age, if you know what I mean."

"A cop? Was she a cop back then?" The wheels are spinning, a poster from that ninety's movie with Jim Belushi and Tupac Shakur floats to mind: *the best place to hide is behind a badge*—that was the tagline.

"Sure. Me and her got into it over a traffic ticket back in ninety-three, maybe ninety-four. She tried to fine me for parking the wrong way on the street out front of Jayce's Bakery—long gone under, Jayce made perfect piecrust—but I was delivering for Folton's Grocery—Safeway nowadays—and bylaws said delivery drivers could park wherever so as to not worry the traffic. Well, she was saying…"

Lewis hasn't been listening, he's been thinking. It all fits, the reason nobody has found Cassandra Wily is that there's a cop getting in the way to protect the perpetrator. Protect a little brother in this situation.

"Maude, thanks. I have to go."

"Oh," is the last thing Lewis hears Maude say before he hits end. It's too late for much of anything by way of discovery and he paces the living room until nine and hops on the internet, again, searching for Laurence LeFleur on Facebook, Twitter, the obits.

Ten comes, ten goes, Lewis knows he should be looking for work, but hasn't been able to focus; first with Lena, now with the missing girl.

He strips to his boxers and slides in next to Lena. She's quiet and momentarily, he wonders about the call, *has it come?* Then the note again. The note is twice as ravenous as the cancer in Lena's cells.

Six o'clock: Lewis jerks upright. Lena is gone and he closes his eyes trying to recall where she'd be. He's losing his grasp on her schedule, she must've had another test, maybe it's a results thing and she took the car without him. *Yeah*, results because treatment means he'd have to drive.

Okay.

Up, showered, dressed, fed, he has the map in his hands and he's following it to the former LeFleur household. The sun is high somewhere, but Wee Georgia is all shadows. The birds in the trees have gone silent watching him walk, as if they know how close he is, as if they sense a conclusion in the works.

He tries the handle of a rundown redbrick bungalow. The door is locked, no surprise. Lewis starts around the home, through the overlong grass, windblown to lean southbound. At the back of the house, there are windows about eight feet from the ground, but breaking a window seems like crossing a line. Lewis looks to the long, empty backyard, thinking. His lips motorboat and his eyes wander.

Thirty feet from where he's standing is a bald patch amid the high grass. He starts walking. Awakened crickets bounce off his arms and legs, his soft stomach and soft chest. Quickly, he sees the pale wood. Bubbling whitewash finish. The padlock on the door handles is rusty with a light blue, rubber bottom.

Standing on those doors, Lewis bends and gives the lock a tug. It's solid, but… he takes off for home. He'd seen a video on YouTube, a life hack he figured he'd never need to use.

✗   ✗   ✗   ✗

He's sent four texts to Lena and she hasn't answered, he focusses on the task. He has a flashlight, a ballpeen hammer, and the steel wrapper from a double-A battery. The hack, if it works, he'll shout it from the digital roof-tops, give it five stars on Yelp… or wherever.

The thin steel slips in around the locked arm. Lewis begins to turn, he squeaks when the arm bounces out of the padlock, freeing the handles. He tosses aside the lock and opens a befittingly creaky door. He has the flash-light in one hand and the hammer in the other. The stairs down are poured cement. The room is skinny and longer than his light will reach, but he's in far enough to see.

"Oh. My. God."

✗   ✗   ✗   ✗

"And why couldn't you call the police?" The reporter is named Bo Jensen, she's young and carries her cellphone like she's trying to sell it on a TV ad. The video recorder is active and the lens is trailing Lewis.

"Because, this is a cop's brother's old place and she, LeFleur something, must've, at minimum, turned blind to her brother."

They get to the bottom and the flashlight lands on the first hairy skull.

The reporter gasps through her nose. "I wish you'd told me that part. Oh, hell."

"Why?"

"I called them… you're some weird dude. People have seen you. You at the library. You talking to Maude. It's a small town. The missing girl… I called the cops."

"You what?" Lewis clenches his jaw.

"I called the—"

"The police." The figure standing at the storm doors is obviously a woman, though shadows shroud her front. "Come up out of there."

"Who are you?" Lewis is shaking, the flashlight glow dances on the steps and floor. He doesn't dare lift the beam to enlighten—probably—the face of a murderer, or at least an accomplice.

"Detective LeFleur. Come out of there."

The reporter starts up, she's unsteady, but she can move, which is more than Lewis can do. He whispers, "Run."

"Don't do that." LeFleur is so solid Lewis feels like liquid by compari-son. "Just come on up out of there and explain what you're doing here."

"No." Lewis can hardly believe this word is coming out of his mouth.

"Why not?"

Lewis feels his tongue go dry as he says, "Your brother."

"Laurence? What could he have to do with this?" LeFleur sounds genuinely confused.

"Kill... killer. He's... Bodies."

"Bodies?" LeFleur reaches for her belt as she steps down into the shadows.

✗   ✗   ✗   ✗

The cemetery is somber, and everyone is sad, this despite the closure offered when Lewis discovered the nine bodies buried in the cellar behind Peter Ronson's former home. Maude's memory wasn't quite what she offered and she confused three of the owners, even if she recalled where the homes were.

In reality, Lewis' amateur sleuth act saved the life of a twenty-nine-year-old prostitute nine states away. Peter Ronson's statement upon capture was, simply, "About time."

The FBI is busy searching properties that had ever been attached to the man while Lewis swipes at a tear slipping from his right eye. Lena's casket is cheap and looks it. Plain stainless steel. It has dents from showroom use, from visitation traffic. People opting for cremation are still shown in a big steel or wooden box; people need to say goodbye. These caskets are inexpensive, but not cheap, like buying a third-hand Lincoln.

"I love you," Lewis says under his breath.

The day they'd moved to Wee Georgia the update from the doctor came and she didn't tell him until she wrote the note, which she left in her coffee mug on the counter the morning she took the car and drove to hospital and then overdosed in the basement washroom on the painkiller cocktail she'd been hoarding. The doctor had said more chemo, low chances, tough battle, and she said thanks, but no thanks.

Lewis wishes she would've done it at home. Dying in a public toilet is a lonely idea. Though thoughtful, since he didn't need to discover her himself.

✗   ✗   ✗   ✗

Wee Georgia is down to one resident. Lewis Tooney is in the ancient phone booth with the receiver to his ear, listening for Lena, but hearing nothing.

✗

Eddie Generous lives on the west coast of Canada with his wife and their three cats. He is the author of close to 40 standalone books, has edited six anthologies, and has put together 19 issues of *Unnerving Magazine*. More than 100 of his short stories have seen print in anthologies or magazines. He created and operates Unnerving Books, a small press responsible for publishing close to original 100 titles. Visit jiffypopandhorror.com for more info.

THE ADVENTURE OF
THE SOLITARY CYCLIST
Sir Arthur Conan Doyle

From the years 1894 to 1901 inclusive Mr Sherlock Holmes was a very busy man. It is safe to say that there was no public case of any difficulty in which he was not consulted during those eight years, and there were hundreds of private cases, some of them of the most intricate and extraordinary character, in which he played a prominent part. Many startling successes and a few unavoidable failures were the outcome of this long period of continuous work. As I have preserved very full notes of all these cases, and was myself personally engaged in many of them, it may be imagined that it is no easy task to know which I should select to lay before the public. I shall, however, preserve my former rule, and give the preference to those cases which derive their interest not so much from the brutality of the crime as from the ingenuity and dramatic quality of the solution. For this reason I will now lay before the reader the facts connected with Miss Violet Smith, the solitary cyclist of Charlington, and the curious sequel of our investigation, which culminated in unexpected tragedy. It is true that the circumstances did not admit of any striking illustration of those powers for which my friend was famous, but there were some points about the case which made it stand out in those long records of crime from which I gather the material for these little narratives.

On referring to my note-book for the year 1895 I find that it was upon Saturday, the 23rd of April, that we first heard of Miss Violet Smith. Her visit was, I remember, extremely unwelcome to Holmes, for he was immersed at the moment in a very abstruse and complicated problem concerning the peculiar persecution to which John Vincent Harden, the well-known tobacco millionaire, had been subjected. My friend, who loved above all things precision and concentration of thought, resented anything which distracted his attention from the matter in hand. And yet without a harshness which was foreign to his nature it was impossible to refuse to listen to the story of the young and beautiful woman, tall, graceful, and queenly, who presented herself at Baker Street late in the evening and implored his assistance and advice. It was vain to urge that his time was already fully occupied, for the young lady had come with the determination to tell her story, and it was evident that nothing short of force could get her out of the room until she had done so. With a resigned air and a somewhat weary smile, Holmes begged the beautiful intruder to take a seat and to inform us what it was that was troubling her.

"At least it cannot be your health," said he, as his keen eyes darted over her; "so ardent a bicyclist must be full of energy."

She glanced down in surprise at her own feet, and I observed the slight roughening of the side of the sole caused by the friction of the edge of the pedal.

"Yes, I bicycle a good deal, Mr Holmes, and that has something to do with my visit to you to-day."

My friend took the lady's ungloved hand and examined it with as close an attention and as little sentiment as a scientist would show to a specimen. "You will excuse me, I am sure. It is my business," said he, as he dropped it. "I nearly fell into the error of supposing that you were typewriting. Of course, it is obvious that it is music. You observe the spatulate finger-end, Watson, which is common to both professions? There is a spirituality about the face, however"—he gently turned it towards the light—"which the type-writer does not generate. This lady is a musician."

"Yes, Mr Holmes, I teach music."

"In the country, I presume, from your complexion."

"Yes, sir; near Farnham, on the borders of Surrey."

"A beautiful neighbourhood and full of the most interesting associations. You remember, Watson, that it was near there that we took Archie Stamford, the forger. Now, Miss Violet, what has happened to you near Farnham, on the borders of Surrey?"

The young lady, with great clearness and composure, made the following curious statement:—

"My father is dead, Mr Holmes. He was James Smith, who conducted the orchestra at the old Imperial Theatre. My mother and I were left without a relation in the world except one uncle, Ralph Smith, who went to Africa twenty-five years ago, and we have never had a word from him since. When father died we were left very poor, but one day we were told that there was an advertisement in the *Times* inquiring for our whereabouts. You can imagine how excited we were, for we thought that someone had left us a fortune. We went at once to the lawyer whose name was given in the paper. There we met two gentlemen, Mr Carruthers and Mr Woodley, who were home on a visit from South Africa. They said that my uncle was a friend of theirs, that he died some months before in great poverty in Johannesburg, and that he had asked them with his last breath to hunt up his relations and see that they were in no want. It seemed strange to us that Uncle Ralph, who took no notice of us when he was alive, should be so careful to look after us when he was dead; but Mr Carruthers explained that the reason was that my uncle had just heard of the death of his brother, and so felt responsible for our fate."

"Excuse me," said Holmes; "when was this interview?"

"Last December—four months ago."

"Pray proceed."

"Mr Woodley seemed to me to be a most odious person. He was for ever making eyes at me—a coarse, puffy-faced, red-moustached young man, with his hair plastered down on each side of his forehead. I thought that he was perfectly hateful—and I was sure that Cyril would not wish me to know such a person."

"Oh, Cyril is his name!" said Holmes, smiling.

The young lady blushed and laughed.

"Yes, Mr Holmes; Cyril Morton, an electrical engineer, and we hope to be married at the end of the summer. Dear me, how *did* I get talking about him? What I wished to say was that Mr Woodley was perfectly odious, but that Mr Carruthers, who was a much older man, was more agreeable. He was a dark, sallow, clean-shaven, silent person; but he had polite manners and a pleasant smile. He inquired how we were left, and on finding that we were very poor he suggested that I should come and teach music to his only daughter, aged ten. I said that I did not like to leave my mother, on which he suggested that I should go home to her every week-end, and he offered me a hundred a year, which was certainly splendid pay. So it ended by my accepting, and I went down to Chiltern Grange, about six miles from Farnham. Mr Carruthers was a widower, but he had engaged a lady-housekeeper, a very respectable, elderly person, called Mrs. Dixon, to look after his establishment. The child was a dear, and everything promised well. Mr Carruthers was very kind and very musical, and we had most pleasant evenings together. Every week-end I went home to my mother in town.

"The first flaw in my happiness was the arrival of the red-moustached Mr Woodley. He came for a visit of a week, and oh, it seemed three months to me! He was a dreadful person, a bully to everyone else, but to me something infinitely worse. He made odious love to me, boasted of his wealth, said that if I married him I would have the finest diamonds in London, and finally, when I would have nothing to do with him, he seized me in his arms one day after dinner—he was hideously strong—and he swore that he would not let me go until I had kissed him. Mr Carruthers came in and tore him off from me, on which he turned upon his own host, knocking him down and cutting his face open. That was the end of his visit, as you can imagine. Mr Carruthers apologized to me next day, and assured me that I should never be exposed to such an insult again. I have not seen Mr Woodley since.

"And now, Mr Holmes, I come at last to the special thing which has caused me to ask your advice to-day. You must know that every Saturday forenoon I ride on my bicycle to Farnham Station in order to get the 12.22 to town. The road from Chiltern Grange is a lonely one, and at one spot it is particularly so, for it lies for over a mile between Charlington Heath upon one side and the woods which lie round Charlington Hall upon the other. You could not find a more lonely tract of road anywhere, and it is quite rare to meet so much as a cart, or a peasant, until you reach the high road near Crooksbury Hill. Two weeks ago I was passing this place when I chanced to look back over my shoulder, and about two hundred yards behind me I saw a man, also on a bicycle. He seemed to be a middle-aged man, with a short, dark beard. I looked back before I reached Farnham, but the man was gone, so I thought no more about it. But you can imagine how surprised I was, Mr Holmes, when on my return on the Monday I saw the same man on the same stretch of road. My astonishment was increased when the incident occurred again, exactly as before, on the following Saturday and Monday. He always kept his distance and did not molest me in any way, but still it certainly was very odd. I mentioned it to Mr Carruthers, who seemed interested in what I said, and told me that he had ordered a horse and trap, so that in future I should not pass over these lonely roads without some companion.

"The horse and trap were to have come this week, but for some reason they were not delivered, and again I had to cycle to the station. That was this morning. You can think that I looked out when I came to Charlington Heath, and there, sure enough, was the man, exactly as he had been the two weeks before. He always kept so far from me that I could not clearly see his face, but it was certainly someone whom I did not know. He was dressed in a dark suit with a cloth cap. The only thing about his face that I could clearly see was his dark beard. To-day I was not alarmed, but I was filled with curiosity, and I determined to find out who he was and what he wanted. I slowed down my machine, but he slowed down his. Then I stopped altogether, but he stopped also. Then I laid a trap for him. There is a sharp turning of the road, and I pedalled very quickly round this, and then I stopped and waited. I expected him to shoot round and pass me before he could stop. But he never appeared. Then I went back and looked round the corner. I could see a mile of road, but he was not on it. To make it the more extraordinary, there was no side road at this point down which he could have gone."

Holmes chuckled and rubbed his hands. "This case certainly presents some features of its own," said he. "How much time elapsed between your turning the corner and your discovery that the road was clear?"

"Two or three minutes."

"Then he could not have retreated down the road, and you say that there are no side roads?"

"None."

"Then he certainly took a footpath on one side or the other."

"It could not have been on the side of the heath or I should have seen him."

"So by the process of exclusion we arrive at the fact that he made his way towards Charlington Hall, which, as I understand, is situated in its own grounds on one side of the road. Anything else?"

"Nothing, Mr Holmes, save that I was so perplexed that I felt I should not be happy until I had seen you and had your advice."

Holmes sat in silence for some little time.

"Where is the gentleman to whom you are engaged?" he asked, at last.

"He is in the Midland Electrical Company, at Coventry."

"He would not pay you a surprise visit?"

"Oh, Mr Holmes! As if I should not know him!"

"Have you had any other admirers?"

"Several before I knew Cyril."

"And since?"

"There was this dreadful man, Woodley, if you can call him an admirer."

"No one else?"

Our fair client seemed a little confused.

"Who was he?" asked Holmes.

"Oh, it may be a mere fancy of mine; but it has seemed to me sometimes that my employer, Mr Carruthers, takes a great deal of interest in me. We are thrown rather together. I play his accompaniments in the evening. He has never said anything. He is a perfect gentleman. But a girl always knows."

"Ha!" Holmes looked grave. "What does he do for a living?"

"He is a rich man."

"No carriages or horses?"

"Well, at least he is fairly well-to-do. But he goes into the City two or three times a week. He is deeply interested in South African gold shares."

"You will let me know any fresh development, Miss Smith. I am very busy just now, but I will find time to make some inquiries into your case. In the meantime take no step without letting me know. Good-bye, and I trust that we shall have nothing but good news from you."

"It is part of the settled order of Nature that such a girl should have followers," said Holmes, as he pulled at his meditative pipe, "but for choice not on bicycles in lonely country roads. Some secretive lover, beyond all doubt. But there are curious and suggestive details about the case, Watson."

"That he should appear only at that point?"

"Exactly. Our first effort must be to find who are the tenants of Charlington Hall. Then, again, how about the connection between Carruthers and Woodley, since they appear to be men of such a different type? How came they *both* to be so keen upon looking up Ralph Smith's relations? One more point. What sort of a *menage* is it which pays double the market price for a governess, but does not keep a horse although six miles from the station? Odd, Watson—very odd!"

"You will go down?"

"No, my dear fellow, *you* will go down. This may be some trifling intrigue, and I cannot break my other important research for the sake of it. On Monday you will arrive early at Farnham; you will conceal yourself near Charlington Heath; you will observe these facts for yourself, and act as your own judgment advises. Then, having inquired as to the occupants of the Hall, you will come back to me and report. And now, Watson, not another word of the matter until we have a few solid stepping-stones on which we may hope to get across to our solution."

We had ascertained from the lady that she went down upon the Monday by the train which leaves Waterloo at 9.50, so I started early and caught the 9.13. At Farnham Station I had no difficulty in being directed to Charlington

Heath. It was impossible to mistake the scene of the young lady's adventure, for the road runs between the open heath on one side and an old yew hedge upon the other, surrounding a park which is studded with magnificent trees. There was a main gateway of lichen-studded stone, each side pillar surmounted by mouldering heraldic emblems; but besides this central carriage drive I observed several points where there were gaps in the hedge and paths leading through them. The house was invisible from the road, but the surroundings all spoke of gloom and decay. The heath was covered with golden patches of flowering gorse, gleaming magnificently in the light of the bright spring sunshine. Behind one of these clumps I took up my position, so as to command both the gateway of the Hall and a long stretch of the road upon either side. It had been deserted when I left it, but now I saw a cyclist riding down it from the opposite direction to that in which I had come. He was clad in a dark suit, and I saw that he had a black beard. On reaching the end of the Charlington grounds he sprang from his machine and led it through a gap in the hedge, disappearing from my view.

A quarter of an hour passed and then a second cyclist appeared. This time it was the young lady coming from the station. I saw her look about her as she came to the Charlington hedge. An instant later the man emerged from his hiding-place, sprang upon his cycle, and followed her. In all the broad landscape those were the only moving figures, the graceful girl sitting very straight upon her machine, and the man behind her bending low over his handle-bar, with a curiously furtive suggestion in every movement. She looked back at him and slowed her pace. He slowed also. She stopped. He at once stopped too, keeping two hundred yards behind her. Her next movement was as unexpected as it was spirited. She suddenly whisked her wheels round and dashed straight at him! He was as quick as she, however, and darted off in desperate flight. Presently she came back up the road again, her head haughtily in the air, not deigning to take any further notice of her silent attendant. He had turned also, and still kept his distance until the curve of the road hid them from my sight.

I remained in my hiding-place, and it was well that I did so, for presently the man reappeared cycling slowly back. He turned in at the Hall gates and dismounted from his machine. For some few minutes I could see him standing among the trees. His hands were raised and he seemed to be settling his necktie. Then he mounted his cycle and rode away from me down the drive towards the Hall. I ran across the heath and peered through the trees. Far away I could catch glimpses of the old grey building with its bristling Tudor chimneys, but the drive ran through a dense shrubbery, and I saw no more of my man.

However, it seemed to me that I had done a fairly good morning's work, and I walked back in high spirits to Farnham. The local house-agent could tell me nothing about Charlington Hall, and referred me to a wellknown firm in Pall Mall. There I halted on my way home, and met with courtesy from the representative. No, I could not have Charlington Hall for the summer. I was just too late. It had been let about a month ago. Mr Williamson was the name of the tenant. He was a respectable elderly gentleman. The polite agent was afraid he could say no more, as the affairs of his clients were not matters which he could discuss.

Mr Sherlock Holmes listened with attention to the long report which I was able to present to him that evening, but it did not elicit that word of curt praise which I had hoped for and should have valued. On the contrary, his austere face was even more severe than usual as he commented upon the things that I had done and the things that I had not.

"Your hiding-place, my dear Watson, was very faulty. You should have been behind the hedge; then you would have had a close view of this interesting person. As it is you were some hundreds of yards away, and can tell me even less than Miss Smith. She thinks she does not know the man; I am convinced she does. Why, otherwise, should he be so desperately anxious that she should not get so near him as to see his features? You describe him as bending over the handle-bar. Concealment again, you see. You really have done remarkably badly. He returns to the house and you want to find out who he is. You come to a London house-agent!"

"What should I have done?" I cried, with some heat.

"Gone to the nearest public-house. That is the centre of country gossip. They would have told you every name, from the master to the scullery-maid. Williamson! It conveys nothing to my mind. If he is an elderly man he is not this active cyclist who sprints away from that athletic young lady's pursuit. What have we gained by your expedition? The knowledge that the girl's story is true. I never doubted it. That there is a connection between the cyclist and the Hall. I never doubted that either. That the Hall is tenanted by Williamson. Who's the better for that? Well, well, my dear sir, don't look so depressed. We can do little more until next Saturday, and in the meantime I may make one or two inquiries myself."

Next morning we had a note from Miss Smith, recounting shortly and accurately the very incidents which I had seen, but the pith of the letter lay in the postscript:—

"I am sure that you will respect my confidence, Mr Holmes, when I tell you that my place here has become difficult owing to the fact that my employer has proposed marriage to me. I am convinced that his feelings are most deep and most honourable. At the same time my promise is, of course, given. He took my refusal very seriously, but also very gently. You can understand, however, that the situation is a little strained."

"Our young friend seems to be getting into deep waters," said Holmes, thoughtfully, as he finished the letter. "The case certainly presents more features of interest and more possibility of development than I had originally thought. I should be none the worse for a quiet, peaceful day in the country, and I am inclined to run down this afternoon and test one or two theories which I have formed."

Holmes's quiet day in the country had a singular termination, for he arrived at Baker Street late in the evening with a cut lip and a discoloured lump upon his forehead, besides a general air of dissipation which would have made his own person the fitting object of a Scotland Yard investigation. He was immensely tickled by his own adventures, and laughed heartily as he recounted them.

"I get so little active exercise that it is always a treat," said he. "You are aware that I have some proficiency in the good old British sport of boxing. Occasionally it is of service. To-day, for example, I should have come to very ignominious grief without it."

I begged him to tell me what had occurred.

"I found that country pub which I had already recommended to your notice, and there I made my discreet inquiries. I was in the bar, and a garrulous landlord was giving me all that I wanted. Williamson is a white-bearded man, and he lives alone with a small staff of servants at the Hall. There is some rumour that he is or has been a clergyman; but one or two incidents of his short residence at the Hall struck me as peculiarly unecclesiastical. I have already made some inquiries at a clerical agency, and they tell me that there WAS a man of that name in orders whose career has been a singularly dark one. The landlord further informed me that there are usually week-end visitors—'a warm lot, sir'—at the Hall, and especially one gentleman with a red moustache, Mr Woodley by name, who was always there. We had got as far as this when who should walk in but the gentleman himself, who had been drinking his beer in the tap-room and had heard the whole conversation. Who was I? What did I want? What did I mean by asking questions? He had a fine flow of language, and his adjectives were very vigorous. He ended a string of abuse by a vicious back-hander which I failed to entirely avoid. The next few minutes were delicious. It was a straight left against a slogging ruffian. I emerged as you see me. Mr Woodley went home in a cart. So ended my country trip, and it must be confessed that, however enjoyable, my day on the Surrey border has not been much more profitable than your own."

The Thursday brought us another letter from our client.

"You will not be surprised, Mr Holmes," said she, "to hear that I am leaving Mr Carruthers's employment. Even the high pay cannot reconcile me to the discomforts of my situation. On Saturday I come up to town and I do not intend to return. Mr Carruthers has got a trap, and so the dangers of the lonely road, if there ever were any dangers, are now over.

"As to the special cause of my leaving, it is not merely the strained situation with Mr Carruthers, but it is the reappearance of that odious man, Mr Woodley. He was always hideous, but he looks more awful than ever now, for he appears to have had an accident and he is much disfigured. I saw him out of the window, but I am glad to say I did not meet him. He had a long talk with Mr Carruthers, who seemed much excited afterwards. Woodley must be staying in the neighbourhood, for he did not sleep here, and yet I caught a glimpse of him again this morning slinking about in the shrubbery. I would sooner have a savage wild animal loose about the place. I loathe and fear him more than I can say. How *can* Mr Carruthers endure such a creature for a moment? However, all my troubles will be over on Saturday."

"So I trust, Watson; so I trust," said Holmes, gravely. "There is some deep intrigue going on round that little woman, and it is our duty to see that no one molests her upon that last journey. I think, Watson, that we must spare time to run down together on Saturday morning, and make sure that this curious and inconclusive investigation has no untoward ending."

I confess that I had not up to now taken a very serious view of the case, which had seemed to me rather grotesque and bizarre than dangerous. That a man should lie in wait for and follow a very handsome woman is no un-heard-of thing, and if he had so little audacity that he not only dared not address her, but even fled from her approach, he was not a very formidable assailant. The ruffian Woodley was a very different person, but, except on one occasion, he had not molested our client, and now he visited the house of Carruthers without intruding upon her presence. The man on the bicycle was doubtless a member of those week-end parties at the Hall of which the publican had spoken; but who he was or what he wanted was as obscure as ever. It was the severity of Holmes's manner and the fact that he slipped a re-volver into his pocket before leaving our rooms which impressed me with the feeling that tragedy might prove to lurk behind this curious train of events.

A rainy night had been followed by a glorious morning, and the heath-covered country-side with the glowing clumps of flowering gorse seemed all the more beautiful to eyes which were weary of the duns and drabs and slate-greys of London. Holmes and I walked along the broad, sandy road inhaling the fresh morning air, and rejoicing in the music of the birds and the fresh breath of the spring. From a rise of the road on the shoulder of Crooksbury Hill we could see the grim Hall bristling out from amidst the ancient oaks, which, old as they were, were still younger than the building which they surrounded. Holmes pointed down the long tract of road which wound, a reddish yellow band, between the brown of the heath and the budding green of the woods. Far away, a black dot, we could see a vehicle moving in our direction. Holmes gave an exclamation of impatience.

"I had given a margin of half an hour," said he. "If that is her trap she must be making for the earlier train. I fear, Watson, that she will be past Charlington before we can possibly meet her."

From the instant that we passed the rise we could no longer see the ve-hicle, but we hastened onwards at such a pace that my sedentary life began to tell upon me, and I was compelled to fall behind. Holmes, however, was always in training, for he had inexhaustible stores of nervous energy upon which to draw. His springy step never slowed until suddenly, when he was a hundred yards in front of me, he halted, and I saw him throw up his hand with a gesture of grief and despair. At the same instant an empty dog-cart, the horse cantering, the reins trailing, appeared round the curve of the road and rattled swiftly towards us.

"Too late, Watson; too late!" cried Holmes, as I ran panting to his side. "Fool that I was not to allow for that earlier train! It's abduction, Watson— abduction! Murder! Heaven knows what! Block the road! Stop the horse! That's right. Now, jump in, and let us see if I can repair the consequences of my own blunder."

We had sprung into the dog-cart, and Holmes, after turning the horse, gave it a sharp cut with the whip, and we flew back along the road. As we turned the curve the whole stretch of road between the Hall and the heath was opened up. I grasped Holmes's arm.

"That's the man!" I gasped.

A solitary cyclist was coming towards us. His head was down and his shoulders rounded as he put every ounce of energy that he possessed on to the pedals. He was flying like a racer. Suddenly he raised his bearded face, saw us close to him, and pulled up, springing from his machine. That coal-black beard was in singular contrast to the pallor of his face, and his eyes were as bright as if he had a fever. He stared at us and at the dog-cart. Then a look of amazement came over his face.

"Halloa! Stop there!" he shouted, holding his bicycle to block our road. "Where did you get that dog-cart? Pull up, man!" he yelled, drawing a pistol from his side pocket. "Pull up, I say, or, by George, I'll put a bullet into your horse."

Holmes threw the reins into my lap and sprang down from the cart.

"You're the man we want to see. Where is Miss Violet Smith?" he said, in his quick, clear way.

"That's what I am asking you. You're in her dog-cart. You ought to know where she is."

"We met the dog-cart on the road. There was no one in it. We drove back to help the young lady."

"Good Lord! Good Lord! what shall I do?" cried the stranger, in an ec-stasy of despair. "They've got her, that hellhound Woodley and the black-guard parson. Come, man, come, if you really are her friend. Stand by me and we'll save her, if I have to leave my carcass in Charlington Wood."

He ran distractedly, his pistol in his hand, towards a gap in the hedge. Holmes followed him, and I, leaving the horse grazing beside the road, fol-lowed Holmes.

"This is where they came through," said he, pointing to the marks of several feet upon the muddy path. "Halloa! Stop a minute! Who's this in the bush?"

It was a young fellow about seventeen, dressed like an ostler, with leath-er cords and gaiters. He lay upon his back, his knees drawn up, a terrible cut upon his head. He was insensible, but alive. A glance at his wound told me that it had not penetrated the bone.

"That's Peter, the groom," cried the stranger. "He drove her. The beasts have pulled him off and clubbed him. Let him lie; we can't do him any good, but we may save her from the worst fate that can befall a woman."

We ran frantically down the path, which wound among the trees. We had reached the shrubbery which surrounded the house when Holmes pulled up.

"They didn't go to the house. Here are their marks on the left—here, beside the laurel bushes! Ah, I said so!"

As he spoke a woman's shrill scream—a scream which vibrated with a frenzy of horror—burst from the thick green clump of bushes in front of us. It ended suddenly on its highest note with a choke and a gurgle.

"This way! This way! They are in the bowling alley," cried the stranger, darting through the bushes. "Ah, the cowardly dogs! Follow me, gentlemen! Too late! too late! by the living Jingo!"

We had broken suddenly into a lovely glade of greensward surrounded by ancient trees. On the farther side of it, under the shadow of a mighty oak, there stood a singular group of three people. One was a woman, our client, drooping and faint, a handkerchief round her mouth. Opposite her stood a brutal, heavy-faced, redmoustached young man, his gaitered legs parted wide, one arm akimbo, the other waving a riding-crop, his whole attitude suggestive of triumphant bravado. Between them an elderly, grey-bearded man, wearing a short surplice over a light tweed suit, had evidently just completed the wedding service, for he pocketed his prayer-book as we appeared and slapped the sinister bridegroom upon the back in jovial congratulation.

"They're married!" I gasped.

"Come on!" cried our guide; "come on!" He rushed across the glade, Holmes and I at his heels. As we approached, the lady staggered against the trunk of the tree for support. Williamson, the ex-clergyman, bowed to us with mock politeness, and the bully Woodley advanced with a shout of brutal and exultant laughter.

"You can take your beard off, Bob," said he. "I know you right enough. Well, you and your pals have just come in time for me to be able to introduce you to Mrs. Woodley."

Our guide's answer was a singular one. He snatched off the dark beard which had disguised him and threw it on the ground, disclosing a long, sallow, clean-shaven face below it. Then he raised his revolver and covered the young ruffian, who was advancing upon him with his dangerous riding-crop swinging in his hand.

"Yes," said our ally, "I *am* Bob Carruthers, and I'll see this woman righted if I have to swing for it. I told you what I'd do if you molested her, and, by the Lord, I'll be as good as my word!"

"You're too late. She's my wife!"

"No, she's your widow."

His revolver cracked, and I saw the blood spurt from the front of Woodley's waistcoat. He spun round with a scream and fell upon his back, his hideous red face turning suddenly to a dreadful mottled pallor. The old man, still clad in his surplice, burst into such a string of foul oaths as I have never heard, and pulled out a revolver of his own, but before he could raise it he was looking down the barrel of Holmes's weapon.

"Enough of this," said my friend, coldly. "Drop that pistol! Watson, pick it up! Hold it to his head! Thank you. You, Carruthers, give me that revolver. We'll have no more violence. Come, hand it over!"

"Who are you, then?"

"My name is Sherlock Holmes."

"Good Lord!"

"You have heard of me, I see. I will represent the official police until their arrival. Here, you!" he shouted to a frightened groom who had appeared at the edge of the glade. "Come here. Take this note as hard as you can ride to Farnham." He scribbled a few words upon a leaf from his note-book. "Give it to the superintendent at the police-station. Until he comes I must detain you all under my personal custody."

The strong, masterful personality of Holmes dominated the tragic scene, and all were equally puppets in his hands. Williamson and Carruthers found themselves carrying the wounded Woodley into the house, and I gave my arm to the frightened girl. The injured man was laid on his bed, and at Holmes's request I examined him. I carried my report to where he sat in the old tapestry-hung dining-room with his two prisoners before him.

"He will live," said I.

"What!" cried Carruthers, springing out of his chair. "I'll go upstairs and finish him first. Do you tell me that that girl, that angel, is to be tied to Roaring Jack Woodley for life?"

"You need not concern yourself about that," said Holmes. "There are two very good reasons why she should under no circumstances be his wife. In the first place, we are very safe in questioning Mr Williamson's right to solemnize a marriage."

"I have been ordained," cried the old rascal.

"And also unfrocked."

"Once a clergyman, always a clergyman."

"I think not. How about the license?"

"We had a license for the marriage. I have it here in my pocket."

"Then you got it by a trick. But in any case a forced marriage is no marriage, but it is a very serious felony, as you will discover before you have finished. You'll have time to think the point out during the next ten years or so, unless I am mistaken. As to you, Carruthers, you would have done better to keep your pistol in your pocket."

"I begin to think so, Mr Holmes; but when I thought of all the precaution I had taken to shield this girl—for I loved her, Mr Holmes, and it is the only time that ever I knew what love was—it fairly drove me mad to think that she was in the power of the greatest brute and bully in South Africa, a man whose name is a holy terror from Kimberley to Johannesburg. Why, Mr Holmes, you'll hardly believe it, but ever since that girl has been in my employment I never once let her go past this house, where I knew these rascals were lurking, without following her on my bicycle just to see that she came to no harm. I kept my distance from her, and I wore a beard so that she should not recognise me, for she is a good and high-spirited girl, and she wouldn't have stayed in my employment long if she had thought that I was following her about the country roads."

"Why didn't you tell her of her danger?"

"Because then, again, she would have left me, and I couldn't bear to face that. Even if she couldn't love me it was a great deal to me just to see her dainty form about the house, and to hear the sound of her voice."

"Well," said I, "you call that love, Mr Carruthers, but I should call it selfishness."

"Maybe the two things go together. Anyhow, I couldn't let her go. Besides, with this crowd about, it was well that she should have someone near to look after her. Then when the cable came I knew they were bound to make a move."

"What cable?"

Carruthers took a telegram from his pocket.

"That's it," said he.

It was short and concise:—

"The old man is dead."

"Hum!" said Holmes. "I think I see how things worked, and I can understand how this message would, as you say, bring them to a head. But while we wait you might tell me what you can."

The old reprobate with the surplice burst into a volley of bad language.

"By Heaven," said he, "if you squeal on us, Bob Carruthers, I'll serve you as you served Jack Woodley. You can bleat about the girl to your heart's content, for that's your own affair, but if you round on your pals to this plain-clothes copper it will be the worst day's work that ever you did."

"Your reverence need not be excited," said Holmes, lighting a cigarette. "The case is clear enough against you, and all I ask is a few details for my private curiosity. However, if there's any difficulty in your telling me I'll do the talking, and then you will see how far you have a chance of holding back your secrets. In the first place, three of you came from South Africa on this game—you Williamson, you Carruthers, and Woodley."

"Lie number one," said the old man; "I never saw either of them until two months ago, and I have never been in Africa in my life, so you can put that in your pipe and smoke it, Mr Busybody Holmes!"

"What he says is true," said Carruthers.

"Well, well, two of you came over. His reverence is our own home-made article. You had known Ralph Smith in South Africa. You had reason to believe he would not live long. You found out that his niece would inherit his fortune. How's that—eh?"

Carruthers nodded and Williamson swore.

"She was next-of-kin, no doubt, and you were aware that the old fellow would make no will."

"Couldn't read or write," said Carruthers.

"So you came over, the two of you, and hunted up the girl. The idea was that one of you was to marry her and the other have a share of the plunder. For some reason Woodley was chosen as the husband. Why was that?"

"We played cards for her on the voyage. He won."

"I see. You got the young lady into your service, and there Woodley was to do the courting. She recognised the drunken brute that he was, and would have nothing to do with him. Meanwhile, your arrangement was rather upset by the fact that you had yourself fallen in love with the lady. You could no longer bear the idea of this ruffian owning her."

"No, by George, I couldn't!"

"There was a quarrel between you. He left you in a rage, and began to make his own plans independently of you."

"It strikes me, Williamson, there isn't very much that we can tell this gentleman," cried Carruthers, with a bitter laugh. "Yes, we quarreled, and he knocked me down. I am level with him on that, anyhow. Then I lost sight of him. That was when he picked up with this cast padre here. I found that they had set up housekeeping together at this place on the line that she had to pass for the station. I kept my eye on her after that, for I knew there was some devilry in the wind. I saw them from time to time, for I was anxious to know what they were after. Two days ago Woodley came up to my house with this cable, which showed that Ralph Smith was dead. He asked me if I would stand by the bargain. I said I would not. He asked me if I would marry the girl myself and give him a share. I said I would willingly do so, but that she would not have me. He said, 'let us get her married first, and after a week or two she may see things a bit different.' I said I would have nothing to do with violence. So he went off cursing, like the foul-mouthed blackguard that he was, and swearing that he would have her yet. She was leaving me this week-end, and I had got a trap to take her to the station, but I was so uneasy in my mind that I followed her on my bicycle. She had got a start, however, and before I could catch her the mischief was done. The first thing I knew about it was when I saw you two gentlemen driving back in her dog-cart."

Holmes rose and tossed the end of his cigarette into the grate. "I have been very obtuse, Watson," said he. "When in your report you said that you had seen the cyclist as you thought arrange his necktie in the shrubbery, that alone should have told me all. However, we may congratulate ourselves upon a curious and in some respects a unique case. I perceive three of the county constabulary in the drive, and I am glad to see that the little ostler is able to keep pace with them; so it is likely that neither he nor the interesting bridegroom will be permanently damaged by their morning's adventures. I think, Watson, that in your medical capacity you might wait upon Miss Smith and tell her that if she is sufficiently recovered we shall be happy to escort her to her mother's home. If she is not quite convalescent you will find that a hint that we were about to telegraph to a young electrician in the Midlands would probably complete the cure. As to you, Mr Carruthers, I think that you have done what you could to make amends for your share in an evil plot. There is my card, sir, and if my evidence can be of help to you in your trial it shall be at your disposal."

✗   ✗   ✗   ✗

In the whirl of our incessant activity it has often been difficult for me, as the reader has probably observed, to round off my narratives, and to give those final details which the curious might expect. Each case has been the prelude to another, and the crisis once over the actors have passed for ever out of our busy lives. I find, however, a short note at the end of my manuscripts dealing with this case, in which I have put it upon record that Miss Violet Smith did indeed inherit a large fortune, and that she is now the wife of Cyril Morton, the senior partner of Morton & Kennedy, the famous Westminster electricians. Williamson and Woodley were both tried for abduction and assault, the former getting seven years and the latter ten. Of the fate of Carruthers I have no record, but I am sure that his assault was not viewed very gravely by the Court, since Woodley had the reputation of being a most dangerous ruffian, and I think that a few months were sufficient to satisfy the demands of justice.

✗

www.ingramcontent.com/pod-product-compliance
Lightning Source LLC
Chambersburg PA
CBHW011502170626
46814CB00008B/3004